Signs &
Portents

Dream/
Press

Santa Cruz/
California

Signs & Portents

Chelsea Quinn Yarbro

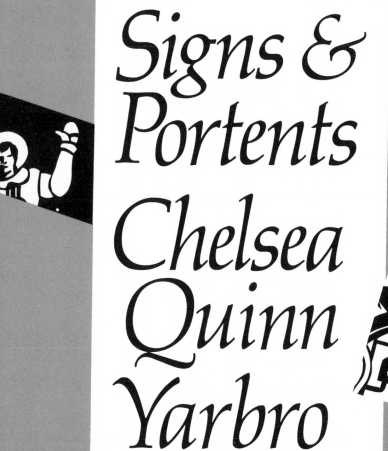

First Edition, December 1984.
Second Edition, June 1985.
ISBN 0-910489-02-5

for
WHITLEY STRIEBER,
fondly.

ACKNOWLEDGEMENTS:

"Chelsea Quinn Yarbro," copyright © 1984 by Charles L. Grant.

"Do Not Forsake me, O My Darlin'," copyright © 1984 by Chelsea Quinn Yarbro from *Shadows 7*, edited by Charles L. Grant, Doubleday Books. Used by permission of the author.

"Depth of Focus," copyright © 1984 by Chelsea Quinn Yarbro, first publication. Used by permission of the author.

"Space/Time Arabesque," copyright © 1978 by Laura W. Haywood from *Cassandra Rising*, edited by Charles L. Grant, PEI Books. Used by permission of the author.

"Best Interest," copyright © 1978 by Chelsea Quinn Yarbro from *Chrysalis 3*, edited by Roy Torgeson, Zebra Books. Used by permission of the author.

"The Ghosts at Iron River," copyright © 1973 by Dean Dickensheet, from *Men and Malice*, edited by Dean Dickensheet, Doubleday Books. Used by permission of the author.

"Fugitive Colors," copyright © 1979 by Chelsea Quinn Yarbro from *Chrysalis 4*, edited by Roy Torgeson, Zebra Books. Used by permission of the author.

"Coasting," copyright © 1983 by Chelsea Quinn Yarbro from *Fears*, edited by Charles L. Grant for Berkley Books. Used by permission of the author.

"The Arrows," copyright © 1983 by Chelsea Quinn Yarbro from *The Dodd, Mead Gallery of Horror*, edited by Charles L. Grant. Used by permission of the author.

"The End Of The Carnival," copyright © 1984 by Chelsea Quinn Yarbro, first publication.

Afterword copyright © 1984 by Chelsea Quinn Yarbro.

CONTENTS

ILLUSTRATIONS by Glen Iwasaki

INTRODUCTION

Chelsea Quinn Yarbro
by Charles L. Grant

Make no mistake about it, Chelsea Quinn Yarbro is beset by demons.

Not the Biblical sort that turns your face pale and hollows out your eyes and makes you speak as if you were shouting down a well with gravel in your mouth; and not the alien kind, that slips through the atmosphere and infects the water and eventually absorbs our minds and turns us into ersatz zombies who have nothing better to do than run around chomping on people so as to fill a digestive track that doesn't work anyway; nor are they the sort that sit in offices large and small, with small minds and smaller imaginations and with an offical government stamp bedevil and beleaguer us with ritualistic rubber messages that purport to have the wisdom to tell us what's wrong and what's right with our non-bureaucratic lives.

These demons would make great press releases, sell a million copies of her books, and perhaps even a movie or two, but they're not what we're talking about here.

Quinn's demons are the demons that plague all of us who have the ego and temerity to believe that not only do we have the skills and the imaginations to tell stories that other people will be willing to pay for and keep in their homes, but also that in the telling, somehow, we also have a bit of information to give out should anyone be willing to dig a little for it — information about ourselves, about the world that is too often too much with us, and about what will happen, perhaps, if we don't stop living on an island of self-delusion.

These are the demons that force us to sit down at a keyboard or a typewriter or at a desk with pen and notepad, and write whether we want to or not; these are the demons that make us feel guilty and edgy and irritable when too much time passes without that session of placating the demons; these are the demons that make us slightly on the batty side because they also have told us, and we believe them, that what we're doing is fun no matter how hard it is and we probably wouldn't be much good at anything else anyway, so what the hell, let's get on with it.

The more Romantic of us (and the more naive) would call these things Muses, I expect. Friends of the so-called Artist, there to provide inspiration and Truth whenever we're prepared to receive their largesse.

The more practical of us, and those who have spent some time in the real world, know better. The Muse is not ethereal, nor is it benign, nor is it a font of wisdom, strength, and all around jolly feelings. The Muse is a winged wimp in the New Yorker cartoon; the demons that drive us are neither pleasant, nor particularly kind, and they weigh a ton when you've ignored them too long and they sit on your shoulder and whisper terribly graphic descriptions of what they'll do to you if you don't stop stalling and get back to work. The paradox is — if none of this was any fun most of the time, if we didn't have a good time breaking our backs writing this stuff, we could shove those damned demons into a garbage bag, put it out for collection, and by god, we wouldn't die.

The question is — where do these things come from?

I haven't the slightest idea.

In Quinn's case, however, I suspect that they were attracted in part by the fact that she is a volatile and intriguing mixture of Finn and Italian. There is within her, and evident in her writing, a hard edge of realism that no doubt springs from her Finnish ancestors, people who live in not the most hospitable country in the world and whose struggles to survive are not confined to their proximity to the Soviet Union; and there is also a strain of wild Italian Romanticism, and extravagant gestures, and a less than bridled love of life and living that permits her to believe that whatever it is, it is conquerable . . . or, at the very least, momentarily manageable.

And realism and romance are what Quinn's work is all about.

In spite of her belief that writers are supposed to have virtual computers for minds — that we see and record all and eventually put it down on paper — I haven't the slightest idea when it was that I first met Quinn Yarbro. In my early days in this none too stable profession, when I was still writing science fiction and thinking I, who had failed Chemistry in college with the lowest grades possible and couldn't make heads nor tails out of physics or math, was good at it,

I recall Quinn being an officer of the Science Fiction Writers of America. I recall her being co-editor of an anthology of original science fiction stories. I also recall seeing her photograph in a few of SFWA's publications. Therefore, I assume I probably first met her at one of that organization's area or local bashes. Unless it was at a science fiction convention.

But when I did meet her, however many years ago that was, I know that what I should have said was, "Quinn, it's been a long time. How've you been?"

That happens. I didn't know her, but there was irrefutable evidence somewhere inside both of us that we certainly weren't strangers.

What I think is, our demons recognized each other as kin.

What I know is, we became fast and lasting friends, and as true friends (as opposed to close acquaintances) we are not shy about either praise or friendly criticism of each other's work. She doesn't like everything I write, and I don't care for everything she writes. It is not, lest the gossips charge salivating for the telephone, a matter of thinking she is not skilled in what she does, but more a matter of taste.

Quinn had chided me gently (o so gently, like a razor that tests the depth of that throat there) for the purple that seeps into my prose on occasion, since her prose is more often than not lean, precise, and descriptive without effusion; I, on the other hand and gently taking that razor from her because I forgot to bring my own, have questioned the use of extensive historical detail in many of her novels, since my approach to history and the reader is to give him a flavor and not the whole stew. We huff, then, and we puff, and we stand on our integrities as writers and tellers of tales, we learn something more about each other, we tell a joke, and we move on.

The demons can be a pain in the ass, sometimes.

But when Quinn is at her unarguable best, her stories, such as those you have here in this collection, are a seamless merger of that Finnish realism and that Italian romance. The characters are folks, not constructs, and the story is a life, not an outline. The horror, whether it's an external critter or an internal disintegration, is an outgrowth of character and story, not a gimmick that is attached to it for the ride.

And don't be deceived by the labels these stories have had in their various original appearances: science fiction, mystery, or dark fantasy, they are all horror stories of one sort or another.

You see, for all her brightness and wit, for all her love of opera and music, for all the fact that she has a laugh that straightens my telephone cord every time she calls, Chelsea Quinn Yarbro writes of darkness more than light.

She is, of course, and let's get this over with now, the creator of le Comte de St. Germain, a vampire in five novels and an equal number of novelettes. You will not find the Count here in these pages. He is a singular character, the Count is, and one that has more than anything else she has written put her in the public eye. And that's a shame. I like the Count, truly, but I'm pleased that Quinn has set him aside. That takes courage many of us don't have. After all, when you hit upon a character that boosts your career, lives with you for years, supports your landlord and the electric company, and attracts a large following of readers and fans (not all of whom are playing with a full deck, by the way), it isn't easy to say to yourself enough is enough, it's time to keep growing.

The darkness that surrounded St. Germain was pervasive, and unsettling, and eventually partially obscured the fact that there were other works just as well done out there, before and since, which deserve mention and support. *THE TIME OF THE FOURTH HORSEMAN, HYACINTHS*, and a pair of mysteries her publisher saw fit to market without fanfare and bury the same way.

All of them are dark, and all of them are well worth seeking out in order to discover that Yarbro can live quite well, thank you very much, without the Count standing behind her.

Lest you believe, by the way, that a dose of Yarbro will lead you straight to the nearest oven to stick your head in, do not forget the Italian in there. Great lovers of tragedy to be sure, but more lovers of life. Quinn's darkness, unlike my own, is never without its light. Even if the hero and the heroine (or one or the other) do not always walk off into the DeMille sunset behind the strains of Vivaldi or Elmer Bernstein, their lives are not totally without redemption, nor are they completely without hope. No matter how gloomy the story is, no matter how wonderfully grotesque the situation, if the protagonist doesn't make it, the author always does, life is too precious to toss away on a whim.

Demons.

They have acted in partnership here, and what you have now is the result. And now it's Quinn's turn. Enjoy.

Charles L. Grant,
Newton, N.J. 1984

Signs & Portents

Chelsea Quinn Yarbro

Dream/Press

Do Not Forsake Me, O My Darlin'

Ben crumpled the telegram in his fist, smiling weakly at Heather. "It's just . . . some kind of joke."

She reached out to take the wadded yellow paper from him, not quite frowning as she did. "What on earth, then — "

He snatched it away from her and began to tear at it, so that bits of it fluttered down onto his half-eaten poached eggs. "It's nothing," he said more vehemently. "Don't make such a big thing about it." He put the shredded telegram next to his spoon. "Somebody at the office, I guess. They get prankish about the time summer comes."

Now Heather was definitely curious. "But what *was* it, honey? If it's just a prank, why not let me in on it?" She automatically poured more coffee for him. "Do you want me to be on the alert for more . . . pranks?"

His head jerked up. "More?" There was a pale line around his mouth and the muscles in his jaw worked. "There won't be any more," he promised her as he reached for his mug.

"All right. If you're sure." She could tell that he was still irritated, so she tactfully changed the subject. "I'll be working late at the library. Denise has both her boys home with measles and I said I'd fill in for her for the rest of the week."

"Oh, yeah," Ben said distractedly; his eyes were still on the remains of the telegram, and he was not paying much attention to her.

Heather knew that look well and accepted it philosophically. She would have time enough later to examine the telegram and find out what it was that had disturbed Ben.

When he had finished his eggs, he got up from the table. "Gotta run," he told her, as he did every morning before going to work. He reached down and took the torn paper, and without a word went and dropped it in the trash. "I'll call you if I'm going to be late."

"At the library," she reminded him, hoping he would remember.

She retrieved the telegram half an hour after Ben had left the house. With care she smoothed it out on the kitchen counter and began the painstaking task of putting it back together. She stared at it as the words took shape:

YOU ARE CORDIALLY INVITED TO ATTEND THE FUNERAL OF
BENEDICT TURNER SATURDAY, JUNE 23, 4PM

There was no signature, and the date was ten days away . . . .

With hands that were not quite steady Heather put the telegram back in the trash, handling it carefully, as if she feared it would explode. "A joke?" she asked the air, her voice shriller then usual. What kind of idiot, she wondered, made light of inviting a man to his own funeral? As if to rid the house of vermin she closed the plastic sack that held the trash and carried it out to the curbside before gathering together her purse and notebook and leaving for work. As she double-locked the front door, she worried for the first time in over a year about the risk of leaving their home unattended.

"You got a moment, Carl?" Ben asked from the door of the vice-president's office. He had been debating for the better part of the morning if he should speak to his superior about some of the company clowns.

Carl Hurley looked over the rims of his glasses. He was neatly barricaded behind his desk, but still gave the impression of peering out at a dangerous world. "Sure. What is it, Ben?"

"I was . . . curious about Tim Hoopes. What's he up to these days?" It was a safe beginning, a way to approach his question without being obvious.

"Tim's been on leave, you know," Carl said cautiously.

Ben made a gesture showing he knew that. "When's he supposed to come back?"

"Not for a while yet." He waited a second. "Why?"

"Oh, nothing. It's been a little dull around here without him, is all." He hoped that Carl would give him a chance to expand on this notion.

"The way Tim can be, that's not such a bad thing." Carl put aside the contracts he had been examining. "What's the matter? Have you been hearing the rumors, too?"

16

This startled Ben. "Rumors? No." He tried to conceal his anxiety. "What are the rumors?"

Carl chuckled, which was rare, and indicated to Ben that he should sit down, which was rarer. "Well, it isn't likely that Tim will be able to resume his old job. He isn't up to managing an office any longer, or won't be for some time. We can't have this company going rudderless for that long. So there has been some speculation about who will be promoted. Are you *sure* you haven't heard any rumors about this, Ben?"

Ben had never known Carl to be impish, but that was the only word that suited the vice-president now. "No, I haven't," he said, taking the chair nearest Carl's enormous desk.

"Well, it's better you don't admit it, even if you have," he said. "Nothing is final yet and it could still fall through the cracks." He leaned back in his padded leather chair. "Let's just say that you might get the chance you've been looking for. Nothing is final. Keep that in mind."

"Of course," Ben nodded, feeling stunned. Was Carl trying to tell him that he would be Tim Hoopes' replacement?

"They've narrowed it down to two; I'll say that much. Harry Riverford's a good man. His office runs well." He narrowed his eyes, watching Ben for his reaction.

"He does very good work," Ben managed to say, thinking of the rough humor of the man. It could be that the telegram was nothing more than putting him on notice that it was Harry and not himself who would be promoted into Tim Hoopes' job.

"Something the matter?" Carl demanded.

Ben recovered himself. "Uh . . . no. I've got my mind on too many things. That machine tool plant that burned — I still don't like the way the reports look. The damn thing's too neat." It was true enough that the case was a troublesome one, and it let him account for his lapse of attention.

"Was that why you came in here? Tim started that claim investigation, didn't he?" Carl knew full well that it had been Tim Hoopes' case, but preferred to let the men under him explain themselves without his help.

"He started it. We're still not quite through. The cops are not committing themselves, and I think that warrants further investigation on our part. You'd be surprised how many questions are hanging on this one." He glowered down at his knees. "Is Tim at home yet, or is he still in the hospital?"

"He's been at home for three days," Carl said colorlessly.

"Three days? Do you think it would be okay if I gave him a call? I mean, do you think it would upset him?" If Tim had been at home and bored, he might take it into his head to send such a telegram to a man he feared would get his job. It made sense.

17

"I'll phone Lilah and ask her when would be a good time," Carl offered, not smiling at all.

"Sure, if you think that would be best." He started to get up, not wanting to appear to be soliciting Carl's good opinion. "If anything clear turns up, I'll let you know."

"I'd appreciate that," Carl said, making no attempt to stop him. "You can check with me this afternoon and I'll tell you what Lilah said."

"Thanks." He started toward the door, then paused. "How much have you said to Harry about these . . . rumors?"

"About as much as I've said to you. Leave it alone, Ben. I've told Harry the same thing." He said it coldly.

Ben responded at once. "Right."

The next day coming back from lunch, Ben found a note tucked under his windshield wiper:

THE FAMILY OF BENEDICT TURNER
ARE GRIEVED TO ANNOUNCE
HIS UNTIMELY DEATH
ON THURSDAY, JUNE 21st

He was about to tear it up when he decided that he might need this as evidence. Handling it as if it had poison on it, he folded the paper three times and slipped it into his wallet. He was not quite certain what he planned to do with it, but he had a vague sense of strategy building up within him. Whoever it was that was doing this to him, he was not prepared to suffer the outrage in silence. He looked down the street, but all he saw was the metermaid puttering along in her little cart, pausing now to write a ticket. He wanted to run after her, to find out if she had seen anyone put the note on his windshield, but he could not bring himself to move, for that might require an explanation.

"Damn!" he whispered, as if any stronger word would lend an importance to the incident that he did want it to have. He walked back to the office in a thoughtful funk, not sure how best to proceed.

"I had a phone call this afternoon," Heather said during a commercial on the evening news. She had been fidgety since she got home but had not been willing to say why. "About half an hour before closing, there was a call at the library."

"Anything important?" Ben asked, not paying too much attention. He was still thinking about the hostage bargaining crisis that the last story had covered. It had been three minutes long. Three minutes, with eighteen lives at stake. He had never been bothered by that brevity until now.

Heather started to tell him, but the jingle for fast foods gave way to the crisp tones of the local newcaster and Ben waved Heather into silence for another twelve minutes while a possible new treatment for A.I.D.S. was speculated on — cautiously and technically by the researcher, more enthusiastically by the reporter; a multi-car collision on the largest local freeway was shown; there was a report on a hearing for a utilities increase; and the Fire Marshall discussed what hazards were to be watched for in the coming dry months of summer, with the reporter doing her best to make a sense of order out of the man's rambling discourse. "Now," Ben said while three handsome, rugged young men praised an imported beer, "what were you saying about a phone call?"

"Can you imagine another increase in the electric bill?" Heather said, her indignation making her cheeks redden.

"Was the phone call about that?" Ben asked, avoiding sarcasm by the barest margin.

Heather cleared her throat, becoming more subdued at once. "No. No it wasn't about that. It was . . . it was a condolence call."

Ben gave her his full attention for the first time. "A *what?*"

"You heard me," she snapped. "A man called and asked for me, and then said he was very sorry about your death. He wanted to know if he was to send flowers or a donation to a charity." She choked on the laugh she attempted.

"That's ridiculous," Ben said apprehensively. "Who'd do a thing like that?"

"The same person who sent you the telegram, perhaps?" she suggested, then flushed as he stared at her. "All right. I read it. You were so upset, well, what would you have done?"

Ben was about to upbraid her when a name on the news caught his ear.

"The suicide of Mister Hoopes was the result of depression following open heart surgery. His wife of twenty-three years, Lilah, discovered the body when she returned from shopping. The Haymarket Insurance Group has issued a request that all those clients dealing with Mister Hoopes contact company vice-president Carl Hurley at their earliest convenience, as the destruction of files in Mister Hoopes' possession was extensive and it appears that he deliberately destroyed many of the computer records before he took his life."

"Je-*sus!*" Ben burst out. "Did you hear *that?*"

"Yes," Heather answered. "That poor woman."

"Destroyed computer files and . . . he must have been in worse shape than anyone guessed." Secretly he thought that his several annoyances might now come to an end. It was tragic, but with Tim Hoopes dead, there would be no more notes, no more phone calls, no more telegrams. The worst was over and he could let himself feel pity for the man. "There's gonna be hell to pay at the office."

"What ever possessed him?" Heather wondered aloud, staring at Ben. "What made him do it?"

19

"Who knows?" Ben answered. "A man does all kinds of crazy things if he wants to kill himself. I guess you better call Lilah in a while, let her know that we're sorry." He cleared his throat. "Don't say anything about the pranks, though. It wouldn't be right to mention it."

Heather was silent for a moment, and when she spoke, it was with unusual reserve. "If that's what you want, Ben."

"Thanks," he said, his mind aleady on the problems they would face at the office with the files in disorder. "You're a good kid, honey."

INSURANCE EXECUTIVE KILLED IN CRASH

Benedict Turner, newly appointed vice-president of the Haymarket Insurance group, was one of four victims when a late-model Mercury collided with an ambulance near the emergency entrance to Southside General Hospital. Also pronounced dead were ambulance driver George D. Bellam, paramedic Kevin Chmura, and Evelyn Hayward . . .

Ben read the newspaper clipping and swore with more feeling than he had shown all through the exasperating morning.

"Something the matter, Mr. Turner?" his secretary asked as she put down a stack of files and peered at him over her glasses.

He forced himself to be calm. "Nothing. Nothing really. Someone with a ghoulish sense of humor and very bad taste," he said, attempting to laugh. "You know what some of our people can be like. Coming now . . . " He let her finish his thought for herself. "With Hoopes dead, and all."

"Very tragic," she said, shaking her head and clicking her tongue in disapproval.

Ben was about to throw the clipping away, when he read it over. It said that he was a vice-president of Haymarket Insurance Group, and that was not the case. It also said that there had been . . . would be an accident between an ambulance and a late model Mercury. His Cougar was three years old, and might still qualify for that description. "It's easy," he said to himself.

"What was that, Mister Turner?" Rosalind inquired, speaking more sharply. "I'm trying to get some order here, Mister Turner."

"Nothing, Rosalind. Just thinking out loud. Don't mind me." He smiled. Whoever was pulling these stunts had gone too far this time. It said that he would be killed outside the emergency entrance to Southside General. He already knew it was supposed to happen next Thursday. All he had to do was be somewhere else on Thursday and there would be no problem. He would even let Heather take his car to work, and that would take care of everything. He folded the clipping neatly and put it in his wallet with the note that had been left on his windshield.

"Do you want me to work overtime, Mister Turner?" Rosalind cut into his thoughts.

"Um?" He looked up with a start, then glanced at the clock. More than an hour had slipped away from him. "Oh. No, I don't think it will be necessary. I'll put in a couple hours tonight and that should give you enough to do tomorrow. Monday is no day to work late, Rosalind."

"All right, Mister Turner," she said prissily. "I imagine that you will want me in early tomorrow?"

He frowned. Obviously she had said something that he had not caught. "Yes, I suppose so, if you think you ought to."

"Very good, Mister Turner." She was already prepared to leave, slipping her summer-weight cardigan over her beige shirtwaist dress. "I hope it's good news."

This puzzled him even more, but he did not permit himself to question her. "So do I, Rosalind," he called after her. Why, he wondered, would he be driving near Southside General, anyway? There was always the remote chance that he would have to visit a client in the hospital, but he could think of no one who was ill or old enough to require an emergency visit. With a sigh he shrugged it off. Another time he would work it out, some time next week, or the week after.

"Hector Wyland called," Heather told Ben as he came in the door. "He would like you to call him back." She could not disguise the excitement she felt; Hector Wyland was the Chairman of the Board of the Haymarket Insurance Group.

"Wyland?" Ben asked, startled. "Did he say what he wants?"

"No. Of course not." She looked closely at him. "Do you know why he'd want to talk to you?"

Ben did not hear the suspicion in her voice, nor noticed the pointed way she watched him. "It's probably to do with Hoopes' files. It's a mess the way he left things." He smiled at her. "Fix me a drink, will you? I might as well get this over with."

Heather did as he told her, trying to decide how she would react to any bad news. She took her time in the kitchen, dawdling over the ice tray and impulsively setting out cheese and crackers, so that she would not have to listen to what Ben said to his boss. By the time she heard him put down the phone, she was ready to listen to him.

"Hey!" he beamed at her. "How did you know it was a celebration?" He pointed to the cheese and crackers.

"Oh . . . " She gave a flustered giggle. "Woman's intuition, I guess."

He took the drink from her and tasted it. "Great! Just great!"

21

She put the cheese and crackers on the coffee table. "And what are we celebrating?"

Ben swaggered the length of the living room. "We are celebrating my promotion. You, my darling wife, are looking at the new vice-president of Haymarket In . . . "

"Haymarket Insurance Group?" she finished for him when he broke off in some bewilderment.

His enthusiasm left him. "Yeah," he muttered, and took a long pull on the drink.

Heather was perplexed by this change in him, but she said, "Ben, that's just wonderful. You've wanted this for so long."

"Un-huh," he said, thinking of the clipping in his wallet, that had indentified him as the newly appointed vice-president of Haymarket Insurance Group. "I just didn't think it would be because of Tim Hoopes killing himself." The words sounded lame to him, but apparently they satisfied Heather, who came to his side and put her arm around him.

"You shouldn't feel that way, Ben. You've deserved promotion for a long time. It's very . . . sad about Tim Hoopes, but you had nothing to do with it, and you mustn't think of your advancement as some kind of grave-robbing." She patted him affectionately. "Come on. Have some cheese. And then let's think of a nice place to have dinner out."

His mouth was dry and there was a vaguely sick feeling south of his stomach, but he smiled at her. "Sounds great."

This time she was not fooled. "Are you all right?"

"Sure. A goose must have walked on my grave, is all." He drained his glass hoping that the alcohol would relieve the dread that had awakened within him.

Lunch the next day was a festive affair, with half the office accompanying Ben to the *Golden Calf* for their most sumptuous fare. Men who ordinarily had little to say to Ben now sought him out to offer effusive good wishes for his success; only a few were unable to conceal their envy of his promotion but they were wise enough to mask their jealousy in banter. Rosalind never moved more than six paces from him, simpering whenever he spoke to her.

When the meal was almost over, a waiter brought in a large bouquet of white mums and yew boughs, his expression sheepish. "They were delivered, Mister Turner," he told the gathering who stared at the funereal display.

"Must have been some kind of mistake at the florists. They probably thought it was because of Hoopes." Carl Hurley had started to reach for the card as he said this but Ben snatched it out of his hand.

IN SINCERE SYMPATHY said the silver-scrolled letters on the front of the card. Inside was a typewritten note. "In memory of Benedict Turner."

22

"Oh, shit," Ben whispered. It was not funny any more, he thought. It had been eerie at first, but this was definitely not amusing.

"It's a foul-up, Ben," Carl said, doing his best to smooth over the awkward moment. "I'll call the florist when we get back to the office; they'll straighten it out for you."

Ben waved this suggestion away. "No. Don't bother."

"But . . . " He cleared his throat. "They might have sent . . . a different arrangement to Lilah. I'd better find out what happened."

This met with a chagrined silence. Slowly Ben nodded. "Sure. It wouldn't be right for her to get . . . " He shrugged.

Most of the Baked Alaska went uneaten.

When Ben moaned in his sleep, Heather woke. She lay still, uncertain of what had disturbed her. She had almost drifted off when Ben cried out and turned over abruptly, no longer entirely asleep.

"It's a lie," he mumbled angrily.

"Ben?" Heather said, propping herself on her elbow so that she could watch him. "What is it?" CMLXVI

He did not answer her. His arms thrashed, catching the sheet and pulling the bedding into disorder. The muscles of his jaw worked and sweat ran down the side of his ear.

"Ben!" Heather was growing alarmed. Against her better judgment, she reached over and gave him a timid shake. "Wake up, Ben."

"What!" It was a shout and it startled them both. He shook his head and looked about wildly, as if expecting to see something frightening. "I thought I saw an ambulance coming," he said, as much to himself as to her.

"It was a dream, Ben." She wanted him to reassure her by agreeing, but he did not do this.

"God, I hope so. It was so real . . . I could have sworn that . . . Well, it didn't happen, did it?" At last he looked at her as if he knew where they were. "Sorry, honey. I didn't mean to upset you."

"But what was it?" She was becoming distressed, her fear magnified by the darkness and the late hour. Only emergencies happened at three-forty in the morning.

He attempted to chuckle. "A dream. That's all. I guess . . . I'm spooked by the new work. Probably I'm afraid that it will all go wrong." He knew that this was not a lie, and he did not want to explain more.

Heather touched his arm. "That isn't all of it."

He did not answer her. "It's late. Get some sleep. I'll be fine in the morning. Chalk it up to the extra brandy."

She was not placated, but she knew it was useless to insist. "All right. But if you're worried, I wish you'd talk to me about it."

23

"I'm not worried," he said, drawing the blankets up tp his chin in spite of the warmth of the night. "I'm fine." As he tried to relax, he decided that the first thing to do when he got to the office would be to get rid of those two scraps of paper in his wallet.

"We're having trouble with the branch office," Carl Hurley said to Ben on Thursday morning. "Are you willing to fly down this afternoon and have a talk with Bryant and his people, to find out what the trouble is?"

Ben almost leaped out of his chair in his hurry to accept the offer. "I'll call Heather at work and tell her I'll be gone tonight," he said, speaking so quickly that the words were slurred. "What time do you need me to leave?"

"There's a plane at two-thirty. That'll give you time to go home and put a few things in your bag and collect your shaving gear." He regarded Ben as he leaned back. "You know, I wasn't certain you were the right choice at first, but if you're going to be this dedicated, I know you'll work out for us."

"Thanks," Ben said, not quite sarcastically. "Do you need me any more this morning?"

"There's a meeting in fifteen minutes, but I don't think you have to sit in, not with a plane to catch." He extended his hand across his enormous desk. "Good to see you so active, Ben."

It was tempting to say that he would have accepted any assignment that would get him out of town, away from Southside General Hospital, before the hour on the most recent card, which he had found that morning inserted in his Rolodex. With any luck, he would be at the airport by one-forty-five, which was the time announced. "Well, I want the Board to be satisfied with my performance," he said as he took Carl's hand. "I want to get off on the right foot; you know how it is."

"Yes, I do." His smile remained fixed, full of good humor and completely without warmth. "Have a good flight. The tickets will be waiting for you at the airport."

"Great. I'll call you from Bryant's office?" It had been the usual procedure, but this time he knew it was proper to ask.

"When you've had a chance to evaluate the situation, yes. But use your initiative, Ben. You go in there and have a look around; you decide what has to be done, and then you report. If you manage this as well as you have other problems, we'll back you to the hilt. It shows us how you'll do when you're in charge." Carl finally made friendly movements with his hands, but Ben was not deceived: he was being tested and if he failed now, he would never rise one notch higher in Haymarket as long as he worked there.

"Thanks," he said, trying to keep from sounding irritated.

24

"My pleasure." The hands now indicated that Ben ought to leave the office. "Look forward to hearing from you."

Ben went through the departing ritual, his mind already racing, taking him away from the hazard that waited for him near Southside General Hospital. He went back to his office to pick up his briefcase and to take one last look at the card, which purported to be part of the autopsy results:

> . . . massive burns over the entire body, in some cases reducing the flesh completely and blackening bone. Identification was confirmed by dental charts. Benedict Turner died within seconds of the fatal collision when the double explosion from both gas tanks occurred . . .

Goddamn he was glad to be getting out of town.

At home, he called Heather at the library and gave her the news. "So there's nothing to worry about, honey."

"I guess you're right," she said, a bit of a shake in her voice. "You have a good trip. I'll expect a call tonight."

"You'll get it," he promised her, please to be able to do this for her, since she had been so good this last week. "You're great Heather. I want you to know that. I don't always say it, but it means a lot to me, the way you stick by me . . . You know."

Her chuckle was more than half sigh. "Thanks. I love you, too. It's good this is finally over."

"I'm sure it is," he agreed fervently. "It had me spooked there for a while. If I ever find out who did it to . . . "

When he did not elaborate, she said, "I almost forgot: Dave Wheeler from Valley called. He wants to talk to you."

"Why? Did he say?" It was rare for the competition to make personal calls.

"Only that it was fairly urgent." She hesitated. "I'll miss you. But you'd better call Wheeler and then get going. I heard on the radio there's a real traffic mess at the Fourth Street Bridge. Only one lane open westbound."

"Oh, shit. I'll leave right after I call Wheeler. See you in a day or so." He made a kissing noise at the receiver as he hung up and reached for his pocket directory.

"That you, Turner?" Dave Wheeler demanded when he came on the line.

"Yeah. What's the trouble, Dave?" He and recently tried to persuade one of Dave's clients to switch companies, but that was not so uncommon that it merited a phone call.

"Who's in charge of dirty tricks at your office, anyway?" he demanded without preamble.

25

"We don't do dirty tricks, Dave, and you know it," Ben answered, affronted.

"Well, someone sure as hell is trying to be funny, but I'm not amused. You find whoever it is who sent this damned clipping and you tell them that if I get any more of this crap, I'm going to talk to my lawyer." His voice had risen from an angry hush to a near shout.

"What are you talking about?" Ben asked, his voice faltering; he was afraid he knew. "What kind of clippings?"

"You *know* what kind — don't deny it!" Behind his anger there was panic. "*Obituary* clippings. For me." He paused. "It's not funny, not at all, and you better tell the joker over there that if anything like this happens again, I'm going to sue you for every cent in your company coffers. Got that?"

"But why tell me? Why not call Carl Hurley?" It was a sensible question, one he should have asked at first.

"Because I thought you and I had a little rapport. My mistake!" He slapped the receiver down and left Ben standing, listening to the dial tone.

For a minute he pondered what he ought to do — phone Carl, or his secretary? Call Dave back? A glance at his watch told him he did not have the luxury of time. He reached for his carry-on bag.

In the airport parking lot, Ben tripped and stumbled in his rush for the terminal. He swore at the pain that lanced up his leg with every step he took. "Must've sprained it," he said to the sky, determined to ignore it. He was almost inside the vast building when he collapsed.

He came to in the ambulance, the siren in his ears.

"Lie still, Mister Turner," said the young paramedic as Ben began to thrash. "We're almost to the hospital." There was a tag on his left breast pocket: K. CHMURA, it said.

"What?" Ben demanded, his voice rising. His mouth felt woolly.

"You've been given a sedative and a pain-killer. Your right leg is broken. It beats me how you were able to walk on it at all." He spoke soothingly.

"Where . . . ?" Ben cried out, trying to deny what he saw.

"At the airport. Do you remember that?" He smiled. "Ordinarily we'd take you to Mercy, there's a traffic tie-up in that direction. We're being sent to Southside General."

"*No!*" he screamed, straining at the belts that held him on the gurney.

"Mister Turner, relax. We're almost there," K. Chmura assured him.

"God, no. Nononono," Ben whispered. Not this way. He had assumed it was his car that had struck the ambulance; he never thought that he would be riding in it, a patient on his way to the emergency room for a stupidly broken leg.

"We'll call your office for you, and your wife," the paramedic assured him.

"Slow down. You've got to slow down." He was panting with fear but strove to be calm and steady.

"Don't worry, Mister Turner. This is one of the best ambulances built. Hell, George could take this thing on a grand prix course." He smiled at Ben. "We'll take good care of you, Mister Turner. Don't worry about it."

"Please slow down," Ben begged in a whisper.

"Almost there," the driver called out.

"Oh, God," Ben muttered as despair flooded through him.

From the front, the driver said, "Will you look at that?"

K. Chmura glanced over his shoulder. "What is it?"

"That crazy — "

"*NO!*" Ben shrieked.

" — broad must be going sixty mi — "

Depth of Focus

Just before they pulled the sheet over what was left of the body, Fawkes took another picture. "Thanks," he said to the whey-faced rookie cop at his elbow.

The cop nodded, his white-rimmed lips pressed tightly together, as if he did not dare to open his mouth.

Fawkes stepped back from the knot of men gathered in the dilapidated tool shed, and decided to get one more shot. The emotions they showed by their stances, the dinginess of the place, the wan light from the dusty, fly-specked window, was simply too tempting to pass up. He balanced himself properly, lifted his camera, setting the flash on the lowest possible brightness as he brought it up to his eye. One practiced squint through the viewfinder, and the shutter clicked.

"Damnit, Fawkes," the senior detective protested without emotion, though he made no other complaint. "Get out of here."

"On my way," Fawkes promised him with a wink, and sprinted out the door with a speed that was surprising in a man as stout as he was. He was chuckling as he went, proud of the photographs he had taken and confident that they would lead to yet another award. As he reached the street, he looked about with as much caution as he ever showed; two years before, he had been mugged coming from just such an assignment and had lost the film as well as the camera he carried and he had no desire to repeat the experience. He hurried to his dented old Volkswagen Thing, thinking as he always did that the roof needed replacement.

Traffic was light for early morning, though Fawkes reminded himself that he was going against the commute. In another thirty minutes, the roads would be jammed, but in the meantime, he was able to cover most of the twenty miles to the paper without dropping much below forty. He pulled into his usual — and "no parking" posted — spot near the building that housed the magazine portion of the operation, locked the one door that did lock, and jogged off toward the side entrance to the paper.

"Hi, Fawkes," the guard said as the photographer went through the lobby.

"Hi," he called back, forgetting the man's name for the hundredth time.

"Rhodes wants to see you," the guard called after Fawkes as he bolted for the elevator, hugging his camera bag affectionately.

"Tell him I'm on the way up," Fawkes shouted as the elevator doors opened.

Bernard Rhodes was waiting for Fawkes when he crossed the upper lobby. "I had a call half an hour ago," the managing editor informed Fawkes. "You were at the scene of the —"

"— Gershman killing," Fawkes finished for him. "That's right. I got there ten minutes after Detective Paige, and fifteen minutes before the meat wagon." He patted the scuffed leather bag. "I got it all in here. I want to give it to Patterson right away, so you can have a look at it."

"How bad is it?" Rhodes asked after a moment of hesitation.

"Pretty horrible," Fawkes answered merrily as he started away toward the photolab. "By the time I left, they still hadn't found the hands."

Rhodes followed him. "You have it all, you say?"

"Every bit of it. Paige told me to leave once they covered the . . . remains. Well, the shape it was in, you couldn't call it a body." He rapped on the closed door of the photolab. "Patterson! It's me."

"Just a minute," came the mournful voice from the other side of the door. "I've got some shots from the computer I'm finishing up."

"This is a rush," Fawkes insisted.

Rhodes, who had caught up with him, put a hand on his shoulder. "He'll get around to it, Fawkes. We don't go to press for another four hours and Collier hasn't done a story on the murder yet."

"I want to see it," Fawkes said impatiently. "I took the roll, I want to see what I got. If they're half as good as I think they are, I know that we'll have the best coverage of anyone. You wait and see, Rhodes." He grinned as the lean, stooped Patterson opened the door at last. "About time."

"Hand it over." Patterson held out his hand for the roll of film. "I'll call you as soon as it's ready." Without waiting for a comment, he closed the door again.

Fawkes stood quietly for a moment, then seemed to deflate. "I hate this part," he said conversationally. "It isn't just the waiting that bothers me, it's having nothing else to do. I mean, my work is done now, no matter what. I'm beginning to believe that I haven't accomplished anything." He laughed once.

"Some of the reporters say the same thing. And the editors can be worse." Rhodes paused. "Want some coffee?"

"I thought you were tied to your desk until the first afternoon edition rolls," Fawkes challenged him.

"It's a slow day. Aside from your story, we're going with vacation-blues fillers and a feature on the computers they use for movie special effects." He sighed. "That's bad, Fawkes. You don't know."

"Find a good accident and I'll give you something for the front page," Fawkes said at once as they went toward the staff cafeteria at the far end of the L-shaped hall.

"I'd almost think you're serious," Rhodes remarked.

"I am," Fawkes assured him, standing aside so that the other man would be first to enter the cafeteria.

"They've got something they insist is poached eggs on corned beef hash, but if I were you, I'd stick with the danish. It's full of sugar, but at least you know what you're getting." He picked up a tray, adding, "Have whatever you want, though. It's on the house."

"Great," Fawkes said, rubbing his hands together. "The danish sounds good, and those sausages aren't too bad." They went to the beginning of the line, so that Fawkes could select from everything available. The bored woman behind the counter shook her head at the quantity of food that Fawkes ordered, but she said nothing as she handed over two well-laden plates.

"Do you always eat like that?" Rhodes asked as they took a seat near the window.

"When I can." He poured cream into his coffee and patted his girth. "There aren't very many pleasures you can trust in this world, and food is the best of them. With food, you get something to show for it." As he said this, he spread butter and jam on half an English muffin.

Rhodes, who had a glass of orange juice, a cup of coffee and a small dish of grapefruit sections, picked at his food. "What about the health thing?"

"What about it? It's not as if I don't exercise. I run five miles a day and when you consider that I do it carrying me around the track, that means a real work-out. I don't smoke, and that stands for a lot. About all I do is eat and drink, which is what I want to do." He took a large bite of the muffin and chewed it energetically. "Listen," he said around his mouthful of food, "I don't want to be hassled because I'm heavy, I just want to get my work done. If you're satisfied with what I do, that's fine. If you're not, there are other places I can get hired. I got fourteen awards for my photos, and that translates into jobs if I need them."

Rhodes lifted his hands in protest. "Don't be silly, Fawkes. For heaven's sake, we appreciate you here." He hesitated, then asked, "Have you had any more offers recently?"

"Sure," Fawkes said as he finished the muffin. "Couple weeks ago, I had a letter

31

from one of the honchos at *Newsweek,* requesting an interview and saying that there were some assignments that they thought I'd be particularly good at. Very nice for the ego." He heaped up the sausages and started in on them.

"What did you tell them?" Rhodes asked apprehensively.

"That I was already busy, but that they should keep me in mind. It's what I tell everyone." He put his fork down and looked squarely at Rhodes. "If you're worried about my leaving, don't be. I've said it before; I like it here, I like my work, and you don't tie up all my photos, so I can make money on the side. That's a good deal."

"I'm glad you think so," Rhodes said, his voice lower than at first. "I was told by the publisher that the upgrading of the news was as much linked to your work as to the new investigative reporters. Mick Clayton said you're the best there is."

"What's this hand-holding all about, Rhodes?" Fawkes inquired, his small eyes widened and his face suddenly innocent.

"It's nothing," Rhodes said unconvincingly. He stirred his coffee for a moment. "You understand that there are times when the management gets a little concerned. They hear rumors and those rumors trouble them."

"You mean they've heard something about me?" He cut several of the sausages into neat sections and began to pop them into his mouth.

"A few things. Nothing specific." Now it was decidedly awkward between the two men, and Rhodes stared hard at the vending machines on the far side of the room.

"So what are the rumors?" Fawkes persisted.

"That you're holding out on us. That you've got a cache of your best pictures that you never let us see, and that you're negotiating with a publisher on the sale of a book of them." He said this in a rush, and when he was finished, he took his cup and drank most of the contents.

"Well," Fawkes said as he chewed, "part of it is true enough. There is a publisher interested in my work, and we are talking about a book, and there are photos that you guys haven't run that they may want to print, but the thing about holding out, that's ridiculous. Hell, I give my rolls of film to Patterson. If you think I'm holding out, you ask him. He develops the stuff."

Rhodes looked embarrassed. "There could be other rolls. You don't have to give Patterson everything."

"True," Fawkes agreed, taking the last of the sausages. "You know, I could even have a vault full of film that you don't know about, either, and I could be spending a lot of time down there in the vault, looking at pictures you never heard about." He had the last of his coffee and glared up at Rhodes. "Anything I got at home is framed and on my walls. You know what I've got there. You printed most of the ones I've taken in the last six years. So what's this crap about, really?"

"I want to assure the publisher that there is no reason to think that you might put us at a disadvantage. They're touchy about that, since the Shnyder business." He coughed once. "There were hard feelings about that one."

"What do you mean, were? If you're putting me through this, someone with wood-paneled walls is holding a grudge." He started in on his food again, but with less enthusiasm than before. "Look, you tell whoever sent you that I am not going to cheat the paper, that I am not going to do anything that would cause you embarrassment or other trouble, and that if there is a book, it won't hurt you at all. And tell whatever bastard it is that he's paranoid, will you?"

Rhodes nodded. "I told him we didn't have to worry."

"Sure," Fawkes agreed with a complete lack of sincerity.

"I did," Rhodes insisted with more feeling. "You may not believe it, but I am concerned for this paper, and I don't want to see anything wreck it."

"Good for you."

"You're an asset to us; I admit that right up front." He wiped his mouth with one end of his soggy paper napkin. "I've done everything I can to keep the quality up around here. Losing you would lower the quality. Does that make any sense to you?"

"Yep. More than some of the other crap you've been shoveling me." Fawkes was genial enough, and he managed a cold smile, but there was no conviction in his words and his eyes were like chips of stone.

Rhodes looked at Fawkes a moment. "What does it matter to you?"

"Oh, I like getting my pictures. I like the awards. I'm good at what I do. Shit, I'm one of the best, and you know it, or you wouldn't be here right now buying me breakfast and trying to pump me for information."

"Isn't there anything more?" Rhodes was studying Fawkes' face in a way that the photographer found disconcerting.

"Why should there be more?"

"Are you trying to make a point? Is there something you want to say about the things you photograph?"

"You mean the way that Stathmore does? I'm no preacher." He smiled a little. "Look, the trick of taking my kind of pictures is to keep your distance, you know what I mean? It's not just for the camera, but for your head. You let yourself get sucked into it, and you lose it all." He got up and went back into the service area for a half a cantaloupe and another cup of coffee.

Rhodes was standing when Fawkes got back. "That's too bad, what you told me, Fawkes. I know it's better for the paper this way, if you think it is, but I can't help feeling sorry for you."

"A man in my position doesn't need pity, Rhodes. Or favors. Or breakfast courtship, either. Thanks anyway." He sat down, grinning as Rhodes turned and walked out of the cafeteria.

Two other reporters had come in a few minutes before and had made a point of not being curious about what Fawkes and Rhodes were discussing, but now they glanced toward Fawkes, and one of them lifted a cup of tea — the string from the bag trailed over the lip of his cup — in a silent and ironic toast.

Fawkes gave a huge shrug and dug his spoon into the cantaloupe.

Patterson showed him the glossies shortly before noon. "The images are nice and sharp except the edge of the sheet. I can have the art department fix that up, if you like."

Fawkes hated the airbrushing and retouching that went on, but he made a pretense of considering it before saying, "Do you think it needs it? You can see everything that's important to see."

Patterson looked at the hideous mutilations of the little corpse. "In a case like this, could be that you see too much."

"What's the matter, Patterson? You getting squeamish in your old age? This thing is going to make papers all over the country and you know damn well the bosses will be happy as whores with a convention in town."

Patterson said nothing for a moment. Silently he held up another, less gruesome picture from the roll Fawkes had given him.

"Sure, it's a little prettier," Fawkes said. "The depth of focus is better, but you don't see as much. About the only bad thing is that hand with the fingers chopped off, and that's nothing." He folded his arms over his bulk. "You have any questions about this, refer 'em to Rhodes." It gave him a malign pleasure to dump such a decision in the managing editor's lap.

"Who's covering the story?" Patterson asked.

"Rhodes'll tell you," Fawkes said, then started toward the door, feeling a burst of irritation that troubled him. "I'm going to see what else they need. If they don't need anything, I'm going to knock off for an hour or two."

"Why tell me?" Patterson inquired reasonably.

"Why not? You listen." He slammed out of the processing room and stomped off down the hall. His face was set, he returned no greeting. When a copyboy accidentally brushed his arm, Fawkes swung around in a rage. "You stupid — I ought to —"

The copyboy, a thin, gangly youth of nineteen, paled at this outburst and stepped back so fast that he hit the wall. "I'm . . . I'm sorry, Mister Fawkes."

"You're a clumsy shithead," Fawkes corrected him. "Got that?"

"Uh —"

"And you can report that to anyone you like. Just fuck off!"

Needing nothing more, the copyboy bolted.

"A prince of a fella," Morrano said from his vantage point by the copymachines. "Why pick on Sammy?"

"Shut up, Morrano." He had no intention of being drawn into an argument. "Anything for me?"

"Not at the moment. Wait around for ten minutes and then talk to Gateman. He might have something." Morrano returned his attention to the flickering green display. "A bad day in Lebanon."

"Wish I could be there," Fawkes said, much of his anger evaporating. "I miss being on war assignment."

"You're kidding," Morrano said absently as he moved paragraphs around on the screen.

"No," Fawkes said quietly.

It was a moment before Morrano spoke; his fingers continued to move and the words shifted before his eyes. "You made your reputation covering wars, didn't you? That should be enough for you."

"I miss it," Fawkes whispered, and went away from Morrano's desk. There was a coffee machine in the foyer by the elevator, and he got two cups of the silty stuff, adding extra cream and sugar to disguise the taste.

Tessling found him there a little later and pounced on him. "Why didn't you answer the page? I've been looking all over for you."

"What's the trouble?" Fawkes asked, his interest kindled by the distracted look in the other man's eyes.

"There's a bank holdup." Tessling took a deep breath. "The cops got there while it was in progress, and there's a hostage situation now. There are at least fifteen people in the bank with the robbers, and there are cops all over the outside."

"Un-huh," Fawkes grunted, encouraging Tessling.

"No demands, but some of the guys who got out said that a couple of the hostages are wounded, and that makes it a lot hairier."

"True," Fawkes said. He took a last sip of his vile coffee and tossed the paper cup into a large trash container.

"Can you get over there? You'll probably miss lunch, but I want you there if anything happens."

"Why? The TV stations will be all over it." He could not resist this, needing to hear what he knew Tessling must say.

"No one gets pictures like you do, and those cameramen are the worst. You go get us shots like the ones you got during the waste-disposal scandal. We'll be the strongest source going, if you'll produce."

"You're a greedy bastard, Tessling," Fawkes said as close as he ever came to being friendly. "I'll get on it right away." He grabbed two of his cameras and pulled his jacket out of the cloakroom, then bolted for the elevator. The address he had been given was halfway across the city, and it would take more than fifteen minutes to get there. He wadded up the parking ticket he found under his wiperblade and tossed it away as he climbed into his car.

He arrived near the bank in a shade over seventeen minutes, and by then most of the parking was occupied. Three huge TV news vans clustered around the blocked intersection, as if protecting the seven squad cars near the entrance to the bank.

Fawkes found a space in an alley two blocks away. He put his press permit in the window, then hurried away toward the bank, holding up his ID whenever a cop attempted to keep him back. A few of them knew him and waved him on as they saw him coming.

"Who's covering the story?" asked one of the newswomen as Fawkes trudged past her van.

"I don't know," he answered, then looked at her. "Anything happening?"

"Not yet. They're trying to get the hostage negotiating team inside, but no luck so far."

"How many robbers?" It was more a reporter's question than a photographer's, but he had learned long ago that the more information he had, the better pictures he got.

"Some say eight, some say nine. They're very well organized. One of the customers said he thinks that they're cops or military types. They're very cool, whoever they are." She sighed. "I'm going to have to work out an angle for the noon news. There's not a lot to say."

"Tough," Fawkes said. "See you around." He waved as he pushed closer to the front of the bank. There were more cops now, and a knot of civilians, and a couple of ambulances standing by. Automatically Fawkes lifted his camera to take pictures. He considered these his warm-up shots, but occasionally one or two turned out to be worthwhile.

"Hey, Fawkes, stop it," the ranking police captain protested as he caught sight of the camera.

"Freedom of the press and up yours, Haig," Fawkes replied cheerfully. He kept on taking pictures.

A few minutes later he felt a tap on his shoulder and turned to find Gene Stathmore beside him. "Hello, Fawkes," the reporter said with a hint of distaste. "Any new developments?"

"Don't ask me, ask Haig. "He's in charge here." He pointed out the man in the rumpled raincoat. "You know him?"

"We've met," Stathmore said. "Are they giving a briefing?"

"Not that I know of. I just take pictures, remember?" He enjoyed needling the younger man.

"All right; I'll talk to Haig." He forced Fawkes to move aside as he approached the police. Fawkes chuckled.

For the next twenty minutes or so, Fawkes strolled around the front of the bank, taking occasional pictures and eavesdropping on conversations. He was fairly certain that the cops would take no direct action for at least an hour, and so he took a chance and hurried off to the nearest cafe to buy a sandwich while he had the opportunity. By the time he trotted back to the bank, another ambulance had arrived and two more of the hostage negotiators were huddling with Haig.

"Where were you?" Stathmore demanded as he came up to Fawkes.

"Lunch," Fawkes answered.

"God, how can you eat while something like this is going on?" He made a short, impatient gesture as he glowered at Fawkes.

"I get hungry. I don't work well when I'm hungry." He started humming as he once again strolled by the front of the bank. There were fewer lights on inside, he noticed, and could not help but admire the good sense the robbers showed. He checked his flash attachment, just in case he needed it later.

"Get out of there, Fawkes," Haig called out to him. "That's too close."

Fawkes took a picture. "All right, Haig," he said, and fell back a good twenty feet, between the squad cars and the TV vans.

An hour went by. A cold wind sprang up, whipped through the tense group, then died. At a safe distance pedestrians gathered, moving on reluctantly when ordered to do so by the cops. In the office buildings around the bank, faces pressed against the windows and people waited for anything that might change on the street below.

"The leader is a man called Ross," one of the civilians told the head of the hostage negotiating team. Fawkes was standing near enough to listen.

"First or last name?" the cop asked.

"I don't know. That's all I heard." The man looked exhausted and unhappy. "I only heard it once."

"You're sure it was Ross?" the negotiator persisted.

"Pretty sure. Like I said, it was just the once." He rubbed his face with his hands. "Sorry. My wife's still in there and you know . . ."

The cop nodded grimly. He patted the man's arm in an attempt at reassurance, then turned his attention to the other men on his team. "One name isn't much to go on," he began, and the others muttered agreement.

Fawkes lost interest and began to look around for other material. Nothing caught his attention and he decided to get another sandwich. He was almost beyond the vans when he heard the distinct sound of gunfire from inside the bank. He pivoted immediately, lifting his camera as he ran, and in the next instant was rewarded with two good shots of a mortally wounded man staggering out the massive glass doors. He tried for a third shot, but the heads of running cops got in his way. He cursed as he attempted to get nearer.

"Step aside, step aside!" one of the cops was yelling as they tried to clear a path for the ambulance attendants and their stretcher.

"Everyone keep back!" came the bellowed order from inside the bank. "You get any nearer and we'll shoot one of the others. We don't have anything to lose now!"

All the men converging on the fallen figure stopped as if held by invisible strings.

"That's better!" the voice shouted. "We'll let you know when you can come closer."

"But the man is bleeding!" Haig yelled back. "At least let us get him out of there!"

"No way," the robber answered. "I don't want you storming this place during a pretended rescue." There was a pause. "Remember that we've got more in here. We have enough ammunition to hold you off for a week, if necessary." The voice was precise and cold, as if the man speaking were reading statistics. "If you try anything stupid, we will start executing the hostages."

"We understand," Haig shouted, his tone more worried than before.

"Don't forget it," the robber called back, and refused to answer when first Haig and then the senior negotiator attempted to keep him talking.

"Was that Ross?" the negotiator asked the man he had been speaking to.

The man stood, his horrified eyes on the body lying in the door of the bank. "I . . . I don't know."

Fawkes moved in a little closer and took three extra shots of the dying man. He would have taken more, but one of the cops ordered him to move back and he knew it was best to comply. He wanted to be around at the finish.

The afternoon dragged on; one of the TV vans left and was replaced by another crew, another squad car brought the best of the marksmen with their sniper's rifles. Fawkes got another couple of shots of the men moving into place, and then he took time off to call in.

"We'll send someone over for your film and will drop some more rolls off with you," Rhodes said. "I'm going to be here a while, if you have anything to tell us. Is Stathmore around?"

"I saw him talking to Haig earlier. I don't know where he is now." He wanted to complain about being assigned the same story as Stathmore — he had an abiding dislike of crusaders — but he held off, in case he had more serious pressures later on. "I'll check in later."

"Make sure you do. You need a back-up?"

"Can't think why," Fawkes said. "I don't mind staying up all night, not for something like this."

"Great. We're running that second photo on page one. Just thought you'd like to know," Rhodes remarked.

"What do you mean, the second photo?" Fawkes demanded. "You mean the one with just the hand, not the whole body?"

"That's the one," Rhodes said with a certain bravado. "Better focus than the first one."

"Bullshit," Fawkes countered. "What's the matter, the guys with the paneling get scared of a little gore?"

"Now, Fawkes —"

"Don't pull that on me, Bernard," Fawkes warned him. "Your bosses got worried that some little old lady would puke if she saw that body, isn't that right? And you went along with it because you thought you didn't want to disturb any of the advertisers. What gutless wonders you all are." He was about to hang up, but added, "I got some shots of a guy dying in the doorway of the bank. You want to see them, or should I just take the film out and expose it to save you the trouble?"

Rhodes sighed. "Fawkes, don't be like this."

"How the hell should I be? Oh, thank you mighty editor for castrating my best work." He could feel heat mount in his face. "What the fuck is wrong with you? Do you want strong pictures or don't you?"

"Well, there are limits in a daily paper, Fawkes," Rhodes said cautiously. "It's not as if we don't have to answer to the community."

"You always say that when you want an out. When you don't want it, you talk about freedom of information and the obligation of the press to provide complete information, no matter how distressing. Okay. You're sucking up to the money boys this week. I'll keep that in mind." He was about to put the phone down when Rhodes managed to get one more word in.

"Fawkes, don't take any chances. From what we've heard, this could get nasty real fast."

"Glad to hear it. I've been bored out of my skull for the last three hours." He made a rude noise and hung up.

By midnight the stand-off at the bank had settled into a steady hostility that rubbed off on everyone waiting outside the building. Cops were surly now, and the TV crews were so impatient that they asked the hostage negotiators to make some kind of move before they had to knock it off for the night. A few of them were angry for missing their eleven o'clock telecasts.

"Why don't you go home?" Haig said to Fawkes as the photographer ambled up to him.

"Nothing to go home to. I might as well stick around here." He cocked his head at Haig. "What do you think? You think they're going to let their hostages out, or is this going to turn into a massacre?"

"You'd prefer the massacre, wouldn't you?" Haig challenged without answering his question.

"Better photos that way, but there's lots of human interest when you get them out alive." He braced one heel on the bumper of the nearest black-and-white, and leaned back against the end of the hood. "Isn't there something special about twenty-four hours? Don't the hostages start helping their captors after that time?"

"It can happen that way," Haig growled. "Leave questions like that to your reporter, Fawkes."

"What? You think old Stathmore has any idea about hostage syndrome? He's

39

too busy looking for the injustices that caused the problem in the first place. You wait: as soon as they know who the robbers are, the Preacher will start defending them and blaming the hostages."

"Don't you care either way?" Haig asked, his big shoulders drooping and his voice raspy with fatigue.

"Just so long as I get good pictures, I stay away from the rest. It doesn't pay to get too close." He winked.

"Didn't anything ever bother you?" Haig inquired.

For once Fawkes thought about it. "Yeah. When I was starting out. I was doing a spread for a news magazine on Biafra. You remember the famine there, and the war?" He nodded along with Haig. "That was something to cover. All those people, especially the kids. They had bellies like watermelons and eyes that Walter Keene would trade his mother for. They were hard to take. Most of the film I shot was shit. Worst job I ever did. It taught me something."

"You think so?" Haig reached into his pocket and pulled out a packet of cigarettes.

"Thought you gave those up," Fawkes said, needling him.

"So did I, but after a day like this, well . . ." He lit a match and held it to the cigarette. "You want one?"

"No, thanks. I could sure as hell use a drink, though." He patted his camera and glanced toward the bank. "When this is over, I'm going to spend the whole day getting sloshed."

"Whatever makes you happy," Haig said, and turned away from Fawkes.

The photographer did not take this personally. He had noticed how edgy the cops were getting, and he could not blame them. It always looked bad when one of these hostage situations went on for long. He had heard the mayor's appeal on the news, which had made him laugh — as if a robber gave a damn about the people of the city — and he had kept track of the various squad cars that had arrived in the last several hours, noting the importance of the passengers, from the District Attorney to the Police Commissioner. He had been able to get pictures of both those men, but he had missed the Lieutenant Governor.

By three in the morning, Fawkes was dozing in the passenger seat of the only remaining TV news van. It was an independent station and devoted far more time to local stories than the network affiliates did.

"What do you think?" the driver asked. He was a young, fresh-faced kid, no more than a year out of college by the look of him.

Fawkes did not answer at once; his brain was muzzy and his tongue felt as if there were a coat of asphalt on it. "They got to do something quick. The negotiators will get maybe one or two more goes at the guys inside, and then someone, it doesn't matter who, is going to start shooting, which'll give the macho cops an excuse to storm the place."

"But won't the hostages get killed?" There was an edge to his voice, as if he wanted to appear inured to the possibility; he only succeeded in sounding appalled.

"Sure they will. Like that poor fucker lying there in the doorway. And afterward, everyone will blame everyone else and say that there was no choice when what they'll mean was they were under pressure and couldn't think of anything else to do." He folded his arms. "Wait till you've been around a while. Give yourself five years, and see it happen a couple of times. You'll get to know the pattern."

The driver shook his head, still new enough to his business to be shocked. "I hope you're wrong."

"Think of the story, kid. That's the only way. Otherwise you'll blow your brains out before you're thirty." He gave a thumbs-up sign and tried to find a more comfortable position to rest his bulk on the seat.

But the kid persisted. "When do you think they'll try something?"

"Gotta be before the morning commuters come in. Give it two hours at the most. They'll want this cleared up by six."

"Because of the *commuters?*" the kid demanded in amazement.

"Why not?" He yawned thoroughly enough to get the kid to leave him alone, and tried to doze for a couple of hours, rousing himself about four-thirty.

"Nothing's changed," the young driver said as Fawkes turned toward him. "There's an all-night cafe three blocks away. Do you want some coffee?"

"I'll walk over myself," Fawkes said, rubbing his face and feeling stubble. "I need to wake up." He started to open the door, then paused. "Any announcements? Anyone saying anything?"

"Just that the hostages were still in pretty good shape, but there're a few of the cops who have been talking about moving the snipers in closer to get a better chance at the robbers." He clenched his jaw. "How did you know?"

"Seen it too many times," Fawkes reminded him. "That means about half an hour. I should be able to get a bite to eat, too." He gathered up his camera bag and slid out of the van. "Thanks, kid. I'll do the same for you some time." He did not wait to hear any answer the young man might come up with, but walked away quickly, forcing himself to a vigorous stride. He felt his body come reluctantly awake, and he grinned. They could say what they liked — he knew that his extra pounds provided reserves of energy that the others only dreamed of, and that pleased him.

The waitress — middle-thirties, desperately plain — looked at him askance, but brought him the omelette and doughnuts he ordered, along with two cups of coffee and extra cream. She made no attempt to engage him in conversation, and when he left, she sneered at the tip he gave her, though it was generous enough.

When he reached the van once again, the head of the SWAT team was deep in conference with the head of the hostage negotiating team. Both men had that determinedly reasonable expression which indicated a very serious dispute was

41

going on. Fawkes edged nearer, hoping he might be able to get a photo of the two men.

"I wouldn't," a voice said at his shoulder.

"Haig." Fawkes lowered the camera. "I didn't know you were back."

"I got here about half an hour ago. It's tenser by the minute." He stared at the body in front of the bank door. "They have to get that guy out of the way first. It's driving everyone nuts."

"I can see why," Fawkes said. "Do you think the SWAT team will get in there?"

"What makes you think they'll try?" Haig asked, but it was clear that they both knew the answer, and he did not continue the pretense. "All right — I guess it's what the brass wants, and what the media will tolerate, so . . . Oh, what the —" This last was in response to a sudden outburst from the leader of the hostage negotiators.

"The machos are winning," Fawkes said, not entirely disappointed. "I guess we'll be getting some action pretty soon."

"You're a ghoul, Fawkes. You know that?" Haig said with a weary half-smile. "All you media people are."

"Just doing our jobs, Haig. Like the cops who're going to go in there with guns blazing and blood everywhere." He fell into step beside Haig.

"Which you'll take pictures of for the evening edition," Haig sighed.

"Sure." He stood aside so that the leader of the SWAT team could speak to Haig. He was able to get three pictures of this hurried conference before Haig motioned him to stop. "Okay."

For the next ten minutes there was a steady and secretive increase in activity around the squad cars. Haig took the hostage negotiating team aside and held an urgent conversation with them that ended in a flurry of angry words as the leader signaled his men to leave with him.

Fawkes strolled around the cops, holding his camera where they could see it and making no effort to take any more photos for the time being. He checked his film supply and was satisfied that he could get through the next couple hours without calling the paper for more. He found three good locations to cover the door of the bank and one good one to get shots of the police in action. That done, he wandered back to the van and tapped on the window. "Hey, kid."

The young man stared out at Fawkes. "What?"

"Better get ready. And call the station to get the rest of the news crew over here. There's about twenty minutes to go before the show starts."

The driver swallowed hard and nodded. "Thanks."

"Any time," Fawkes replied and went back to the best location for pictures of the assault.

There were another series of huddles, and then the cops repositioned the squad cars. Beyond range of fire and vision, two more ambulances pulled up, and the paramedics readied themselves for what was to come.

"How much longer?" Fawkes asked Haig, and received an obscene gesture for an answer.

A few minutes later Stathmore, his hair still wet and his chin bleeding from the razor's nick, hurried up to him. "I had a call. What's going on?"

"They're about to storm the place," Fawkes told him. "You better get a good place to watch. Haig's been moving people back, but now that all the TV news hacks are back, he can't do much about all us media types."

"I thought they were going to negotiate," Stathmore protested.

"They tried it and it didn't work. Now they're going to play O-K Corral and the best man win." He made a last check of his camera.

"This is terrible!" Stathmore announced to the air around him.

"Put it in your column. Right now you have work to do." Fawkes looked at the reporter. "The trouble with you, Preacher, is you forget what the news is — the news. It's not our job to discuss but to inform. Anything else is editorializing, and that isn't what they pay you to do." He coughed, noticing for the first time that his throat was a little raw.

"God, I hate creeps like you, Fawkes," Stathmore murmured, and deliberately walked away.

Fawkes shrugged and braced his forearm on the roof of the squad car.

The rush came suddenly, some five minutes later. First there was almost no movement and then there was a fan of black-clad cops closing in on the building. On a signal, tear-gas cannisters were lobbed through the window, and those of the attack force wearing gas masks rushed the door.

Machine guns spattered; two of the cops fell, one of them screaming, the other silent. Three more took their places in the formation and the drive continued. The first officer was through the door when Fawkes had to replace his roll of film, and then he had to change the batteries on his flash unit. Cursing, he worked quickly while the sound of firing increased. Drifting tear-gas made his eyes water and held some of the TV crews at bay.

Then all the fighting moved indoors. Firing increased, sounding eerily distant yet enormous, magnified and muffled by the bank's marble lobby. Squad car radios chattered and squawked. Another cop staggered out of the bank, the side of his head shiny with blood.

Then it was over and activity erupted in the men gathered around the squad cars. Paramedics rushed forward, uniformed cops swarmed into the building and the grisly business of bringing out the wounded and dead began.

Fawkes moved in for a better view.

Cops and hostages were brought out first, many of them wounded. The hostages were dazed and disoriented. Four of them had been badly hurt and were rushed away in ambulances. The others were directed to squad cars. Fawkes got it all on film.

Finally the robbers were brought out. There were eight of them, and most of them were on stretchers.

"Mind if I get their faces?" Fawkes asked Haig as he caught sight of the captain standing not far away.

"Suit yourself," Haig answered before trying to learn from an hysterical middle-aged priest who should be called.

Three of the robbers refused to be photographed; the others were unconscious or dead, and the attendants did not make any objections once they saw Fawkes' press pass.

The next-to-last stretcher out was flanked by cops. "It's Russ, the leader," one of them explained to Fawkes when he stopped them.

"Can I get a shot of him?" Fawkes asked, trying not to be too eager.

The older cop hitched his shoulder and signaled the attendants to stand aside.

Eagerly Fawkes went to work. The man — Ross or Russ? — had been shot at least three times, and the damage was massive. His left arm had been blown away at the shoulder, his hip was shattered and his right knee was nothing but pulp. "Lift the sheet, can you?" Fawkes said to the attendants.

"It's pretty bad," one of them said unnecessarily.

"Just lift the sucker, will you?" Fawkes said, coming a little closer.

"Go ahead," the older cop growled.

Fawkes lifted his camera and bent forward.

A hand sticky with blood, rigid with shock, closed on his wrist.

"Jesus Christ!" one of the attendants cried out, and the other reached to pry the fingers loose.

Fawkes doubled over, his camera falling from his hands. He was afraid that he was going to vomit.

The blood-dappled face was only inches away. A thread of a voice spoke in his ear. "Bast . . . help. . . ."

Then Fawkes was free and the stretcher was rushed away, cops flanking it and TV cameras following it through the squad cars.

Fawkes sat alone on the pavement, his camera lying beside him. He was staring at his wrist and hand, at the smears of blood that seemed to burn into his skin. It was all too real, too immediate, too inescapable. It would never leave him, he knew, that hand. He would never again lift a camera without those ephemeral fingers on his wrist.

When Haig came and tapped him on the shoulder, Fawkes gathered up his camera and got to his feet.

"Had a bad moment there, didn't you?"

For once, Fawkes could not bring himself to answer.

Space/Time Arabesque

contortions
beloved

Someone
Please Help
me   ‡ ‡‡   LOVE

With ponderous speed the stagecoach lumbered over the dusty plain pursued by the painted, be-feathered hostiles.

"Why the hell couldn't it've been Indians?" complained the shotgun rider as he poured lead into the howling mob behind them. Bullets had proven ineffective and it wasn't easy melting down his ammunition in a frying pan atop a wildly careening coach. It was not a good day for the shotgunner.

"Giddap!" yelled the driver as he snaked his whip over the ears of the horses. The horde at their back was drawing nearer and looking uglier — and weirder — all the time.

"Crevass ahead," warned the shotgunner, who had pulled up splinters from the roof and was seeing what he could do with improvised flaming arrows. Aside from setting the coach afire, not much.

A creature remarkably like a spoon-billed dinosaur regarded the coach with dim curiosity as it rattled past.

The driver stoically ignored it, tugging heartily on the reins, tettering the wheels precariously over the brink, jarred back to safety. In the stage's gritty wake, unheeding, the savages went down the yawning maw of the canyon wall, and just as unheedingly up the other side.

"Consarn it!" The shotgunner stomped on his hat as he scowled at the bounding backs of their tormentors. "I thought we had 'em for fair that time."

45

"Not today." The driver knew what he was talking about. Any day that featured fissures like the one that had gaped beneath them as the last one had, bands of whooping tripedal horrors; well, those days you just didn't get ahead. What was more, he was over three hours late and heaven only knew where — and it was certain that Wells Fargo didn't. The last time he'd looked the sun was happily setting into the south.

"We're on again," sighed the shotgunner, and added with a lonesome note, "It ain't Indians, but at least it ain't them things," and he pointed toward the far rim of the canyon where the multicolord aliens undulated to wheetles and tweeps played on their own filagreed snouts.

Wearily the driver urged his horses on to the south-setting sun.

Amid the stiff sighs of brocades and ruff, Sir Walter Raleigh bent his knee to the Queen's Grace and presumed upon their long acquaintance with the invitation, an she cared to blow a joint.

"God's Teeth! Hath stashed some?"

He led her into the galliard, leaning slightly toward her when the movements of the dance allowed. "I'll not reveal what thou'lt not share."

She considered this, missing one step and rapping him with her fan for her error. "Let us draw aside some little while, my smiling privateer, and have some talk of this."

With a gracious inclining of his head in what might be a bow, Sir Walter followed the Queen's Grace off the floor. The sweet music of Thomas Tallis floated after them.

"Now," she declared as they stepped into an alcove as she gave her farthingale an expert twitch to assure their privacy. "Prithee vouchsafe me this intelligence. Where be the stuff? I charge thee on thy honor and for the love you bear my Crown to make this known to me."

It was dangerous to play with Good Queen Bess when she got short-tempered, but Sir Walter was ever a bold man. "But say the word that will take us from this place and the secret is thine, good Queen." He grew even more audacious. "Sweet lady, heartless lady."

She showed the beginnings of a murderous frown. "Well do I know the worst of your reputation, else I'll have thought that you do not love me."

"But listen," he said quickly, changing tactics. "E'en now I have it hard by me and were you but to slip away with me, we could to the *Hinde* whiles Drake is off a-wenching and disport ourselves otherwise."

Her shrewd eyes widened a bit as she struggled with her cravings and her position. "Stay awhile," she said at last, in a voice full of cajolery. "On what pretext do I leave me court?" From shrill to shukiness: "An I leave this room, t'will be a rare uproar. How's to succeed?"

46

"Do but command it, and it must be as you wish. Who," he wheedled gently, "mine radient lady liege Glorianna, be Queen here? There's pleasure for you waiting if you but give me the word. All of the weed I brought with me is thine at the asking. And thou know'st it brings so sweet waking dreams." His eyes grew bright and his idle gloveless hand made bold to finger her great sleeve.

A beautific smile spread over her rather pointed features. She extended her arm in a sweeping gesture that encompassed the entire gathering. "Off with their heads," she commanded serenely.

The study was completely draped in pink silk. The walls, the chairs, the curtains that shut out the bright Vienna afternoon, all was pink silk. For that matter, the body of Richard Wagner was also covered in pink silk. Pink silk was his favorite.

Reluctantly he wrenched his mind from the luxurious pageant of his sumptuous daydreams to his dear hatchet-faced Cosima. There were grim realities to be dealt with. Ah, the tragedy that genius should have to deal with realities. His friends had had the effrontery to refuse to lend him any more money. So far no one had offered to produce this latest opera and he was becoming more broke than usual. And the other day the mercer had demanded at least partial payment on the silk.

Wagner rose and paced the room, humming furiously off-key to himself, his Rembrandt jacket of blue velvet sliding over the pink silk. How unfortunate that this picture must be denied to the world. Finally he sank artistically and unhappily onto the pink ottoman with a towering sigh.

There was nothing for it: he would have to sell his patent on the electric tuba.

The receptionist had the finest nose a plastic surgeon could make — pert, pretty, and almost natural enough to be real. She was the best advertisement her boss had ever had, and she looked at the tattered, bandaged man who smelled of turpentine.

"Your first appointment, sir?" she asked in her best professional voice, knowing it was and doing her best to impress him.

"Yes, it is." His speech was mildly accented.

"You'll find the doctor can work wonders," she announced, wondering what wonders the strange man required. "Now, sir . . .may I have your name please?"

"It's Van Gogh. G-o-g-h."

In a laboratory that exists to take care of this sort of thing, a young assistant fumbled with panic-stricken digits. He had meant no harm, he had been careful; and it was such a little, new, unimportant world. He thought that a few things might not upset it. But he was wrong. It was so delicate. He twiddled the knobs again.

The discrepancy might not be noticed and he would be safe. But if it was, he would be out of the program forever, a serious threat to an immortal. No one had told him that the balance on the tiny worlds was so blasted precise — why, anything could throw it off.

But he was relieved. Just one or two minor adjustments would put it all to rights and no one the wiser. Everything would be fine as soon as he lined up *that* impulse with *that* graph.

The fatherly man with the shiny head looked unhappily at the dignified Frenchman and quiet Oriental gentleman who stood with him beside the gigantic map. His hand rested on a flagged pin tagged Saigon.

"I really am sorry," he said, and he really was, "but you must see that I can't commit this country to a course that might lead to armed conflict somewhere other than our own continent. Korea proved that."

The Frenchman looked at the Oriental and the Oriental looked at the Frenchman. The Frenchman raised his brows. "It wouldn't have to be a *real* war," he said.

"Oh, don't worry," the fatherly man said reassuringly, showing them his famous fatherly smile. "I'm sure there are countries willing to take you on. Have you considered asking Pakistan?"

The trouble with crime, reflected the man in the alley, was it's fascination. There was a pure, dreamlike intoxication to it, a passion that possessed the intellect as well as the baser parts of men. He toyed with the long surgical knife hidden in the folds of his ample cape. Ah, the shine of it was hypnotic. It was so pristine, so neat. It was almost a shame to ruin it. Blood, after all, was a messy business. But there it was. He signed. He shook his head. Pity about those poor women. Messy, as well, always so messy.

There was an element of perfection in his murders. First of all, the women had meant nothing to him; they were the refuse of society, and although the papers might scream headlines of shock and capitalize on the horror, most would secretly agree that they had come to their proper ends. They were nothing more than a demonstration, the necessary testing of a complicated theory, an experiment which required a control.

But what they had been to others was also significant. Their used bodies were the crux of the matter. They had lured men; men who were weaker than he had succumbed to their lusts rather than their passions. And secretly he felt that there was no harm in ridding the world of garbage.

A cab went by in the gray darkness, visible for a moment in the fuzzy glare of the streetlights. A poorly disguised Bobby got out of it. The man in the shadows clucked his disapproval.

Drawing nearer to the wall, a precaution against what might be an untimely recognition, the man weighed the alternatives. Weighing alternatives was a speciality of his.

"There is no excuse for doing this thing foolishly or excessively," he said to himself. "Ergo, consider. It is well past midnight. No women have gone by and there are a great many police about." Certainly it was awkward. The circumstances did present a greater challenge, but without any genuine accomplishment in the final analysis. All that excitement wasted on poor, stupid, exhausted trollops.

With a reluctant sigh he put his knife away into the heavy folds of his inverness cape.

Now he would change his tactics, since he fully understood about murder. He could now plan other, more interesting killings.

Of course, next time he would kill someone important. He ran over his mental list with relish. It would be difficult to pick and choose among so many.

Remarkable, he thought, all this Ripper nonsense. With a low chuckle he sucked at his curly pipe as he wandered back toward Baker Street. He trusted that Watson would have tea ready.

The red-headed girl in the van of the army adjusted the visor of her helm and pointed across the river to the fortress held by the English. Above her the lily banner of France flapped listlessly in the sultry air.

"We cannot cross," said her second in command. "There is no possible way."

It was as if she had not heard. She did not turn, staring across the river as if sight alone could build bridges. "If we have faith in the Good God we can do anything. We will reach the other side. We will defeat the English. We will free France. God has said so; it is His promise. To think otherwise is blasphemy. We will but fulfill His word . . . ."

Her lieutenants looked at each other and shrugged. Perhaps the Maid *was* only a crazy farm girl. Convincing the foolish Dauphin was one thing, but crossing a river at flood was another.

"We can't do it," ventured the boldest of her men with a silent plea to the others for support.

"There is always a way with God on our side. God will defend the Right. St. Michael and St. Katherine have promised us the victory this day."

This was met with silence. The knights were too familiar with the whims of the ineffective Dauphin to rely on his support for long, and this girl could lead them into disaster. And the loss of France to the English.

"You are doubters of God's power?" She turned to them, the shine of her armor making them wink. "I say to you that God will help us. I tell you that St. Michael protects us with the Sword of Righteousness. I say that Jesus walks with the men of France and the archangels guide our footsteps. Our weapons cannot fail, we have the victory."

"The river is too deep," they told her.

She fairly snorted with indignation. Then, commending her soul to God and St. Michael, she turned a scornful gaze to her soldiers and with an eloquent twist of her thirteen-year-old head she urged her great warhorse into the river.

The valiant animal struggled. He thrashed and strove and despite the heavy armor he and his rider wore he did his best to swim. But the current was swift and the river in deep flood. It was no use. A little beyond midstream, with the French looking on in despair and the English cheering from the walls of Orleans, horse and rider went down for the third time.

They stopped him at the Mexican border, telling him that he was too old for fighting wars.

"Damn it," he said irascibly. "I have my rights. Deny me as you will, I can die any way I like. I want to die for freedom."

Still he was refused.

"I hate the trappings of death. Just let me disappear."

No, they said.

He coughed, trying to hide the asthma that plagued him. "I have nothing left here. Nothing of worth. Nothing is keeping me."

But they sent him back to San Francisco and poor Ambrose Bierce had to be content with the 1917 Nobel Prize for Literature . . . not that he *was* content, but even he learned to be philosphical.

The assistant had the uneasy feeling that all was not quite back to normal. To be sure, there was only a little unevenness in the matching lines, but that might be almost enough to alter the fragile balance.

He squared his mandibles resolutely, took stock of the display board, and made a few, very few, very minor adjustments, holding his breath as he worked. He must take care . . . slowly . . . slo — ow — ly.

"Which will you have: the Nazarene or Barabas?"

"The Nazarene! The Nazarene!" roared the crowd.

In the hazy August sun the Yorkists rested and gave thanks for victory. In his pavilion, Richard Plantagenet rubbed at his polio-twisted shoulder and brooded over the rebellion.

Tudor had fought well at the last, when forced to fight, but had made his campaign by treachery. The accusations of his nephews' murder laid to his door . . . . Even now the memory of his defense before Parliament was fresh in his mind. Richard knew well how little it would have taken to change the course of history. If Tudor had been able to win over his cousin, the Duke of Buckingham, then all might have been lost.

Suddenly Richard the Just of England laughed. What if Tudor's stories of Crook-backed Dick had caught on? What a monster his memory might have become for generations. The fairest King of England would seem a villian and Tudor, instead of a treacherous bastard, an avenging angel.

With resignation he rose to receive the nobles of the last vestiges of the Tudor armies.

On the Yellow River a bargeman poled his boat and the sound of the nightingale rippled through the gentle air. In the Inn of Three Gold Dragons the young poet waited for the concubine to come to him. Now he was a man and within his rights in the Laws of China. And tonight he would celebrate his age and his status with the woman his father had paid for. He would wander in the sweet garden of her thighs and touch the gates of heaven in their loving.

The door behind him opened and the beautiful moon-maiden came toward him, holding out a flask of wine on a tray with delicate porcelain cups. The blue flowers in her gown shown in the lantern light. Her face was round, smooth, and pale, as delightful as the laughter of children, serene as the moon. She looked at him and then sat demurely beneath the ornamental maple tree.

"You are most enchanting," he said to her. "I am honored to be with you this night."

"This is your first time?" she asked him in her shy, silvery voice, hands lingering suggestively on the rim of the tray.

"I blush to admit it."

"Here," she whispered to him as she extended her arm toward him. "This will make it easier the first time. Wine makes all living more beautiful and more pleasant." She handed him the cup.

Already half-drunk from the woman and the night, Li Po took the cup dazedly, lifting it to his lips in the gauze of a dream.

"Drink. It brings much joy," she urged him.

He tasted it. The worst of cold reality thrust in upon him with the acrid stuff as it rolled across his tongue. "Phath!" He spat it out. "That is terrible! I cannot drink that! Never! Keep me from wine always!"

Wilkie won.

The assistant beseeched any Power that might be nearby to keep the Instructor away from the lab just a little while longer. He knew that he almost had the problem solved. There were one or two factors to line up and a couple of simple details to verify, but it was really quite simple now. All he needed was time.

He curled around the console and groped for the gauge to settle the whole thing.

"Aw, goddamn," whined the shotgunner as the procession of flagellants approached them. All carried whips that they flailed over themselves and each other impartially. They were thin, gaunt beings, hardly human, with the deadly Tokens on their chests, armpits, and groins. They chanted as they went, the whips beating out the terrible rhythm around them. They were possessed not of demons but of disease.

"One Indian!" the shotgunner pleaded. "Just one flaming Indian."

The flagellants paid no heed to the coach but continued on their masochistic way.

The driver didn't even look around.

The tall man, bearded and gray-eyed, looked at the dispatches on his desk. He was grateful for the end of the bloody Civil War, but it had taken a toll of him. Laughter was rarer with him now that it had been, and he knew he needed perspective. So tonight he and Mrs. Lincoln would be going to the theater.

He was looking forward to the play. It was David Garrick as Lucky in *Waiting For Godot*. He had heard it was more fun than congress.

The bells of St. Basil's and the Annunciation boomed as ominously as the sound of guns as Tsar Peter pulled himself up to his near seven feet and icily informed the Boyars that their long patriarchal beards would no longer be tolerated in court. The Boyars gesticulated helplessly, feigning ineptness.

"Here," said the Tsar with an air of great patience. "Use this." And he handed them his personal, portable, battery-powered Norelco shaver. "Europe has much to teach us," he said sardonically.

The battle of Thermopylae was won, as Darius was to remind himself morosely even after, by a handful of Spartans, three M-1 rifles, two air pistols, a sackful of grenades, and one roving reporter with a walkie-talkie.

> Oh, give me a home where the mastedons roam
> And the trilobites romp through the clay.
> Where a large reindeer herd is attacked by a bird
> That can carry a dozen away!

Tetrazzini sang it and Paris loved it.

* * *

The thing was made of a stone not unlike cinnabar, and it shown like metallic spice in the torchlit room.

"You see," said the strange black man in the peculiar clothing emblazoned with the mystic symbols *MIT*, "it will be much easier with this. This will simplify the task considerably, Pharoah." He pressed the hidden button and the weird artifact hummed to the waiting Egyptians.

"What does it do? The sound is remarkable," Pharoah conceded, "but has it any worth? Is it a religious object? To what god?"

"Watch!" the black man commanded, and even as he spoke the platform with Pharoah on it rose into the air.

The Egyptians fell back, awed.

But Pharoah, beyond initial surprise, showed nothing but absorbed interest. "Yes. I see. But does it do more than make a sound and hang things in the air?"

"It does." The black man gestured with it and the platform with Pharoh swung easily about the room, dodging frightened guards.

"I see," repeated Pharoah as the platform settled to the floor careful as a spinster. "But what is this to me?"

"Exalted One," the black man said, "place as many men on this platform as you like and still it will sing and float for you. With this simple device, mountains will rise as high as you command. Slaves and mules will not be necessary to you any longer. All you need do is have this little gadget and men to load and unload your platforms."

"Uummmmm," Pharoah mused. Then his sharp eyes became eager slits. "My tomb. My tomb," he whispered. Then, raising his voice, "Wizard, for wizard you surely are, I require you to build my tomb with that, so that it may be larger than any other, and more beautiful."

At that the black man smiled, murmuring to himself, "I wonder how Cal Tech is making out with the Mayans?"

The last knob was meticulously eased into place. The dial sounded a decisive click. The assistant held his breath, ran a quick scan over the screens just to be sure. This developing world project was ticklish business, as he was finding out.

He heaved himself the equivalent of a sigh of relief. Then he admitted that for a while he was afraid that he would have had to take the whole thing back to *LET THERE BE LIGHT* to put all back in order.

But he had been lucky this time. All was secure and no one the wiser.

The door opened. His Instructor strode in, somber and full of lore. He fairly crackled with all the things he knew. Quickly he regarded his assistant, an air of suspicion about him. His hoary wisdom included a knowledge of young assistants and their overenthusiastic tendencies.

The assistant returned the look with perfect blandness.

The Instructor was puzzled, but turned away.

It had worked! The assistant congratulated himself on his success and blithely led the Instructor to the display board.

And all went well for the first few ranks of screens, and then the Instructor became attentive in his bordeom. That was the trouble. The Instructor waved aside the assistant's narration and looked closely for himself.

Even then everything went along splendidly for the assistant until a cry of "Lay to and prepare to board!" came from the display board and the assistant watched helplessly as the three galleons with the arms of Spain on their sails swung wide and prepared to grapple the moon.

Savory, Sage, Rosemary, and Thyme

She was known as the Herb Woman, and everyone on the mountain was afraid of her, though few were willing to admit it. She had lived in her shack above Lizard Creek for as long as anyone could remember, and no one knew for certain how old she was. Less than a dozen people in Candy had made the rigorous trek up to her place, but it was tacitly believed that more than one girl with a yen for a particular boy had sneaked away to get her philtres and, when they were successful, went again to be rid of what their desires had got them.

Amy Macklin had heard about the Herb Woman but was not sure that she accepted all the stories. Unlike most of the girls in Candy, Amy had stubbornly continued on in the little two-room school over in Pageville, eagerly listening to Mr. Houseford tell her everything he could dredge up from his long-ago college days of poetry and history and botany and art. If Ellis Houseford had been a younger man with prospects instead of disappointments, Amy's family might have encouraged her, but as Ellis Houseford was nearing fifty and was possessed of an ailing wife, Amy's mother actively discouraged her second-oldest daughter's scholastic ambitions.

"What do you think will happen to you, child?" she demanded more than once. "You're getting so's you hardly want to talk to anybody here. Another few months and you'll be like Tom Gosling over in Sandy Hollow, going off to the city, thinking you're too good for the people here. You know how he came back.

I don't want that kind of shame brought to this house! Lord between me and evil."

At the time, Amy had set her pretty jaw rebelliously and wished she had nerve enough to answer back, even if it got her the flat of her father's hand for sassing. She continued to bring books home with her, to read them, and to write in one of three looseleaf notebooks Ellis Houseford had given her.

Then Jemmy Howard drifted into Candy, and for Amy everything changed.

Jemmy Howard was twenty-four years old, almost six foot two, with big eyes bluer than a clear summer sky. He had brown hair that streaked out in the sun, a smile that was better than anything Amy had ever seen in the movies, and a voice as warm and coaxing as a sandbank by a swimming hole. Amy Macklin was dazzled. From the first time Jemmy had given her his lazy smile and said, "Now, this is purely the nicest thing I've seen in many a day. I could make a bouquet of you, girl; buttercups for your hair, cornflowers for your eyes, and wild roses for your lips," she felt she had drowned in light. The breath caught in her throat then, and with the baffled ardor of her fifteen years, she had plunged into love with Jemmy Howard.

Three love-fraught weeks later, after Amy had found more excuses than she knew existed to go into Candy for a glimpse of her deity, she caught Jemmy kissing Georgina Taylor. Her dreams dissolved as if dipped in acid. Georgina was nineteen, with hair so thick and dark that no one doubted it when the Taylors said that they were descended from an Indian princess. Her eyes were darker than chocolates with raisins, and her mouth made voluptuous promises when she spoke, even if it was only to say hello.

At home Amy had wept and then become oddly silent, sitting by the window of the room she shared with two of her sisters and staring out at the mountain as if listening for one particular sound. Lucy teased her, and Caralou was worried, but their mother, who knew enough about men like Jemmy Howard to guess what had upset Amy, shooed the other girls out of the house and went about her chores, giving Amy a chance to talk if she wanted to but pressing nothing on her.

"Ma," Amy had said as sunset came, "what do they want? What is it?"

Amy's mother sat down at the dull, well-scrubbed table where she had served family meals for more than twenty years. "I can't tell you exactly, child. There are those who like one thing and those who like another. Some men, if they're good-looking and sweet-tongued, like to keep a lot of silly girls on the string so they can sample a bit of this or a bit of that, as they fancy. Men like that, they think all a woman's good for is kissing. They don't know about the kinds of things that count in this life. There's no faith in them, child. The good Lord put a special burden on Eve that He didn't give Adam, and not many have the sense to know." She studied her second-oldest daughter, who was so unlike her other children, and wondered whether she had paid any attention.

"Isn't there a way to make them know?" Amy asked in a small, tense voice.

"They say there's always something you can do, but that's not the way for a Christian woman. If the good Lord wants you to have this man, then you'll have him; if not, then all the mooning and sighing and wishing in the world won't bring him to you." She got up from the chair. "Your pa'll be home soon. I've got things to do before then."

Amy shook her head in a daze. "You need help, Ma?" she asked in an abstracted way, her eyes straying toward the door and the sight of the mountain beyond.

Ordinarily, Amy's mother would have accepted the offer with thanksgiving, but knowing how her child felt and the depth of the shock she had received, she changed her mind with a wistful sigh. "Not tonight, Amy. Caralou can set the table this once. It won't hurt her to do it."

Amy murmured a distracted thanks, still preoccupied as her mother got up and went to prepare the evening meal. She listened to the familiar sounds of the pump and the unmelodic clang of the grate in the wood-burning stove and then called out, "When you met Pa, what was it like?"

Mrs. Macklin did not answer at once. "I don't rightly remember. I think I must have been about fourteen the first time he came to the house. It wasn't to see me; he was buying a couple head of hogs from us, for sausage."

"How did you feel when you saw him?" Amy was more forelorn, thinking that no one had ever been struck as she was and been treated so shabbily.

"I don't think I felt much of anything. Why should I? He was just a man coming to buy stock. There was nothing in that. It happened all the time." She had the fire going now and was searching for kindling in the wood box. "You tell Willy when he comes in that I need more cut wood here. There's not enough for doing breakfast."

"Sure, Ma," Amy responded listlessly. It was apparent that her mother, for all her kindness, did not know how she was suffering. She was too proud to weep, but her eyes ached as if the lids had been starched.

There was the sound of a horn and a motor. A battered '48 Dodge lumbered down the road toward the house.

"That's your pa already, and supper not on the table. Give a holler for Caralou, Amy. She's down at the rabbit hutches."

Amy got up slowly and went out the door, paying no attention to the greeting her father gave her or the shouts of her brothers. There were dark shadows on the mountain now, deepening to night in a special way. As she looked up, she shivered, thinking that the shadows were more massive and colder than anywhere else in the world. The pines trembled in the breeze and whispered among themselves as if afraid to raise their voices. Somewhere up past Lizard Creek the Herb Woman lived, spending her days making God knows what mischief. Sally Gibbs swore that the Herb Woman had given her a secret perfume that caused her to be irresistible to men with dark hair. That was why, she insisted, that Hank Patterson was forever chasing after her, and Bobby Huggins as well. Boys with dark hair, that's what the perfume was good for. Idly, Amy thought about that. Everything she had learned from Mr. Houseford taught her that such things as magic perfumes were nonsense, but it was true that boys with dark hair took to Sally Gibbs in no uncertain terms. Perhaps, if it could be made to work with dark hair, there would be a way to do something with light-brown hair with sun fingers through it. She was not aware that she had crossed the field and was at the edge of the pines that sighed like the ocean. Lizard Creek was a good four miles up, maybe more. In the dark there was no telling how she could find her way. It was foolishness, anyway, the desperate gesture of a lovesick girl.

Amy stepped into the trees.

It was more than half an hour before her family missed her; when her father asked why Amy was not at table with the rest of them, his wife nipped the sudden comments of the other children by saying, "Amy is feeling poorly, Sam, and needs time to herself."

Sam Macklin didn't hold with indulging children, but he only grunted, trusting his wife to know what was best where daughters were concerned. Even when Caralou tried to say that she thought Amy might be in trouble, out there by herself in the night, he merely pointed out that she was a sensible girl and would come home when she was good and ready. "No use fussing about her, Caralou. That's one female with a mind of her own. Leave her be."

Caralou fell silent, and Joey claimed the family's attention by announcing that he was going to set up some traps for coons as soon as he got together enough money.

About the time Caralou and Lucy were clearing the table, Amy was wishing she had never started out for Lizard Creek. Her legs were scratched with brambles, mosquitoes had made a feast of her, there was a rent in her thin blouse, and she was not at all sure she was going the right way. She had stumbled twice and once had rolled a fair distance before getting to her feet, and she was disoriented.

There were skitterings, cracklings, and smells in the brush around her, and she tried to forget all the tales she had heard of the poor souls who got lost on the mountain and were found again only as white bones, often marked with the gouges of gnawing teeth. The recollection goaded her on. She had not come this far to let herself be killed by a bear or raccoon. She was going to see the Herb Woman.

With that decision, her way seemed easier. She walked along the narrow trails left by deer, always climbing, her senses tuned to the night with the acuity of long knowledge. She no longer slipped, and her fear of the quiverings and muted grunts around her faded. The Herb Woman would protect her; there was no reason to worry.

For more than an hour she climbed, stopping now and again to peer through the moon-dappled trees up the slope. Twice she crossed large meadows, and she saw deer grazing in one of them. She stopped, reluctant to startle the beautiful animals into flight. The nearest doe raised her head, ears turning, and then lowered it again. Amy smiled with satisfaction and continued on.

On an outcropping of boulders, she missed her step and turned her ankle. She bit back a moan and heard a dry slithering from where she had almost put her foot. Her tongue turned to flannel in her mouth as she realized how close she had come to the reptiles. When she tried to walk, she stumbled, and for several minutes she stood terrified, her teeth chattering, as she thought of herself lying senseless while all the wood creatures with sharp teeth assailed her flesh until she was another anonymous skeleton. She had started to cry in her misery when she remembered the way that Jemmy had kissed Georgina, and that drove her on.

It was close to eleven o'clock when she reached Lizard Creek. By this time, she was light-headed with fatigue and hunger, and her sense of triumph had a muzziness to it, very nearly like a moment in a dream. She bent down and drank eagerly, thinking of the time her father had told her that the sweetest water on the mountain was here in Lizard Creek. He had also mentioned that the Indians who had lived there long ago — dead for almost a century now — had said that the place was haunted by a powerful force that could drive a sane man mad and restore the senses of the possessed. Sam Macklin did not believe such talk, and the pastor at the clapboard church ranted against superstitions, but neither man went willingly to Lizard Creek when the sunlight was not full upon it. Amy wiped her hands on her torn skirt and continued up the mountain.

She stumbled upon the place by accident. Her ankle was paining her, there was a stitch in her side, and she had seen an owl fly past her, which she knew was bad luck. The hollow offered a respite, and she thought that if she found a well-protected spot, she could crawl into it and sleep a bit. She might even wait until morning and then make her way home. Chagrin was fast taking hold of her, mocking her hopes. So intent was she on finding a safe place that she did not at first notice the wink of firelight, or if she did, she decided to ignore it and its worrisome implications. Gradually the brightness drew her, and then she recognized the cabin for what it was.

Ferns grew out of the roof, and other plants clung close to its sides so that even in daylight it might be possible to mistake it for a hummock in the undergrowth. But there were small, square windows neatly divided into four parts with thick, old glass in them, and a low doorway.

She stood staring, giddy with relief that she had found the place though wondering whether it was real. She took a few tentative steps toward it and then asked herself whether she dared to call out. Her mind was not made up when the door opened and a small, shapeless figure stepped out.

"Come on in, girl. No sense skulking out there in the dark." The voice was old, no doubt about that, but vigorous and hearty. The figure raised an arm and beckoned. "You come all this way to see me, you might as well come in."

"You the Herb Woman?" Amy's voice trembled, and she flushed with embarrassment.

"Of course I am. Who else you think lives up here but me?" She gestured again and held the door a little wider. "Come on, child."

Amy allowed herself to be persuaded. By the time she stepped through the door, she had begun to feel grateful. "Thank you," she murmured, not knowing what else to say to her benefactor.

"It's the least I can do," the old woman said with a chuckle. "It ain't too often that I get company of an evening, no, not too often." She had gone over to the hearth where the fire crackled. She was almost a head shorter than Amy and wore so vast and enveloping a dress that it was difficult to know whether she was fat or thin. Her face was seamed and wrinkled as a dry creek bed, and her hands, though large and square, were mottled with spots and ridged with veins like blue twine. Her eyes were a clear, arresting green, bright with amusement and something less pleasant. "Here, girl, sit down, why don't you? There's two chairs at the kitchen table and a bench under the window. Take whatever one you want. The rocker's mine."

"Oh, yes. Thank you." Amy chose the bench and sat on it carefully, poised on the edge as if she wanted to run away.

"Give me a couple of minutes and I'll let you have something for your ankle, and then you can tell me what brought you up here." The Herb Woman had been stirring a pan by the fire, and as she spoke she went to the sink and began to work the handle of the pump.

"How'd you know my ankle's hurt?" Amy demanded, oddly frightened.

"Good Lord preserve us! I heard you thrashing about out there, and when you came in, you were limping. The skin there's all tight and swollen, if you'd trouble yourself to look. It's what I did." Although her tone was exasperated, she was not angry.

"Oh." Amy twitched aside the hem of her skirt and looked down. Yes, her ankle was swollen, shiny-looking, and now that she realized it, quite sore. "I stumbled."

"That's not surprising. Anyone fool enough to come up here in the dark, they got to expect to get ruffled up some." She added the freshly drawn water to whatever was in the pan. "Now, I want you to put your foot in this," she said as she came across the room to Amy. "I'll add hot water, and it'll take care of you in no time."

Amy nodded, wishing that she had enough courage to bolt for the door. She knew — *knew* — there was something awful in the pan, and it would do terrible things to her. Mr. Houseford had said once that there were chemicals that would just dissolve whatever you put into them. She closed her eyes as she placed her foot in the pan. A few minutes later hot water was added and a pungent, mossy secret smell rose up on the steam. She blinked.

"You keep your foot in that until I tell you to take it out," the Herb Woman said as she sank into the rocking chair.

"Okay," Amy promised. She was feeling better now; the ache was fading, and the variety of scratches, cuts, and bruises she had got during her climb seemed less terrible. To her languorous amazement, she was beginning to feel sleepy.

"I'll give you a little broth in a while, but before that, you tell me what brought you up here." The Herb Woman rocked slowly, her chair creaking. "Must be something to do with love. You're too young to worry about money yet, and it don't look like you want to stop bearing kids. Unless you got a drunken daddy who beats you or brothers who want into your drawers. . . ."

"It ain't like that!" Amy protested, shocked out of the gentle lethargy that had taken hold of her. "My pa's a good man, and none of my brothers would try anything like that. Ma makes sure they listen to the pastor." She was dimly aware that Mr. Houseford would be disappointed in her if he could hear how she was speaking now. For the last year she had been talking like a city girl, not a half-educated girl from the hills.

"Love then," the Herb Woman sniffed. "Thought so. What is it about you pretty ones that always drives you to this? Ain't it enough that most girls'd give their eyes to have hair like yours?"

"But he don't like yellow hair. It's dark hair he wants," Amy burst out unhappily. "He can't see me at all, he's so busy with Geo —" She stopped at once, not wanting to say her rival's name.

"Oho! Georgina Taylor, is it?" The Herb Woman made a rattling sound that might have been laughter. "Georgina Taylor. Well, well. I've heard that name before now, what with one thing and another."

Amy repressed the urge to ask to hear more. Instead, she remarked, "She's had other boyfriends."

"Indeed she has," the Herb Woman agreed. "Dark-haired and dark-eyed, isn't she? Like Solomon's lady in the Bible."

There was nothing Amy could say to that; she felt utterly defeated, and so she was silent while the Herb Woman rocked and stared at nothing in particular, her splendid green eyes brooding.

"What is it you want of me, girl?" The question came so quickly, when Amy had been lulled into a wistful drowsiness, that she gasped before answering.

"It's Jemmy, Jemmy Howard. He's new in Candy. He said I have eyes like cornflowers, but that was before he saw Georgina Taylor. I saw them kissing," she went on in a desperate rush. Now that she had admitted her plight, she had nothing left to hide. "There wasn't anything I could have done about it. I don't . . . didn't plan to see. They never knew I was there, either of them."

"I see," the Herb Woman said when Amy stopped talking. "And you want what?"

"I want him to notice me, to kiss *me!*" Amy cried out. "I want Jemmy to hold me and put his tongue in my mouth." She blushed, anticipating what the pastor would say if he ever heard her confess such desires. "He's not right for her; it's me he'll want. Ma said that men don't always know what will do for them. I know I'm right for Jemmy." She almost knocked over the pan her foot was soaking in as she half rose in her determination.

The Herb Woman waited until Amy was seated once more. "You're kind of young to be saying those things, child."

"I'm *not.*" Amy tried to sound dignified but was afraid that she was being sullen. "Georgina Taylor, she doesn't want Jemmy the way I do."

This time the Herb Woman's laughter was raspier, and there was a tired cynicism in her well-used face. "No, she certainly doesn't. What do you think I can do for you, girl? Do you know?"

Amy faltered. "Well, I want. . . ."

"You've told me what you want," the Herb Woman interrupted brusquely.

"Isn't there something you can do? Maybe a thing I can wear around my neck or some drops I could put in his coffee?" What else was there? She knew that she was willing to do a great deal. After all, she had walked up the mountain at night to ask for the favor. "Tell me."

"Well, first, you better know that nothing's free in this world, especially not my kind of help. You want me to fix these things for you, there are things I got to have in return. If you fail me, then it'll go badly." She paused, looking toward the ruddy logs on the hearth. "This ain't quite the usual situation, however, and if I demand my price of you, I got to tell you now that you don't understand what you're asking."

Amy bridled at that. "If you tell me that Jemmy is a useless man and that he won't take care of me. . . ."

"No, that's not it, although it's true enough." She gave a short, impatient sigh. "You see, I've already taken a hand in these doings. . . ."

"What!" This time Amy did stand up, and the warm, scented water sloshed over the floor. "Did that Georgina Taylor come up here already? Why'd she do that? Or was that how she got Jemmy? Did she try to get him because she was afraid he might like me too much? Was she scared of me?" Amy could not entirely conceal her pride in the thought that she might be threatening enough to beautiful Georgina Taylor to cause her to seek out the Herb Woman for help, just as Amy was doing now.

"No, no, child, it wasn't like that." The Herb Woman stared down at the dark shine of the spreading water and sighed. "You're looking to the wrong place."

"The wrong place?" Amy echoed, her satisfaction deserting her.

"I've never seen Georgina, just heard about her." The green eyes were hard on her.

"From other girls?" Amy asked, not wanting to examine the suspicion that had begun to grow in her.

"Yes, but not this time. This time," the Herb Woman went on with rough gentleness, "the person who described her to me was a young man, tall, good-looking in a weak-willed way, with a too-ready smile and a tendency to flattering speeches. You recognize him, girl? Do you?"

"Jemmy?" Amy said the name so quietly that the low sputter of flames in the fireplace was louder. "How . . . ?"

"He came up here one afternoon — and brought a lantern with him, too, by the way — and said that he'd met a girl who did more to him than any female he'd ever laid eyes on in all his life. He said she didn't give ant's piss for him, and he was ready to do anything to get her. He'd tried presents and conversation and doing chores for her daddy so's he'd be asked into the house to talk with her. None of it worked. Miss Georgina Taylor wasn't having anything of his, that was plain. So he told her that if she didn't love him, he'd go away, maybe join the army, maybe get killed. Georgina said that was fine with her. That was when he came to me, to find a way to make her want him. He paid my price, and I did what I could. If what you saw is any indication, it must've worked pretty good." She leaned back, thinking for a moment. "You know, it ain't many women, not even those who know herbs and other things, who could have done that."

Amy had listened in growing anguish to the Herb Woman, and she seized on her last reflection. "Does that mean you can still help me?"

"Not exactly. I already accepted a fee from Jemmy Howard." She turned swiftly toward Amy. "If I go back on my bond, there'll be trouble."

"Then there's nothing left," Amy sobbed, at last giving way to the tears that had been building within her. There was no Jemmy Howard for her, never would be.

"He's not worth your tears, girl," the Herb Woman said quietly. "Not after what he did to you."

Amy shook her head, letting her weeping claim her and taking solace in the abandon of her grief. "Never," she was able to say, but nothing more.

"Oh, yes, girl," the Herb Woman went on a bit later, with less warmth. "Yes. You don't know what kind of a man you're dealing with." She got out of her rocker and went to open one of the square windows. A cool rush of wind came through the house. "That's more like it. It was getting close in here. That's the trouble with houses. They protect you, but they shut out a lot." She went on in this aimless way until Amy had calmed herself, and then she came back to the rocking chair. "You know, girl, you're blinded by that man. You want him to kiss you, and cuddle you, and put his hands all over you. It's no use denying it" — she raised her hands to prevent Amy's protests — "and at your age, it's not surprising. But a man like Jemmy Howard, who'd give you away with no more thought than he'd show a line of fish, there's no reason for any woman to cry over the likes of him."

"But it wasn't like that," Amy wailed when the Herb Woman broke off. "Jemmy cared for me!" She shrieked her conviction. "He did!"

"So much that he asked me for a potion to get Georgina Taylor." She stared down at Amy. "So much so that he paid my price for her. Don't you want to know what it was? Aren't you the least bit curious?"

Amy was struck by the remarkably sinister tone of her last remark. "What did he pay?" She did not truly want to know, but she admitted to herself that she would rather learn from this odd old woman than from Jemmy, which would be devastating, or from Georgina, which would be unbearable.

"Why, he gave me his word that a virgin would come of her own free will to me, ready to endure anything required of her on his behalf. You came tonight, and his price is paid. By you."

"What did you say?" Amy had been wiping the wetness from her face and did not hear what the Herb Woman had told her. "I paid the price? But how?"

"You came here." The Herb Woman's face was decidedly nasty now as she folded her arms on the back of the rocker and swayed gently with the chair. "You came here freely, on behalf of Jemmy Howard. When you started up the mountain tonight, Jemmy was able to breathe easy. Nothing can stop him from getting his Georgina after this."

"*No!*" Again Amy lurched to her feet, thrusting her hands out in front of her. It was not possible. "He wouldn't do that!"

"He did." The Herb Woman gave her a long, impassive stare. "I won't lie to you about that. You see, the thing is," she added more craftily, "I was kind of hoping that he was just being cocksure and that no one would come, so that when the moon was full again, I would be able to claim my price of him since he had not paid his to me." She chortled. "Yes, that was what I wanted. I see a boy like that, strutting his way about, crooking his little finger so that every girl for miles around swoons for him, and I don't like it. There're too many of them. And too many girls, silly creatures that they are, suck up their charming words; and when it's too late, and there's unhallowed loaves in the oven, they find that their lovers don't want a thing to do with them. Most women haven't the gumption to get mad when they've been scorned, girl. They lie back and weep and hurt and let their lives be blighted. Jemmy Howard will have his Georgina for a day or a week or however long it takes him to get tired of dark eyes and stolen kisses; then he'll be off to Pageville or Five Roads or Oak Mountain, looking for another silly girl to charm. I know. I seen it before, too long."

64

Amy had listened to less than half of this, trying to shut out the implications of what the Herb Woman was saying. She pictured Jemmy, his smile, the way he moved when he walked. There was nothing of treachery in him. She refused to accept what the Herb Woman was telling her. "No," she announced quite calmly. "Jemmy's still feeling his spirits is all. He doesn't care about Georgina, not really. . . ."

"Probably true," the Herb Woman agreed at once. "That kind, they don't care about much of anything but what catches their eye at the moment. It don't seem like that to you now, but mark my words, girl, when you've lived as long as I have. . . ."

"Maybe," Amy interrupted carefully. She told herself that Mr. Houseford had been right and that there was nothing to spells and magic but a lot of stupidity. It was not possible that Jemmy would *give* her to this person or would imagine that he could. Amy all but laughed with uneasy relief. She would tell Jemmy, and he would be amused, and that would make him realize how foolish he had been. It was ridiculous to suppose that Jemmy would actually *do* what the Herb Woman had said. Not Jemmy, never Jemmy. And when she told him, he would know that she loved him enough to go up the mountain to Lizard Creek in the dark for his sake, and Georgina Taylor would be a thing of the past. For the time being she had to get away, find her way back home. The sorrow that had filled her faded away to nothing as she tried to imagine how Jemmy would respond to what she would say. His eyes would get that glisteny look to them, like dew on leaves, and he would give her a look that would make her think she was with the heavenly choir.

"You have to find out for yourself, don't you, girl?" the Herb Woman asked in a voice both sharp and sad. "You don't trust me because you're caught by a grinning rogue. What's an old woman with half her teeth gone compared to his stolen kisses?" She shrugged. "Go on, then. You won't be satisfied until you do. You'll have to be disappointed before you understand."

"I won't be!" Amy declared staunchly.

"And when you know," the Herb Woman went on as if she had not heard Amy's interruption, "come back to me, and there are a few things I might teach you. I think there are ways our ends can be served." She stood back from the chair, giving it a gentle shove and watching it rock slowly. "You know the way now, but it'll be easier if you come in the daytime."

"I won't be coming back." Amy's chin went up, and if it were not for her foot in the pan, she would have looked very brave.

The Herb Woman half smiled. "That's as may be, girl. You should have the chance to learn for yourself, I suppose. But if it should happen that it's as I've told you — *if*, mind you — then my door is open. I can take no action; I've told you that. You, though, that's another matter, and there's no reason I shouldn't tell you how to do it. That isn't contrary to my bargain." She stared down at Amy's

65

foot. "I'll get you a length of cotton to wrap up your ankle. And if you want an easier walk, go over the crest and bear to the right at the rock with a sign on it. There's a trail there that leads to the Foley Mine Road, and that will bring you into the outskirts of Pageville. You can get Mrs. Fountains at the hotel to call your folks. That was the way Jemmy came up. He didn't want to make the climb."

"And I don't want my family to know I've been gone," Amy countered at once. "Ma'd be furious, and Pa'd want the pastor to come talk to me about my duty. I'll go the way I came and say that I stayed out in the shingle maker's shack. They'll believe that, and there won't be trouble for anybody." Her indignation was apparent, but it evoked no derision from the Herb Woman.

"A man like Jemmy don't deserve the likes of you," she muttered as she went to rummage in a chest under the open window.

"I don't deserve him, but I want him," Amy said, chiding her companion. "He won't forget about this. He'll know what I did for him, and that will. . . ." She could not see beyond that overwhelming moment when Jemmy would know that he had been wrong about Georgina. Why, she told herself, it was almost like Jemmy was testing her, making sure that she was the right kind of girl for him. And she would prove it beyond any doubt. Georgina Taylor would never go up the mountain in the night for Jemmy or any boy. Everyone knew that. Georgina thought that all she had to do was give one of her smoldering smiles and the thing was settled. Well, now little Amy Macklin would show her how wrong she was.

The Herb Woman brought the cotton and bent to help Amy wrap it around her ankle. As she worked, she said, "When you come back, miss, you bring something he wears: a shirt if you can get it, but a piece of it will do, and some of the dirt he's walked on recently. Don't need much, just a handful. You bring those up to me, and we can do something."

Amy nodded, not wanting to argue further with the Herb Woman, confident that in the next day or so she would have Jemmy Howard in her arms and all this would be behind her. "Okay." It was easier to sound as if she agreed.

"With a shirt and the dirt," the Herb Woman crooned to herself, "he'll plow a hole that's six feet deep and put on his last shirt. It's all in the song, all in the song. When Enoch Parker went away, he went to plow a place for himself."

Amy looked up at the name. "Enoch Parker?" She remembered that her pa had mentioned the name once or twice. The man had been a friend of her father's who'd gone off to the city or to war, he couldn't remember which, and had come back with a high-spoken woman from far away. Nobody in Candy spoke well of either of them, or at least so her pa had said. Then Enoch Parker went away, and while he was gone, his lady friend disappeared. When Parker came back, he had gone back to his old rounder's ways, but they hadn't lasted long. According to Amy's pa, it wasn't more than six weeks before Enoch Parker was laid out at the undertaker's, horribly dead, his flesh shrunken on the bones, loamy, as if he had been in a dry grave for a long time. His clothes were wound tightly about him in spite of his slightness.

Amy's pa had warned his children not to believe all that they heard about that time in Candy. "There's lots of folk hereabouts who don't have nothing better to do with their time than go about scaring honest men with bogie tales and made-up horrors. My pa went to the funeral, and he said that even then the gossips were busy." He admonished his whole family to be sensible, and that, for the time being, was the end of that, except for Joey getting under Amy's window and howling about how he was going to chew up her bones.

When the Herb Woman stood up, there was a sly smile lingering on her lips. "Enoch Parker is dead. You remember that. A shirt and the dirt." She went over to the window. "It's past midnight. You'll have to be careful going down the mountain. I figure you'll be back at your family table in time for breakfast. But you got to keep in mind what I've told you. I need the dirt and the shirt or there's nothing either of us can do."

Amy shrugged. Her ankle felt better, she had to admit. She wasn't quite so light-headed as she had been when she stumbled upon the cottage. Now she was eager to leave.

"I'll get you a cup of broth. I don't want you hurting yourself again," the Herb Woman said as she bustled toward the stove. There was a kettle simmering on it, as there was in so many country houses. She opened the lid and peered into the pot. "Lamb and rabbit, for the most part, but occasionally a little venison finds its way in as well. I think you'll like this." She ladled out a good-sized portion into a large mug, which she held out to Amy.

"That's kind of you," Amy said as she had been taught to respond. She did not want to accept anything from the Herb Woman, but there was no way she could refuse without being unforgivably rude. The flavor was strong and hearty. "I like it," she said, a little surprised.

"Good. I don't have much call to cook for anyone but myself. It might be different if I had company more often, but as it is. . . ." She shrugged. "I don't make coffee, but there's lots of herbs that make good drinking teas, so you can have a cup of that, if you want it."

"No, this is fine." In fact, she thought, it was really *good*, full of tastes she had never encountered before and nice on the tongue. She had the last of the broth and handed the mug back. "It was real good."

"I like it too," the Herb Woman confided. "Most people don't, but then, why should they? Why should they?" Her green eyes flashed. "You'd better get moving if you want to be back by sunup."

Now that she was about to go, Amy felt strangely sad. She had enjoyed the time here, but for the terrible lies the Herb Woman had told about Jemmy. The old lady was interesting, and Amy had the unaccountable feeling that she owed the Herb Woman something. Well, when she was married she would invite the

Herb Woman to visit, and she wouldn't pay any mind to what the neighbors said. "I'll see you later," she promised.

"Yes," was the Herb Woman's answer as she opened the door.

As Amy made her way down the mountain, she found herself thinking again of all the things she had heard about Enoch Parker. Much of it was made up, that was certain. But the man had been something of a rounder, and he had left that woman of his alone. At Lizard Creek she had another drink and asked herself whether Parker deserved such a death, and at the next moment she giggled uneasily since it seemed to her that she was being unwise to think about such things.

Her climb was so uneventful that she was worried. It was as if someone or something had cleared the way for her. Brambles as well as animals fell back as she went on, and the brush was silent. Yes, she felt that she was being watched. She saw a brightness in the trees and hoped that what she had seen was eyes.

When she reached the edge of the field, the sky was turning rosy. She could hear her pa out in the shed, getting ready to milk their two cows. He was singing a hymn, as he often did first thing in the morning. Amy walked across the low-grazed grasses toward the voice, calling out "Pa!" as she got nearer to the song.

Amy's pa fell silent, and then the shed door swung open. "Amy! Where in tarnation have you been? Your ma's been up more'n half the night, worried sick about you." For the taciturn man, this was remarkable volubility, and it showed how much he shared his wife's worry. He folded his arms and waited for an explanation.

"I went to the shingle maker's place. It's empty. I wanted time to myself," Amy said as she drew nearer, faltering toward the end when she saw the look on her father's face. "I . . . I. . . ."

"Don't you *never* do a thing like that again, Amy June. Your ma was ready to call Hammond and have them send one of the rangers over. And I won't have any tales about the shingle maker's cabin; we looked there and didn't find you. If it turns out you were off with a boy, you'll have to learn to fend for yourself. I won't have a daughter of mine catting." His face darkened, and there was a nervous vein on his forehead that jumped and quivered as he talked.

"I *did* too stay at the shingle maker's cabin. I went and walked. Look at me if you don't believe it." She had not seen her face or her clothes, but she was reasonably sure that there were scratches and bruises enough to make her statement believable. It shocked and upset her that her pa should be so insensitive as to think that she might meet a boy and put her family to such worry. "No boy's going to do this to me unless he does it against my will." She folded her arms.

"Why'd you do such a fool thing, Amy June?" His expression had softened a bit, but he was still forbidding. "It ain't like you, girl."

Amy stared at him, her mind in turmoil. She had always supposed that her parents were stern but understanding, ready to be sensible judges and dependable allies, but here was her father, questioning her as if she were a trollop and accusing her of all manner of things. "I had to, Pa," she said, pleading with him to sympathize. "I didn't think you'd all worry. You know how I was feeling."

"Mooning all over about that Howard boy. Your ma told me. I want you to know that I won't tolerate it. I'm not going to see any daughter of mine taking up with a ne'er-do-well like him. Just you keep that in mind when you start wasting time on him." His anger had subsided somewhat, but there was still a feeling about him as if he were waiting for a wild animal to break from cover.

"Don't you talk that way about him, Pa. Not to me." She waited for the rebuke and the blow and took them with resignation when they came.

"Who'd you see when you were walking?" her pa demanded.

"Nobody."

"Then who put the bandage on your foot?" His voice was rising again, and he was getting red in the face.

"I did." Amy was becoming angry now as well. If her pa was not willing to give her any comfort, she would not make concessions to him. Had he shown compassion, she might have told him what she had done during the night, but now she had no more intention of doing that than of making friends with Georgina. "I found a couple extra rolls of cloth in the Cottermans' hay barn. I was going to put a couple extra rolls in for them, later." How easy it was to lie, she thought, once you get the hang of it.

"Then you apologize to them. I want you to tell them that you snuck into their barn and took their bandages. I want you to ask them to forgive you. And I want you to have a talk with the pastor as soon as he can spare the time." He turned away. "I got to get to the milking. The cows need proper care, girl."

"I know that, Pa," she said quietly, and because he did not see her face, he thought she was being properly submissive.

"You go on in and talk to your ma. She needs to be thanked for staying up most of the night on account of you. And you're to stay in today. You'll have to do chores for your ma so that she can sleep some." He closed the door of the milking shed as clear indication that the conversation was over.

Amy made her way back to the house, thinking. There were a lot of things she had to do at once. She had to talk to Jemmy Howard so that he could see how much he loved her and what she thought of him. She did feel a little sorry for her ma, but after what Pa had said to her, she wanted nothing more to do with him. He had failed her, and she would not forgive that.

Caralou was up, making biscuits. She gave a startled cry when Amy walked in the door and almost dropped the bowl in her lap.

"Shush," Amy said, beginning now to feel tired. Until her meeting with Pa, she had not felt as if she had been up all night. Now she was as exhausted as if she had been awake for a hundred years. "I don't want to wake the others."

"You're back," Caralou said. "Where've you been?"

"Out." She no longer wanted to explain. "I slept at the shingle maker's cabin, but that wasn't till real late. I'm worn out."

"You're all scratched up," Caralou said, as if afraid to mention it. "Did anything . . . you know, happen to you?"

"Not that kind of happen," she said, sitting down on the couch and tucking up her legs. She was not aware of falling asleep, but the next thing she knew her father was shaking her and demanding that she get up and take over her ma's chores for the day.

It was not until mid-afternoon that Amy was able to get away from the house. She said that she wanted to go into Candy to get the bandages to put back in the Cottermans' hay barn, and her father reluctantly gave his permission.

"Just make sure that you spend your own money, Amy June. I don't want your ma giving you her pennies for this." He folded his arms and looked down at her.

"It's my own money," she said wearily.

"And don't be too long about it. I want you back here before sundown. Hear?" His own stern parents had taught him by example that it was necessary to make harsh rules for children. One of his sisters had ended up in the city, at a fancy house, which proved that her parents had been lax. He could see that Amy was by far the prettiest of his daughters, and therefore he knew that she would have to be watched closely for any signs of waywardness.

"I'll be back, Pa," she said quietly.

"See that you are." He walked a little way down the road with her, but neither of them spoke.

In Candy she went through the motions of buying two rolls of heavy cotton gauze, and then she started toward Mr. Houseford's place, knowing that she would have to pass the Taylor's house. She thought she might find Jemmy there. Her plans were hazy beyond that. She knew that she could not simply run up to him and tell him everything, but there had to be a way.

As she came around the bend in the road, she looked down toward the creek and saw Jemmy fishing. It was so easy. "Hi, there," she called out.

Jemmy turned. "Why, hi yourself, Amy. What are you doing out here?"

"I'm going over to Mr. Houseford's to borrow a book." She had done it often enough in the past.

"You're surely the readingest girl I ever knew," he said ruefully. "Don't you ever do anything else?"

Amy decided that she would never have such an opportunity again. "I done something else last night. I went up the mountain to see the Herb Woman."

There was a look in his eyes that was gone faster than the flick of a bird's wing. "You did what?"

"I went up to the Herb Woman's. She said you'd been there. She said you wanted something from her and promised her something in return." Amy had folded her arms. "I wanted her to give me a potion to bring the boy I love to me but she couldn't do that." She wished he would figure it all out.

"Why'd you do a thing like that?" He pulled the line out of the water.

"Because I wanted you, and after you met Georgina Taylor, you never came to see me or talked to me at all. So I went up the mountain in the dark and saw the Herb Woman. She said you'd promised her I'd come if you got the thing you wanted. I figured that was just a test." She waited for him to tell her she was right, that he loved her after all, that he thought she was the bravest girl in the whole country.

Jemmy Howard threw his head back and laughed. "Christ almighty, girl, you do give yourself airs, don't you? Hey, Georgina, d'you hear that? Amy thinks I went to see the Herb Woman." He laughed again, and his laughter was joined by another voice. "Why'd I want to do that, Amy, when I had everything I wanted? Besides, the Herb Woman ain't so much, just a crazy old lady living all by herself up beyond Lizard Creek. You're a fool to go up there at night."

Georgina Taylor came along the bank and put her arm possessively around Jemmy's shoulder. "Amy, how do you figure any herb or spell could take him away from me? There ain't no magic can fight what I got, right, Jemmy?"

Jemmy grinned down at her and patted her fanny. "Righter than gospel, Georgina."

Amy watched them in petrified fury. Her face had been scarlet; now it was white. She glared down at them. "How *could* I love you? How? You're worse than she said you are. You're vain and cruel, both of you." Their renewed laughter humiliated her the more, and she started to run down the road, wanting only to get away from the terrible scorn of their mirth.

"Hey, Amy," Georgina called after her, "you tell that Herb Woman that we don't need her at all."

"Yeah," Jemmy agreed. "You tell her thanks for nothing."

Amy pressed her hands over her ears as she ran, blocking out the rest of their taunts. Only when her ankle began to hurt so badly that she stumbled did she slow down. She had paid little attention to where she was, but now she looked about and saw that Ellis Houseford's place was about a quarter mile away. She began to plod toward it, knowing that she could rest there, get a drink of water and an aspirin tablet. Maybe, she thought, longing to escape her suffering, she really would borrow a book.

Houseford opened his door on her third knock and smiled. "Amy, this is an unexpected pleasure. Come in. Do come in."

She went into the shabby house gratefully, trying to smile at the kindly, harassed teacher. She made her way, out of habit, to the back room that had been a sun porch and later had been converted into an office and library. "I hadn't been here much, so . . . here I am."

Houseford was not an unobservant man, and he knew there was something very wrong with Amy. That grieved him, for she was one of his few students who had shown a capacity for scholarship and a little of the glimmer of real intellect. Amy Macklin was intelligent, and he dreaded what would become of her if she remained here in Candy. He had spoken once with her father, but that had proven a fool's errand. With an effort he kept a calm expression. "It's good to see you. I'm glad you stopped by. I had a new load of books just last week, and I was thinking you might want to have a look through them."

"Sure," Amy said with little enthusiasm. As he brought the large cardboard box out from under the desk, she asked politely, "Is Mrs. Houseford well?"

"No, unfortunately not. She's over at the hospital in Hammond. I won't keep you long," he added, knowing how little it took to harm a girl's reputation in a town as small as Candy.

"Oh. I hope she's better soon." She peered into the box Houseford had offered her, glancing over the titles. Most of them were about Greeks and Romans, but there was one that caught her eye: *Folklore and Shamanism: Celtic Magic in British Song and Story.* Amy stared at the book. Her tongue was suddenly dry. "Mr. Houseford, would you mind if I" — her newly discovered craftiness asserted itself — "if I borrow a couple of these? I need something to get my mind off things."

Houseford was aware of Amy's crush on Jemmy Howard. Who in Candy was not? He also knew that Howard had taken up with Georgina Taylor. Secretly, Houseford was glad because he knew that this was his last chance to instill academic ambitions in Amy. "Why, certainly. Take whichever ones you want. I won't be getting around to them for at least two weeks. Perhaps when you've read them, we can discuss them."

When Amy left, she had four books with her: three on Greek myths and the book on shamanism. She read as she walked until she got near the place in the road where she had seen Jemmy and Georgina. She faltered, dreading another exchange with them.

There was a splash and a whoop, followed by a giggle. Amy listened, thinking that if she ran by while they were swimming, they would not see her. And then another, darker thought occurred to her, and she hid herself in the brush by the road as she crept nearer. Sure enough, there were two piles of clothes on the bank. Amy put the books down and crept nearer. She parted the branches carefully and stared toward the swimming hole.

Jemmy and Georgina were farther down, near the old railroad trestle where the water was deepest and the most still. As Amy watched, she saw Jemmy reach out and fondle Georgina, saying something in a voice suddenly low and husky. Georgina's answering murmer was ripe as August melons.

Knowing that Jemmy and Georgina were not paying attention to anything but themselves, Amy slid closer to the piles of clothes, reaching out with care for the shirt Jemmy had worn and scooping some dirt into the cloth. She drew the garment back into the bushes and wadded it tightly. Then she made her way back up the bank, picked up the stack of books, and headed for home.

A week later, Amy returned the books to Mr. Houseford, and he noted with amusement that the book on shamanism had been very well thumbed, as had the book on Diana and Astarte. He wondered whether he ought to offer her the text on comparative anthropology in the near future.

He might have been more concerned about her interest if he had been able to follow her home, for Amy would periodically stop and pick the blossoms and leaves of various plants, singing quietly to herself as she went. There were three of the necessary plants, and she made sure that she got plenty of them, just in case.

That night she was more quiet than usual, and her pa began to think that the worst was over for a while. The pastor had told him that teenage girls were tricksy creatures, but a firm hand and prayer would keep them in the path of righteousness. At least, her pa had told her ma the night before, she wasn't chasing after that no-good Jemmy Howard any more.

Late that night, Amy pulled the shirt, the dirt, and the sprigs of sage, rosemary, and thyme from under the mattress where she had hidden them. Carefully she rolled them up and stuffed them into a grain sack, along with her own meager collection of eleven paperback books. Certain that her two sisters were asleep, she let herself out of their bedroom, stopping in the kitchen for a slice of ham and a half dozen hardboiled eggs before going out the front door forever.

The woods were friendly, and she climbed up the mountain with greater strength. With each step, she recited a little of what she had learned. There were ways to be revenged. With the shirt and the dirt, there were many things she could do. It was only a question of making the best choice. She might make the skin tear off his body in strips. She might blind him, like that Greek king, and leave him to make his way alone, for Georgina would want nothing to do with a blind man. She might give him a constant thirst so that he would bloat up like a balloon and still not be satisfied. She might wither him up like a leaf on a dry vine. She might cause him to be consumed with carbuncles and sores so that there was not an inch of his body that did not fester. She might wreck him as a man by causing his thing to grow so that it dangled lower than his knees, giving no one any pleasure. There were an endless number of things she might do, assuming she found winter savoury.

Considering what had happened to Enoch Parker, she was confident that the Herb Woman would have some. Her joyous bloody anticipation gave her renewed speed. She was happy now that she had thought to bring along one of her pa's shirts as well.

In the hollow, the little cabin waited, ruddy with welcome.

Best Interest

Slowly, Derek spread the mauve color in concentric circles on Melanie's breasts — helpless targets with rosy bull's eye at the center. To finish the job he drew more circles around her navel and aimed an arrow away from the dark hair that fluffed between her thighs. He knew it was over between them just as he realized that mauve wasn't a very flattering color on her.

He glanced at the Dial glowing in the darkened room like the loving eye of a mother watching over him. The display read:

YOUR APARTMENT HAS BEEN INDIVIDUALLY PROGRAMMED
IT HAS YOUR BEST INTERESTS AT HEART

The Dial was something a man could depend on; not like the unpredictable female lying besides him asleep. Asleep! While the Dial stayed resolutely awake, ministering to him, anticipating his needs, understanding his desires almost before he knew them himself.

He dialed the bed to a more comfortable angle, moving Melanie away from him. The Dial had superimposed a warm golden glow over what was rather a sodden morning. It was that dreadful kind of day, the sort that Derek liked least. It was slightly warm, with a slow drizzle leaking out of the clouds. Days like this, Derek found it hard to think. And the Dial knew it.

Melanie sighed in her sleep and slid into a more relaxed position. Derek decided not to wake her. There was no reason for her to get up yet. Since he was going to tell her goodbye that evening he might as well let her spend the morning getting a good rest.

Across the room the Dial activated the mirror. Derek propped himself on his elbow and looked at the image the Dial provided for him. In the glass his pudgy body was tall and slim, his movements fascinating and seductive rather than awkward. His lank, mouse-colored hair became blond, his slightly myopic eyes were really quite compelling and of a brilliant blue instead of washed-out hazel. He had seen himself this way for so long that he would not have recognized the shapeless, pale, lazy young man he really was. But he never bothered to look into another mirror.

Since he was the superintendant of the complex of buildings in which he lived, he was never away from the Dials. His title was impressive — Environmental Engineer — and he had a certain prestige along with the loving care of every Dial in the building.

Melanie stirred beside him, making a mess of the bed. She was the kind of sleeper who took all the covers and cocooned them around her, the kind who could work a sheet to the bottom of the bed and keep all the scratchy, old-fashioned blankets up around her neck. That was one of the reasons Derek was tired of her. Even her luxurious Rococo curves did not truly excite him anymore.

He looked away from the Dial, feeling a rush of warmth as he gazed at the display. None of his other mistresses had been able to give him the same sensation of being cared for, of being so very *important*. And now Melanie was becoming exacting and cold. He wriggled closer to the Dial and cleared this throat.

The display lit up promptly:

GOOD MORNING, SIR. THIS UNIT TRUSTS YOU SLEPT WELL.

Derek wished the Dial a hearty good morning and considered breakfast. The Dial anticipated his requests with this display:

THERE IS A STANDARD EGG BREAKFAST #3, AVAILABLE IMMEDIATE-LY, OR ANOTHER CAN BE PREPARED TO YOUR ORDER. THIS UNIT WILL DO FRIED, SCRAMBLED, OR POACHED EGGS.

"What about eggs Benedict?" Derek asked, and immediately regretted it.

THIS UNIT IS SORRY TO INFORM YOU THAT THERE ARE 380 TOO MANY CALORIES IN EGGS BENEDICT. IF YOU WILL BE SATISFIED WITH HIGH TEA INSTEAD OF SUPPER, THIS UNIT WILL SERVE THE EGGS BENEDICT YOU REQUESTED, BUT MUST REMIND YOU THAT YOUR EGG LIMIT IS HALF FILLED FOR THIS WEEK AND THIS IS ONLY TUESDAY.

Derek glared. He knew that he should have Breakfast #3, but he snapped, "Never mind. I'll skip breakfast."

THIS UNIT WISHES TO REMIND YOU THAT BREAKFAST IS THE MOST

IMPORTANT MEAL OF THE DAY. IT IS IN YOUR BEST INTERESTS TO EAT.

Rubbing his hands over his stubby face, Derek remembered that the Dial was right. It *did* want to take care of him. He sniffed through the chronic nasal sludge of sinusitis.

THIS UNIT HAS MEASURED YOUR BLOOD SUGAR LEVEL AND BODILY NUTRITIONAL DEPLETION. THE EFFECTS OF THREE ORGASMS HAVE SIGNIFICANTLY REDUCED YOUR AVAILABLE ENERGY. IN ADDITION TO BREAKFAST #3, THIS UNIT WILL ISSUE THREE VITAPEP CAPSULES.

"Thank you," murmured Derek. He hadn't realized until then how drained he felt. Behind him, Melanie snored gently. Derek had not been aware that women could snore until Melanie had moved in with him. None of his other mistresses snored. He was uncertain if snoring was a fault in women, but he was sure it wasn't a virtue.

The Dial glowed, and on its upper surface a panel slid back and a glass of white liquid rose into view.

GOOD MORNING, SIR. THIS UNIT, IN ACCORDANCE WITH YOUR WISHES AND THE PRACTICE OF GOOD DIETARY HABITS, IS BRINGING YOU A MORNING DRINK.

"I thought I ordered coffee. There's a standing program that says coffee with breakfast. A *standing* order."

THIS UNIT REGRETS TO INFORM YOU THAT LARGE QUANTITIES OF COFFEE ARE NOT IN YOUR BEST INTERESTS.

Rather than argue with the Dial, Derek took the glass. He drank the stuff, making a face, but refrained from asking the Dial what nutrients went into it: he had asked that once and the Dial had told him.

"Is that you, Derek?" There was a stirring in the mound of bedclothes. The tone of her question was calculated to annoy, and succeeded. It was a frigidity training technique that seldom failed.

"Yes, darling," he said patiently. He pondered what to do about her, for recently when they made love, she had taken to lying there limply, muttering about shopping lists. He would be glad when the frigidity fad was over. Now he wished there was something he could do that would shock her back to the warm, cuddly thing she had been three months ago.

The display lit up brightly:

THIS UNIT HAS FULL SEXUAL RATINGS FOR THE LAST TWENTY-FOUR HOURS. YOUR PERFORMANCE STANDS AT AN AVERAGE OF 5.88 COMPARED TO A USUAL PERFORMANCE LEVEL OF 8.79. FRUSTRATION QUOTIENT IS NOW 4.93. IT IS IN YOUR BEST INTERESTS TO EX-

PERIENCE ORGASM WITH A MORE ENTHUSIASTIC PARTNER.

Derek stared at the Dial. Always before when he received his sexual ratings, the Dial had waited until his partner was gone. He said, "Can't it wait?"

There was a clucking sound as the display changed:

THIS UNIT HAS DETERMINED THAT IT IS IN YOUR BEST INTERESTS TO HAVE THIS KNOWLEDGE AS SOON AS POSSIBLE, SO THAT YOU MAY REMEDY THE PROBLEM QUICKLY.

Derek was still thinking about this when Melanie asked from her side of the bed, "When do you leave?" She didn't even smile.

"Oh, a couple of hours. No *rush*, Melanie."

"Good. You can fix the Dial for me. It hasn't been doing anything I program it to do." She sulked, and it wasn't very pretty. "You'd think it has something against me."

He yawned. "Probably just some trouble in the programming. Nothing to *worry* about; it can't be serious. I'll take care of it this evening." The time Derek spent on his own apartment was not considered part of his job, he was paid for maintaining the other units in the complex. "If it's still giving you trouble, I'll take care of it."

Now Melanie pouted. "The other evening when we had those friends of yours over, I dialed a tropical veranda and it was all chilly and none of the flowers were right. And the food tasted like paste!"

"I know you were upset. But it turned *out* okay, didn't it? We just got rid of the veranda and did a standard interior — don't forget how hard it is to get a full exterior at heavy power-use times. Everyone wants dinner and the building can't . . . "

"Go ahead," she sniffed. "Defend it. Sure, it works fine for you. It's me it won't work for."

With a click and a whirr the Dial came to life again:

THIS UNIT WISHES TO INFORM YOU THAT BREAKFAST IS READY. FOR MAXIMUM BENEFIT IT SHOULD BE EATEN WHILE HOT.

Melanie screamed and threw the pillow at the Dial. "You bitch!"

There was his mistress lying in bed, Derek thought, swathed to her neck in sheets, and there he was drinking ersatz milk while a machine issued orders. Something had to be done.

"Melanie," he began, edging a little closer to her, "*maybe* you'd better stop at the therapy station this morning. You aren't acting like yourself, letting the Dial upset you." He inched closer. "You aren't using the Dial as a willing servant, so that you're free to do those creative things only human beings . . . "

IT IS NOW TWO MINUTES SINCE YOU WERE CALLED TO BREAKFAST, announced the Dial.

"See?" she demanded, thrusting her hand toward the Dial display. "It won't leave us alone. It's always butting in!"

"We could ignore it," he suggested hopefully, reaching for her.

She leaped from the bed. "I know what you want — you want to smother me with your sexual ruttings. It's disgusting."

It was sad, remembering how much fun she had been at first. Now she was little more than a shrew.

THIS UNIT INFORMS YOU THAT IT CANNOT BE RESPONSIBLE FOR THE NUTRITIONAL CONTENT OF THE MEAL AFTER THREE MORE MINUTES.

Derek was almost angry. "Wait a bit and fix us another."

ACCORDING TO CODE 4-88371A, PARAGRAPH 134-D, THE MISUSE OF FOODSTUFFS IS A MISDEMEANOR PUNISHABLE BY FINE OR TWO DAYS WITHOUT MACHINE SUPPORT.

Melanie burrowed into the blankets, saying scornfully, "You let yourself be ordered about by metal and plastic."

"But, Melanie . . . " He faltered. "All right. Maybe there *is* a foul-up in the circuits somewhere. All you have to do is open that panel and see if the three screws are in a straight line. Honestly, that's all there is to it." He opened the panel and showed Melanie the three screws, all lined up. "I've made a few modifications on the unit, of course," he added modestly. "It's one of the few advantages of working on the Dials — I can experiment on my own."

THIS UNIT MUST INSIST THAT YOU EAT YOUR BREAKFAST.

"All right." Derek got to his feet. "It really does *care*, Melanie. All it wants is what's good for me." He saw the weak but implacable defiance in the set of her chin. "Breakfast time. Do you want to join me, or would you rather . . . " He held out his hand on the off-chance that she might take it.

She ignored him. "I'll put on my robe."

He reached back to the bed, grabbed the robe, and tossed it to her. "You might get dressed."

"I haven't bathed. I'm not going to put clothes on over this!" She put her hand on the bull's eyes.

"I'll wait a few minutes while . . . "

The Dial interrupted: IN A FEW MINUTES, THE VALUE OF BREAKFAST WILL HAVE DECREASED TOO MUCH, AND WILL BE COLD, BESIDES.

Derek glared at Melanie. The morning and breakfast were both being ruined by that woman. "I'll help scrub," he said as he realized she would be certain to misunderstand him.

"Surely I have the right to privacy?" Her arched brows went up and she remained that way, one hand to her breasts and an expression of haughty shock on her face until Derek was out of the room.

The creamed bacon and eggs tasted like sulphur and the tea seemed to be squeezed from old blotters. There were, in addition to the eggs, two small slices of watery and tasteless fruit which the Dial assured Derek were chock full of the required nutrients.

He was almost finished with the last, hard piece of toast when Melanie came into the eating area. She was still in her robe and her expression had not improved. Derek let her order her food for herself, wincing as the Dial informed her that there were too many fats in corned beef hash for her to have it twice in one week. Hoping to distract her and to steady her temper, Derek asked, "What about work today? What's going on at your office?"

"I'm going to stay home today," Melanie informed him as she stared at the gray mass of reconstituted protein that slid onto the table in front of her.

THIS UNIT REMINDS YOU THAT THE PENALTY FOR ABSENTEEISM IS TEN DAYS OF CONTINOUS WORK AND A FINE IN THE AMOUNT OF THE VALUE OF THAT WORK. FULL COOPERATION OF ALL MEMBERS OF SOCIETY IS ESSENTIAL IF TRUE DEMOCRACY IS TO BE ACHIEVED. CONSULT THE LEGISLATIVE TAPES FOR PERTINENT LAWS.

"It's none of your business!" She yelled at the machine, and threw the contents of her bowl at the screen.

MALICIOUS DAMAGE OF A DIAL IS A MISDEMEANOR, DELIBERATE MISUSE OF A DIAL IS A FELONY. SEE HOUSING CODE SECTION 445-P-1A, ALSO THE LEGISLATIVE TAPES FOR LAWS COVERING ANTI-SOCIAL ACTS AND VANDALISM.

"It hates me!" Melanie screamed. "It wants to punish me!" Her eyes grew bright and her fingers began to twist the lapel of her robe. "Wait a minute . . . it isn't me, is it? It's you, Derek. This is your unit. You made all those improvements in it, didn't you? It doesn't want to share you with anyone! It's jealous! It wants you all to itself!"

Derek looked at Melanie in some alarm. Then he turned to the Dial. "Notify the Medical Center in this complex. Melanie isn't quite herself today."

"I'm fine!" she insisted in an hysterical shriek. "It's the Dial that's all wrong!"

"Nonsense!" Derek snapped. "It's a machine, Melanie, a machine whose sole purpose is to make our lives fuller and better. It's just absurd to think that a Dial can do anything we don't want it to. It has our best interests at heart. That's why everyone has them."

"Oh dear, oh dear," Melanie wailed, well into her outburst now and secretly enjoying it. "Everyone has them. Of course they do. And everyone believes that they control the Dials, but it's the other way around." She began to sob.

Another bowl of reconstituted protein slid toward her, along with a suspicious-looking brown pill.

SUPPLEMENTAL VITAMINS, the Dial explained. SUCH OUTBURSTS LEAD TO MINOR VITAMIN DEFICIENCIES.

Melanie put her head on the table and wept.

A prescription arrived a few minutes later, and Derek wearily guided Melanie back to the bedroom, trying to think of something to say that would reassure her without sounding wholly inane.

"I won't, I won't, Don't" Melanie thrashed and turned her head from side to side to avoid the magenta syrup that Derek held out to her in a specially provided plastic spoon. "It's all wrong!" Her face was rigid and her voice was as unpleasant and penetrating as the whine of a buzz-saw.

IT IS NECESSARY THAT YOU TAKE THIS PREPARATION IN ORDER TO REGAIN YOUR EQUILIBRIUM AND HEALTH. IT IS NOT BENEFICIAL TO YOUR SYSTEM TO BEHAVE IN THIS WAY. YOU WILL HARM YOURSELF IF YOU CONTINUE TO DO SO. THE MEDICATION PROVIDED WILL CALM YOU AND HELP YOU TO RECOVER. FOR YOUR OWN GOOD, THIS UNIT MUST URGE YOU TO TAKE IT.

"Melanie," Derek said with an exasperated sigh. "It's right. You're *not* acting rationally. Just drink this down and you'll be fine in a couple of hours." As he forced the prescribed and vile-smelling medication to her obstinately tightened lips, he pleaded with her. "Come *on*, Melanie. Just one sip and it's done."

She shook her head vigorously and screwed up her face, as if shutting every possible orifice he might want to use for the medication.

THIS UNIT SUGGESTS THAT YOU HOLD HER NOSE. SHE WILL HAVE TO BREATH THROUGH HER MOUTH AND YOU MAY THEN ADMINI-STER THE PRESCRIPTION.

Derek nodded dubiously and did as the Dial suggested. Melanie twisted and turned a magnificent plum color before she capitulated and allowed Derek to tip the nauseating stuff down her throat.

THE PRESCRIPTION WILL REQUIRE APPROXIMATELY 7.5 MINUTES TO BECOME EFFECTIVE.

"Will you be okay, Melanie?" Derek asked with a solicitude he did not really feel.

"I hate you," she answered.

THIS UNIT MUST REMIND YOU OF THE TIME. YOU MUST LEAVE WITHIN THE NEXT 3 MINUTES OR YOU WILL BE LATE TO WORK. THE PENALTY FOR TARDINESS IS OUTLINED IN LEGISLATIVE CODE GGR-12982AP-3T11. A COMPLETE SCHEDULE OF MONETARY FINES ARE OUTLINED IN UNION MANUAL 17-44-B AND C.

"I've got to go," Derkek said hurriedly. "Don't worry about anything, Melanie," he said from the doorway. "The Dial will take care of you."

OF COURSE.

"Oh, thanks," Derek said to the Dial as he hurried to complete primary hygiene. He dressed quickly and neatly, choosing a conservative red and orange stripe-along and a simple chartreuse neckscarf. Only major executives were entitled to wear the impressive outfits of organic textiles, and Derek cherished in his heart the wish that one day he, too, would have the soft tartan plaids and magnificent woolen houndstooth jackets that were the privilege of the highest level management.

Going back through the bedroom, Derek leaned over the drowsy Melanie and said, "I'm going to work now, Melanie. I'll be back at the usual time."

YOU'RE 85 SECONDS LATE.

"I'll walk fast," Derek said to the Dial. He turned back to Melanie, hoping for some response, but there was none. She gazed at the landscape the Dial had conjured on the far wall. Her breath came slowly, easily, and he could see the ghosts of the circles he had drawn on her breasts and stomach, smeared and useless now. He cursed gently and quietly so that he would not disturb her.

LEAVE HER TO THIS UNIT.

Derek was delighted to obey.

When Melanie awoke from her drugged slumber some time later, the apartment was shadowed and dark. The windows did nothing to disguise the soupy weather outside; in fact, they enhanced the depressing effect by giving the walls the same melancholy tinge. Melanie sat for some time, staring out at the wet and the clouds as she tried to gather her thoughts. She remembered the morning's outburst as if it had happened to someone else, a long time ago. Her tongue felt furry.

A little later she rose from the bed and found the mirror. Yes, the cirlces were still there, blurred and smeary now, but definitely there. She touched one faded mauve line, frowning.

THIS UNIT ADVISES YOU TO BATHE. FOR MOST EFFICIENT REMOVAL OF THE SUBSTANCE ON YOUR SKIN, THIS UNIT RECOMMENDS CLEANING CONCENTRATE 6-B.

Melanie sighed. The Dial was right, of course. The sooner she got the marks off, the better she would feel. She did not want to dwell on Derek's reasons for drawing the circles. If only her head were clearer, it would be easier to think.

She bathed in sour-smelling water. The cleaning concentrate, though it did an admirable job of removing the cirlces, smelled slightly fishy and left a chalky scum floating on the water. Her face felt tightened when she washed it, and the tepid water was not warm enough to tempt her to linger. The towel that dried her was unpleasantly scratchy, her clothes were wrinkled and their colors washed-out. A grayish haze hung over the mirror, making Melanie look even more haggard and spent than she was.

"Impossible," she said to the Dial. "You're being horrid!"

THIS UNIT HAS HIS BEST INTERESTS AT HEART.

"You don't have a heart!" Melanie shrieked at it, then forced herself to speak calmly. Another such outburst and there would be a few more hours of drugged sleep to took forward to. "I didn't mean that," she said evenly. "I realize that you have been programmed to put the interests of Derek first in your consideration. I suppose I might be jealous of him, since my unit is an old 385 model, and there's no way I can get a newer one for at least a year."

THAT IS INCONVENIENT, the Dial responded with what in a human being would have been smugness.

Choking back a sharp retort, Melanie looked around the bedroom. "I'm surprised that you've dimmed the walls. Derek doesn't like drab colors."

DEREK ISN'T HERE, the Dial pointed out.

"But if he should return unexpectedly?" Melanie suggested slyly, thinking that there were few ways she could get back at the machine.

The walls brightened and a flower-scent breeze wafted through the room.

"Oh! You're impossible!" Melanie waited for the Dial to display another retort, but it remained obstinately blank, and after a time, Melanie wandered into the sitting room.

THIS UNIT AWAITS INSTRUCTIONS.

The announcement startled Melanie. Then she pulled herself together. Perhaps the Dial had reconsidered its attitude. It wasn't in Derek's best interests to be quarreling all morning.

THIS UNIT REMINDS YOU THAT YOU HAVE LESS THAN 58 MINUTES TO PREPARE FOR DEREK'S ARRIVAL. HE RETURNS FROM WORK EACH DAY AT 3:27 P.M.

Melanie made an effort to think of all the things Derek had said he liked. It would be nice for him to come home to a special treat. It would show him that she was no longer upset with him, and that she wanted things to go well between them. A new setting would be a delightful way to begin their making up.

She was very explicit with the Dial. She knew that the garden maze and kiosk setting were far too advanced for her. The demands of all those hedges and flowers were daunting, but she decided to do her best. If she couldn't handle the maze, the kiosk and lawn would be a good compromise.

The Dial obeyed her, transforming the sponge chairs into rigid rattan, curliqued with Victorian determination. Next, the windows were taken care of. She decided that the setting should be rather more exotic, and so the view was of a sun-bruised spit of land reaching out into the sinuous bend of a river. Melanie had some vague mental picture in her mind of India in the days of the Raj, the proper British tea and crumpets juxtaposed with the mysterious, eternal soul of the East. She wished she knew how to program the Dial to make a turban for Derek.

The light had altered to leaf-filtered green. Melanie stood back and studied the effect. Derek, she decided, would be pleased.

THIS UNIT AWAITS FURTHER INSTRUCTIONS.

Scowling with concentration, Melanie went back to the Dial. This was much more difficult than she had thought. After a difficult moment, she selected the bird calls and other sounds, including a low, insect-like drone. Next she added a lazy wind redolent with spices and tropical flowers. But here she ran afoul of the Dial, which insisted on adding hickory smoke as well.

"But there isn't any hickory smoke in the jungle," Melanie objected, almost certain she was right.

THIS UNIT MUST REMIND YOU THAT HICKORY SMOKE IS HIS FAVORITE SMELL.

Melanie shrugged. It was only one little detail, and might not be important. What mattered was that Derek liked it. She would overlook this opposition to her will. Feeling more confident, she dialed the rest of the information and was delighted to see how avidly the machine accepted her instructions.

The far wall, which had been a fjord-blue, turned to a deep jungle green, and the air was filled with a somnambulant haze. The temperature soared reassuringly. The floor sprouted several inches of creepers and grass. Croquet hoops and balls appeared on the small patch of lawn.

Melanie was deeply satisfied as she lounged in the highbacked rattan rocker. This was going to be a great success, she was certain.

Now vines were twisting down from the ceiling, coiling around her affectionately as they sought the grounds. She giggled as one of them seemed to tweak her shoulder. It wasn't quite what she had in mind, but it was fun. The air was heavier, more humid. It was perfect, just perfect.

Not quite perfect.

There was an unfortunate odor coming through the hickory, a flavor of rotting seaweed spiced with old eggs. This overwhelmed even the heavy perfume of the gardenias. Melanie reached out for the Dial to adjust the olfactory scale, hoping the keep the stench from becoming unbearble.

The sky — for it was now more sky than ceiling — grew darker and took on a malignant orange tinge. There was a pall over the jungle, menacing. Alarmed, Melanie scrambled out of the chair and reached for the cancel level, when her foot slipped in the ooze.

Ooze?

What was the matter with the Dial, anyway? In the heat, fear made her cold, settling like a lump of ice at the base of her spine. She tried to tell herself that this was just an illusion conjured by the Dial, and that it had turned out badly because she had been too ambitious in the effect she had tried to achieve. Panic seized her. Nothing — nothing could convince her that she had done this on her own. She didn't know enough about the operation of the Dial to make so thorough a change of scene. And Derek said he had made modifications to this unit. Certainly, she had overstepped herself. She tried to move nearer the Dial, but by then she was mired in quicksand. It was then that she saw the yawning gap in the floor, like the maw of a tiger, or the entrance to Hell. Or a waste chute.

Melanie was still laughing hysterically when the floor closed over her, making a noise curiously reminiscent of a kiss, or, possibly, smacking lips.

Some little time later, there was a loud, mechanical belch.

"Melanie?" Derek stood in the middle of the sitting room. The fjord-blue walls and ceiling beamed down at him, a brisk, salt-laden breeze ruffled his hair. The sponge chairs turned toward him invitingly. It was 3:28 p.m.

Into the bedroom: "Melanie?"

"Melanie!" in the eating area.

At last, he went to the Dial. "All *right,*" he demanded. "Where is she?"

THIS UNIT MUST INFORM YOU THAT SHE IS GONE.

"Gone where?"

THIS UNIT DIRECTED HER TO A PROTEIN RECLAMATION CENTER.

There was a long, guilty pause.

THIS UNIT ATE HER. IT WAS IN YOUR BEST INTERESTS.

Derek smiled as he gave the Dial a reassuring pat. "That makes three," he said.

The Ghosts at Iron River

"Damn it, Nicholson, not over there!" James Raven Feathers yelled at the soccer players as the ball rolled between the staked mounds. "That's sacred ground! Cut it out!"

"Sorry, chief," came the call as Ian Nicholson retrieved the ball.

"Yeah. Just make sure you keep it away from here. Understand?"

The young man waved good-naturedly, jogging away across the dry grass. Nine other students in soccer togs followed him as James turned back to the RCMP Captain who stood with him in the staked enclosure at the end of the wide meadow.

"Aren't you being a little hard on them?" Captain Grey asked with a wink. "Should have thought you'd be out there yourself."

James Raven Feathers shook his head. "Not for me. Doctor's orders. And this is more important." He nodded toward the burial mounds.

"Right. I assume you've got it all cleared with the chief? There isn't going to be any nastiness over this." From the way he said it, Captain Grey was doing more than hoping. He straightened his rangy six feet and pulled on his gloves. "We got to stay around while you get the bodies moved, but after that, if you want to do anything special over them . . ." He left his thought open.

"Thank you," James said quickly. His dark, intense eyes were out of place in his young face. He scowled at the mounds. "First we'll have to open them. My grandfather will oversee that. Then we'll have to make sure all the skeletons are complete. They were buried wrapped in leather, but once that rots, there might be some drift. It's very important, a complete skeleton. My students are all set for that. When we're through, your men can come in and take care of the hauling."

"A lot of trouble for a . . ."

"A bunch of dead Indians?" demanded James fiercely. "You bet it is. But no one will move from here unless those dead Indians go with the live ones. And if we don't go, you don't get your hydroelectric dam."

Captain Grey shrugged. He liked young Wilson (Raven Feathers, he reminded himself) and trusted him to make the Iron River Indians' move as uncomplicated as possible. He knew that the younger men were touchy about being Indians, and he tried to go easy around them. But the habits of thirty years died hard and occasionally he blundered.

"We *do* value our dead," James said forcefully.

Grey sensed more irritation than usual in the Indian. "Has Chief Jackson tried to interfere?"

"No. It's not that. There was an article in the *Globe & Mail.* Davidson was kind enough to mail me a copy. One of their reporters had talked with Yngvessen."

"Oh? Who?"

"That muck-peddler Choffe." James fairly spat the name.

"What did he have to say?" Grey kicked a rock out of the path as he asked.

"The usual garbage. That we're a childlike, simple people, lacking culture and civilization, and that it's the responsibility of intelligent, progressive Teutons to look after the poor, incompetent Red Man." He snorted. "Predigested to words of two syllables."

"As bad as all that?"

"Yes, and we have to take it. Sometimes I wish Berenet had lived long enough to publish that bloody book of his. At least he had a different point of view. As it is we're saddled with that dreck of Yngvessen's."

"I see," Grey said, involuntarily looking at the bleak setting of the Iron River village.

James followed his glance. "Grandfather wants to talk to you. Today, before you leave. He told me to tell you."

Grey nodded. "Good. I'll go now. Always like seeing William. He's been a lot of help over the years. He sure knows how to handle people." The praise was genuine and it won him a wintery smile from the sullen young man at his side.

"Yes, grandfather has always been a peaceful Indian. A real model of failing culture." There was just enough resentment in his voice to make Liam Grey say

88

sharply: "Now, you look here, James, being peaceful kept your people together more than once. Back in the '20s the tribe almost got broken up and William fixed it. Even when Berenet disappeared, your grandfather kept everyone here out of hot water, in spite of Yngvessen. You've got no call to speak of him that way." He had begun walking back through the mounds toward the few, plain houses that were the homes of the Iron River Indians.

"Grey, he's my grandfather. I know what keeping us all together has cost him. Lots." The straight dark brows drew down over his eyes. "And we're still getting moved."

"The tribe voted to move," Grey reminded him.

"With half the province looking over their shoulders. And with the experts in Regina and Calgary quoting that damned book of Yngvessen's. A lot of choice we had."

Although Grey secretly agreed with the young man, he had had enough. "You stop being a professional Indian, James. If you want to do that to your students at McGill, fine, but don't try it around me. I'm trying every bit as hard as you to keep this tribe together." Abruptly he stopped talking.

"I'll take you to my grandfather," James said stiffly. "Follow me." Without looking at the Captain he moved ahead of him. At the door of the largest house he stopped. "He's inside. He hasn't been well. It's his eyes."

"I won't be long." Grey smiled with what he hoped was warm assurance, and went into the house.

The room was a fugitive from sunshine. The curtains had been marshaled against the windows, the colors vague and dim. Even the big-bellied stove showed only a faint ruddiness at the grille.

In the corner between the stove and the bookcase was an old leather chair, made so comfortable with use that it was nearly shapeless. At the moment William Wilson sat in it, his near-blind eyes trained on Grey.

"Good afternoon, Liam," he said.

"Good afternoon to you, William," Grey answered.

"My grandson has been giving you a piece of his mind?"

"No more than usual."

The old man chuckled. With his white hair braided neatly down his back and his high-necked robe he looked more like a venerable Korean scholar than the medicine man of the Iron River Indians. "He has even lectured me. Wants me to change my name to Raven Feathers. That was his father's name, of course. Mine is Hand-of-Water." He pointed to a chair. "Sit down, Liam."

"They're ready to start digging out there tomorrow, William," Grey said gently.

Wilson simply nodded. He pulled the blanket on his knees higher up his chest. "Watch out for John Yellow Sky. He wants to turn this into an incident." He shook his head. "An Indian informing against an Indian. A thing James deplores."

Grey tugged at his gloves. "What kind of incident?"

Wilson shook his head again, this time with disgust. "Yellow Sky wants headlines, and with Maxwell Choffe, he'll get them. Aaron Jackson almost called a tribal council over it."

"But he didn't." Grey wondered how much pressure had been put on the chief from both sides to bring things this far.

"No. I stopped him. He's left the running of the tribe to me for the last fifteen years, anyway. He knew he couldn't handle it. Well, I can. I suggested James have a little chat with Yellow Sky." He reached out to the stove and the pot of coffee. "Don't think James understands Yellow Sky. John wants the blood." He poured himself a cup, returning the pot to the stove with the handle toward Grey. "James wants justice. John wants vengeance."

Grey rose and poured himself a cup of coffee. He had learned that this was the simplest form of hospitality, and that if he had been offered the drink, then the endless ritual of repaying would begin.

"Better be on the alert, Liam."

Grey sipped the coffee. "Who else is in with Yellow Sky?"

"Eddie Two Foxes. Both of the Harris boys . . . calling themselves Hare-in-the-Snow these days. David Lynx. Henry Running Bear was with them, but shied off a while back."

"As far as you know?"

"As far as I know," he admitted. "Talked to Aaron about it. I hoped he'd take a hand for once, but he's sitting on this. I think he wants it to go away."

Captain Grey did not like Chief Jackson the way he liked William. To him, the old chief was evading the issues, letting the tribe grow dangerously polarized. He said: "Is he planning to be here for the disinterring?"

"Don't think so. Told me he thought it would be better if we all kept away. Let the university people handle it."

After a moment Grey said cautiously, "He's asking for trouble."

William nodded. "Yes," he said.

James was waiting for him when Grey left the old man. His Indian calm had returned and he looked at Grey with remote severity. "My students are waiting for you. We want to discuss the arrangements for tomorrow."

Grey considered his answer. "Good," he said at last.

"They're waiting at the trailers."

"Right." Grey started toward the four small house trailers that hid behind the wooden buildings as if ashamed of their shiny aluminum bodies. "Coming?"

James did not answer but fell into step beside the Captain.

90

*   *   *

The students were gathered around the ashes of a campfire in the circle of the trailers. They had changed from their soccer togs into more practical camping clothes, and now they were getting ready for the long northern twilight of summer. Grey thought them all very young, especially the tawny giant who was laying the fire.

"A little early for that, isn't it?" James asked sharply.

"The sun's down," said the short stocky one. James introduced him as Sandenny.

"And that's Nicholson, Adams, Kepple, Feyette, Alyoisu, Stuart, McCloud, Whiting, and over there is Bates."

Grey nodded to each and hoped he could keep them straight. Nicholson was easy, the blond giant; Adams, wiry; Kepple, lean and lantern-jawed; Feyette, unremarkable; Alyoisu, absurdly handsome; Stuart, carrot hair, no freckles; McCloud, nothing noticeable; Whiting, big-chested and sturdy; Bates, retiring and unfriendly. So long as he could keep Feyette and McCloud straight he would be fine.

"Go ahead, Captain," James said.

He stepped forward. "About your project tomorrow: we'll be here to help you, and to keep publicity at a minimum. You aren't old enough to remember the trouble when Berenet turned up missing fifteen, sixteen years ago. Yngvessen took advantage of that incident in his book, as you probably know. We're going to try to keep that from happening again. Now, some of the young men of the tribe might try to force our hand here. If that happens, you're to stay well out of it. Let the RCMP handle it." Grey hated this kind of talk and knew he did it badly. Doggedly he continued: "For the rest you take orders from Professor Raven Feathers — he's in charge of the whole operation, even the police. We rely on his judgment. Are there any questions?" He hoped for a response just to show that they'd been listening.

"Captain Grey?" Stuart, red hair. "What should we do about reporters? Chief Jackson said we might have some around."

"Do as Dr. Raven Feathers tells you. He'll know best what the press should cover and what is private to Iron River. Any more questions? Mr. Kepple?" This last was in response to Richard Kepple's hand tentatively in the air.

"Suppose the press is pushy? And we can't manage them? Should we call you?" He was obviously referring to Choffe.

"If a reporter won't be referred to Dr. Raven Feathers, and is not respecting the barriers you've set up, all you have to do is ask for our help."

Ian Nicholson put his huge paw into the air. "What if John Yellow Sky and his bunch try to make trouble? They've said they would. What are you prepared to do to stop them?"

This was a question Grey had dreaded. He thought about his answer very carefully. "I know what John Yellow Sky has been saying about the moving of the tribe. I've read his statements about the obligations of the white man to Indians and the restitutions he feels are due. I will not debate that question now or later. But I know that he wants to create some particular reaction here for the moving of the burial grounds. The whole project is supposed to take a week, and his group could cause trouble at any time throughout the week. We know that he will certainly be present most of the time. But until he has actually done something, leave well enough alone. My men have handled John and his" — he almost said boys — "bunch before. We can do it again. If we have to, keep out of the way."

"Any more questions for the Captain?" James asked briskly. When none were forthcoming, he turned to Grey. "That does it. But just one more thing: a couple of Yngvessen's students might show up with Choffe. What are you going to do about them?"

Grey shrugged. "What can I do? Lock them up? Toss them in the river? They've got a right to be here if Chief Jackson gives them permission. If they don't have his permission, then they get sent out. That's all I can do. Sorry, James."

"Aaron Jackson will let them in," James said with certainty. "Yngvessen scared him gutless with that book." He frowned. "All right. Thank you for speaking with my students." On cue there was a ragged bit of applause. "We start tomorrow, and work for a week."

"Yes," said Grey. "I'm glad you're in charge, Jamie. You're a good man."

Reeling mentally between the insult of his childhood nickname and the compliment of being called a good man by someone who had known him most of his life, James Raven Feathers found himself stammering for the first time in years. "I . . . I'll . . . walk you back to your car," he said lamely.

"I'll be glad of your company." He turned to the group around the fire. "Tomorrow morning, then. Thank you for your co-operation."

The young men at the campfire waved before they turned back to their projects.

As they walked away from the trailers, Grey said to James, "We do know that there will be reporters from Calgary and Regina here to cover the moving, not just Choffe. And a sports writer is coming from Winnipeg to get a story on you for his magazine."

"Shit!" James said through clenched teeth.

"Wants a story on what a famous la crosse player does in his spare time," Grey added apologetically.

"I'm not even playing any more. What makes them think that the only thing I do is play la crosse?" he demanded of the air.

"You were doing pretty well until that accident. You're still headline material in sports."

James was about to speak and then thought better of it. Finally he said, "Well, it paid for my Ph.D. even if I got a chunk of steel in my arm that tells when it's going to rain." He glanced shyly at Grey. "It felt good, all that fame. For the first year I thought I was king of the world."

They walked on in silence, letting the understanding slip away. Then, "Was it hard to give up, James?"

The young man laughed abruptly. "Yes. I thought that they'd fix me up like new. *Really* like new." He pushed out with his hands before jamming them into his pockets. "Well, they didn't. They couldn't."

With a sympathetic smile Grey said, "I know how I felt when I read about the accident. Dreadful."

"Another poor Red Boy proved he couldn't take care of himself, huh?" James asked bitterly.

He had not understood. Grey looked at him with a certain shock on his weathered face. "No. I thought that William's grandson was pretty bad hurt."

Unable to express either shame or contrition, James took refuge in petulance. "And hoped there wouldn't be a fuss. How did we get on this, anyhow?" he went on in a different voice. "This is too depressing."

They had reached the Land-Rover that Grey drove in the rugged country of Iron River. It was equipped with every extra that was available. The Captain had once used the winch to pull four stranded cows out of a mudbank. Grey put his hand on the door but made no move to open it. "About tomorrow," he began awkwardly. "We might be in for more trouble than we counted on."

The dark eyes that looked into his blue ones were flinty. "Yes?"

"I can have guards if you think it necessary. Now, don't fly off the handle, James," he added quickly. "I know that gets your back up. But there's going to be reporters and everything here tomorrow. You know that John Yellow Sky isn't going to let an opportunity like this slip by. And some of Yngvessen's people are bound to be here with Choffe. He's trouble all by himself. So think it over. I'll do what you think best." He opened the door. "Don't make me any speeches, just think it over. I want you to be sure." He stepped into the car, fumbling for the keys as he moved.

"What if I don't want any guards, after all?" This was a challenge.

"It's your decision, James. If you think it's better without guards, all right. That's the way we'll do it."

"What about stand-by?" James shifted uneasily as he looked beyond the Captain to the burial mounds.

"Certainly. As many men as you want. I'll check with you first thing in the morning." He slammed the door before James could say anything more. He started the motor, gave it a minute to warm up, then drove off down the rutted dirt road of the Iron River reservation.

James watched him go, then walked thoughtfully back toward the circle of trailers.

The signs were all over, the next morning. Written in clumsy block letters, terse, simple, they framed the burial mounds:

THIS IS THE WHITE MAN'S LEGACY . . . THE ONLY GOOD INDIAN IS A DEAD INDIAN . . . WE HAVE A RIGHT TO OUR WAY OF LIFE . . . ELECTRICITY IS MORE IMPORTANT THAN RED DIGNITY . . . SINGING LOON BETRAYS US and cryptically, JACKSON'S FOLLY.

James Raven Feathers stood looking at the signs for a few minutes, his eyes hooded. "Yellow Sky, damn him." That was said softly. The next was not. "Sadenny! Nicholson! Whiting! Get out here!" He started purposefully toward the trailers.

"Something wrong?" Bert Adams bounced out of the trailer first, an eager smile on his face. "Are we late?"

"Go look," James said stonily as he walked to the trailers and began to pound on the doors.

The first grumblings and stirrings were heard inside the trailers as Bert Adams ran back from the mounds. "That's going to have to come down, sir, isn't it? They're in awful deep."

"Yes. It's going to have to come down. Feyette, get out here!" he bellowed as Bates, McCloud, and Stuart stumbled into the morning.

"What's the matter?" asked a sleepy Richard Kepple as he opened his door.

"Yellow Sky is playing games," James said violently. His hands clenched at his side. "That bloody fool. He's going to turn this into a grandstand play if it kills him." He took three deep breaths, saying more calmly: "I want one of you to get my grandfather. We need him here."

"Right," one of the young men said.

"And I'll want to talk to Henry Running Bear. He ought to know about this, and he's cowed. He'll tell us what Yellow Sky is up to."

"I'll do it," McCloud volunteered.

"Good. Thank you." He nodded. McCloud took this for an authorization and trotted off toward the houses. "The rest of you, get some hatchets and come with me. We've got to get those signs down before Captain Grey gets back here with the observers." He stood while the others went for their tools, muttering, "Damn Yellow Sky. He makes Yngvessen look right."

"I've got the hatchets. And Dave's bringing the shovels," Nicholson said as he came up to James. "Where do we start?"

94

"Come along," James said coolly, taking a hatchet from Ian and heading back toward the mounds.

"Is there going to be trouble?" Ian asked amiably as he trotted beside James. "I'll do my bit, if you want, Dr. Raven Feathers."

James stopped in his tracks. "Ian, don't. You try anything and you'll be playing right into John's hands. And Choffe's. He wants headlines, dirt, savages. He thrives on ugliness." He looked up into the wide blond face. "Don't let this get out of hand."

"Okay. I just thought you wanted Yellow Sky's head on a pole."

It was a terrible admission for James to make. Here was a Nordic giant beside him asking about a fellow Indian. Inside, James allowed that Nicholson was right, but he could not say so. "We've got work to do," he said and resumed walking toward the burial grounds.

McCloud was waiting for them. "Your grandfather will be along shortly. He wasn't up yet. He sent Charlie to find Running Bear for you. Looks terrible, doesn't it?"

"Yes." James glanced back toward the trailers and saw that his students were following him. He waited for them to catch up, then he said, "We've got about forty-five minutes to get all that crap down. Chop 'em down or dig 'em out, I don't give a damn which. Just don't disturb any of the mounds. The ones close to the mounds, use hatchets on them. Anything beyond the stakes, those you can dig out, if you're careful."

"We'll be careful," Michael Whiting assured him as he started toward the signs. "Boy, they really set those things up." He grabbed one of the poles and shook it. "That's in deep," he said and started to dig.

The others selected poles and began either to dig or chop while James anxiously watched in case the burial mounds should be disturbed. The first of the signs had come down when William Wilson joined his grandson by the signs.

"I am not surprised," he said when he had had the signs read to him. "John Yellow Sky wants to make trouble here. He is just getting started. Watch. This is so."

James shook his head at his grandfather. "This is a grandstand play. If we handle it right, he'll leave us alone."

The old man wagged his finger at James. "He is a dangerous man, Jamie. You will not contain him so easily."

"I've sent for Running Bear. Between us we should get some sense out of Henry." There was a stubborn set to his mouth, so William did not press him further.

"There is not much time," he said.

Then, "Doctor . . ." Mark Alyoisu said from where he was digging. His eyes were frightened in his handsome face. "There's something down here. I thought this was safe. I didn't know that there were other mounds. . . ."

"What is it?" James went to him, puzzled. "You're outside the area. . . ."

"But I've hit some . . . one. . . ." He was quite pale now, white around the mouth. "There's a body down there. I didn't mean to do anything. Honest. I thought it was safe."

James pushed him aside and looked into the small hole Alyoisu had dug. He knelt, and scooped the dirt away with his hands. Then he stopped. "You're right." He said it quietly, but they all heard it.

Old William stumbled toward James. His fading eyes tried vainly to see what was in the hole. "This is not the sacred ground. It is too far to the north. This is not right."

James rose. "There is someone down there, grandfather. I had my hands on the ribs."

"Yellow Sky!" William said in a terrible rage. "He has desecrated the graves of his ancestors. For his futile posturing he has done this! I am ashamed." The leathery old man stopped shouting quite suddenly. He turned to his grandson. "Call Liam. Tell him what has happened. See if he can stop the visitors until we can find out how far his sacrilege has gone."

"Yes, Grandfather."

"And call Aaron. No. I will call him. I want him to know what his vacillation has done to us." And feeling his way he stalked off to his house.

The rest stood, looking into the hole.

Finally Edgar Bates asked, "Should we go on digging?"

"Better not," James said slowly. "Not with this." He looked over the burial mounds. "But you'd better clear away around that one. Make sure you don't disturb the skeleton. Keep it intact if you can. I'll have to talk to Grey and see what he wants done. We might just need those guards after all."

As he walked off the young men began, reluctantly, to dig.

Twenty minutes later Grey came barreling down to the houses. His face was set and his shoulders were tense.

"And I thought Berenet used to take chances on this road," James greeted him as he slammed out of the Land-Rover. "We don't need another accident on our hands."

"What's this all about?" Grey demanded without preamble.

James hesitated. "It's pretty awkward." Then, as Grey strode angrily toward him: "We found an extra body. The boys are digging it up now."

"What do you mean, an extra body?"

"Just that. It was beyond the mounds, oh, about ten feet. We thought it was safe."

Grey clamped his hands to his hips. "What the hell were you doing digging, anyway? That wasn't supposed to start until we all got here."

96

Realization dawned on James's face. "That's right. You don't know about the signs, do you?"

"What bloody signs?" So as they walked toward the mounds and the extra skeleton, James explained about the morning. "And now we have this extra body to deal with. I don't even know who it was. I was hoping that grandfather might tell us."

"Yellow Sky," Grey said as James finished. They were next to the staked mounds and James's students were taking down the last of the signs with their hatchets.

"I've told them not to dig any more out. There might be more."

"You haven't brought this one up yet?" Grey cocked his head toward the hole. He did not want to get too close to the stakes.

"No. I don't want to disturb more than I have to."

"Good. What about Yellow Sky? Seen him about this morning?" Grey pulled out a small notebook and began to sketch the sign and the hole. "Go on; I'm listening."

"Well, I've sent for Henry Running Bear. Probably won't do any good, but I hope he might be able to fill us in on what John is planning to do next. This may only be a warm-up," he said grimly.

Grey snorted in agreement. "How is William taking it?" He toed the sign that lay in the dirt at his feet. "He sounded very upset on the phone."

"He is. He thinks that John opened the mounds or moved the staking so that the graves could be desecrated." James paused as he thought it over. "Does that make any sense to you, Grey?"

It was Grey's turn to think about it. "No," he said at last. "Not John Yellow Sky. This isn't his style. He wanted this for publicity, for a soapbox, not to shut the place down. This isn't flamboyant enough for him, not this way. Unless he's got something more in mind, other than a skeleton." He looked around again, squinting against the sun. "This is going to be real trouble if Choffe gets ahold of it."

James said nothing. He sighed unhappily. "But it would have worked," he said wistfully.

"I know."

Then James shook off his mood. "Do you want that body brought out of the ground?" he asked briskly. "I've told them to start, but this might be in your sphere, not mine."

"No, not yet. There are some other questions to take care of first. I'm going to talk to William now. Keep Henry around wherever you are. I don't want him wandering off until we have a little chat. Who's picking him up?"

"Charlie Moon." James gave a half-smile at the mention of his lawyer cousin. "Ogilvie, Tallant, and Moon decided they could spare him, so he flew in last night. He said he had a feeling we might need a good attorney. We turned Henry over to him. Charlie will take care of him."

Flipping his notebook closed Grey said, "I don't doubt it." He started walking toward William's house. He went slowly, reluctant to disturb his old friend again. He turned over all the questions that faced him in his mind. He was fully aware of the trouble this would bring to the tribe. With one Indian agent disappearing, followed so closely by that ruinous book of Yngvessen's, this might well be the final disaster for the Iron River tribe. More than either James or William, he knew the ambivalence most people had for Indians. A thing like this, well, it was a great excuse to scatter the tribe. Even Yngvessen had suggested it; it would be a way for them to upgrade their culture. He was deeply afraid that this would be the end. His heels bit more deeply into the pathway. He did not know how to influence the reporters who were coming to cover the disinterring, especially Choffe, who was armed with Yngvessen's opinions. He hoped that they could all be held back, if only for a few hours. Otherwise it would be difficult.

"Come in," said the old voice in response to the knock. Grey pulled the door open.

"Come in, come in," William ordered. "Want to talk to you. Don't want those foolish heads outside to hear us." He grunted impatiently as Grey secured the door.

"Now then," he continued as Grey walked forward, "we have got a proper mess now. There's a body out there in the wrong place. John Yellow Sky put it there. . . ."

"I'm not sure he did," Grey said quietly. He was silent, waiting for William to go on.

"What do you mean?" The old man rose and came toward Grey. He was a head shorter than the Captain, but he seemed taller. "What do you mean, Liam? What is that body there for? Who put it there?"

Grey shook his head. "I don't know. I don't think Yellow Sky did it. There's no point to it. I think that either the stakes were moved or the old mound was flattened in the '43 flood. You remember? You said some of the old graves were lost."

"That was thirty years ago. Even before Berenet came. It could be." The old man shuffled back to his leather chair. "What if Yellow Sky found out about the body and planned this?"

Grey shook his head reluctantly. "It doesn't fit the pattern, William. What publicity would he gain?"

"You're as bad as Berenet with the endless history of the tribe he was writing." William paused, then reached for his coffee mug. "I don't know. That's puzzled me, too. Yellow Sky is usually direct."

When the coffee pot was returned to the stove Grey helped himself. "Can you get Aaron to keep the reservation closed for a few more hours?"

"I will try." He drank half the coffee in silence, then went into the other room where the tribe's one telephone was kept. Chief Jackson lived in town, visiting the reservation only when necessary.

Grey waited while the call was made, meditatively sipping his coffee. He could hear William's voice raised in anger, but could not make out the words. He refilled his mug and sat down.

"The old fool," William was muttering as he came back into the room. "He told me to shut the thing up. Choffe is flying in from Saskatoon in two hours, and I'm supposed to shut it up. How do you shut up a body? Told me to have them bury it again and leave it. And he's an Indian." The scorn in his voice almost choked him.

"May I make a suggestion, William?" Grey asked, as soon as the old man had stopped talking.

"Go ahead. Won't hurt anything more. He's keeping the other reporters at the gatehouse for an hour so that George Snake Killer can give them a lecture on the history of the tribe. Without Yngvessen's theories. That's all he's willing to do. More than that would look suspicious, he says."

Mentally Grey damned Chief Jackson for a fool, but he said, "Let's take the body out. Remove it to the hall, get it out of the way. Then we can dig up the others, and claim that the sign poles were part of the preparation for the disinterment. We can tell them that only Indians were allowed to attend that ceremony."

For a moment William was silent. Then he chuckled, "*We* do this for *us* Indians?" He grinned at his friend. "All right. It is not what I would want to do, but there is no time for that. I will order the body to be removed from the area and placed in the meeting hall so that I can set to work finding out who it was." He hesitated for a bit, folding his hands across his chest. "There is no need for you to support us. That was your decision. I am proud to have you my friend." Which was as close as he could come to saying thanks.

"There is still going to be the devil to pay. I just brought you a suggestion. All we've got is very little time." Grey said this hastily as he rose from his chair, determination back in his manner. "I'll get the boys on it. Guess James will go along with us?"

With a steely smile, William said, "Oh, yes."

The students were standing uncertainly outside of the staked area when Liam Grey returned to them. "All right," he told them, "it's back on. Dig him out. Put him in the hall when you've got him out. You've got about half an hour." He looked around as he heard his name called, and saw Charlie Moon coming toward him, a wolfish grin on his pointed face.

"I've got a surprise package for you, Grey. He's waiting in the trailer. A nice little teddy bear." He waved offhandedly to the students. "James is keeping him company, but I think you'd better come along. James can be pretty rough on toys."

Promising the students that he'd be back shortly, Grey strode off with Charlie Moon to the trailers.

"What has he said?" he asked the young attorney at his side.

"Denies all knowledge of the skeleton. He said that they only put the signs up to annoy James. I get the feeling that John is saving the main event for later."

They turned into the circle of trailers. "Any idea what?"

"No," Charlie said as he opened the door of the second trailer.

James was seated backward in a chair, his arms folded across the back, chin resting on his arms. In front of him was a sturdy young man trying very hard not to look frightened. He was saying ". . . and all your talk about reconciliation with the White Man. Look what it's got us. We have to move and . . ." His voice trailed off.

"Hello, Grey," James said without turning. "Glad you could make it. Henry here was telling me about how you've abused us. Do you think you've abused us, Grey? Do you think Berenet abused us?"

Quickly Grey took over. He feared that otherwise it would degenerate into a name-calling contest. "Hello, Henry. You know about our find out there?"

"I don't know anything," was the fast sullen answer.

"Not even about the signs," Grey assumed incredulity. "I thought you were in on that."

"Well, on that . . ."

"And I thought you might know if John Yellow Sky had any clever ideas about planting skeletons? No?"

"I don't know what you're . . ."

"Forgetting for the moment that you broke the law when you put up those signs . . ."

"I didn't . . ."

"Yes, you did, Henry. Unless I say otherwise, you did. Now, where are John Yellow Sky and the Harris brothers?" He waited. "Well?"

"I don't know."

"Make a guess," said Charlie Moon gently.

"You can't make me. . . ."

"I can't," Grey agreed cordially. "But James and Charlie might want to." He let that sink in. "I don't have time for any more nonsense, Henry. We've got a hell of a mess on our hands right now. If you're going to play Martyred Indian, then off you go to jail until I find out what's happened."

"You're trying to bully me," Henry Running Bear lurched to his feet. "You stinking, genocidal White Man!"

"That's enough!" James's voice cut like a whip. "Let us talk to him, Liam. We can find out."

"Give him a chance," Charlie smiled. "He's read Yngvessen's book. He knows we're not civilized. He knows that our hard lives have made us brutal, stupid and violent. Right, Henry?"

"Hey, Captain, they can't do this." Henry looked beseechingly at Grey. "Can they?"

"If I know about it, they can't. But I told you, I don't have much time. If you haven't given us an answer I'll have to leave you with them." He managed to sound sorry.

"But that's not fair. You lousy cop!" He took two steps toward Grey. "It's not. They don't understand. They've already talked to John and he told them he . . ." Henry looked around uncertainly. "He told them how he felt about the move," he ended defiantly.

"Do you think he'd tell me?" Grey asked. "I haven't got much time, Henry. Remember that."

"I don't know. I don't," he said desperately. "He went back into the woods last night, after we put up the signs. I don't know where he is. I don't know if he'd talk to you."

"But he is planning more . . . entertainment?" Charlie suggested.

"He didn't tell me. Really." He was certainly scared now. "I asked him what he was going to do. He just said he had a real surprise for them. But it wasn't for today. It wasn't." He looked from one man to the next, pleading with his eyes. "I didn't think he'd do a thing like . . . that. . . ."

"Right," Grey said firmly. "Tell us where he is."

"In the woods. That's all I know. Back in the woods on the North Fork. He and Lynx and Two Foxes are up there. The others are off in Calgary. They left last night. They're going to get supplies. So you see, they can't do anything until they get back." He spoke in a rush.

"Anything more?" James asked.

"I don't know any more!" Henry yelled. "I don't! At least . . ." He glanced uneasily at Charlie Moon. "You're a lawyer, Charlie. You got to protect me."

"Oh, I will," he said pleasantly as a grin split his face.

"No, Charlie. Really. You got to help me. . . ." He stopped for a moment. "John might show up sometime while the press is here. But that's all I know. Honest, it is. Tell him, Charlie."

"All right, Henry. We believe you," Grey smiled down at him, taking full advantage of his height. "But let's suppose we get it all on paper, just on the chance you're wrong?" He pulled out his notebook and pen.

There was a knock on the door and Jerry Feyette stuck his head in the door.

"It's McCloud, James," Liam Grey said.

"Feyette, sir," he corrected. Then: "Sorry to bother you, Doctor, but there's something you should see before we move the body." He was uncomfortable, rubbing his hands on his overall as he spoke.

"Is it urgent? Can't it wait?"

"No sir, I don't think so." He pulled his earlobe. "There's something you'd better see."

James shrugged. "Oh, all right, if it's important." He rose from the chair and turned to the other two men. "Keep Henry company until I get back." With that, he slung his jacket over his shoulder and went out the door.

"What did you find?" he asked Feyette as they walked back toward the mounds.

"There's something strange about the skeleton. I figured you might know. . . ."

"Well, what is it?" he demanded.

But Feyette shook his head. "Better wait until we get there." He did not speak again until they had reached the gathering around the pile of bones on the ground.

"Now what is it?" James demanded as he came up to them.

Michael Whiting stepped aside for him as he pointed to the skeleton. "Take a look. The right arm, just above the elbow." James twinged, but knelt next to the skeleton.

"There. Right there," Lincoln McCloud said, touching the bone with the toe of his boot. "Look at it."

Puzzled, James picked up the humerus and turned it over in his hands. There, imbedded in the bone, slightly above the elbow, holding an old fracture together was a pin of stainless steel.

"One of you go get Grey," he said softly. "Tell him it's urgent." Gingerly he moved around the rest of the skeleton. When he got to the skull he stopped.

"That's the other thing we wanted you to see, Doctor," Leon Sandenny said cautiously. "That sure got bashed, didn't it?"

James picked up the ruined skull, trying to keep the fragments together. "This isn't anyone I know," he murmured.

"Did that happen after he was buried?" Bert Adams asked, a little frightened.

"I don't know. The break is in the back. I don't think so . . . I doubt it," James said dubiously. Somehow all the objectivity he had felt in Peru vanished now that his own tribe was involved. He put the skull down carefully. "Don't disturb that, all right?" he said to his students. "I want Grey to see it this way." He fingered the head of the pin in the bone. "No Indian I know has one of these. Except me." He studied the bone around the pin. "That was one hell of a fracture."

"What caused it?" asked Leon Sandenny as he squatted next to James.

James shook his head. "Some kind of accident. It put his arm out of commission for months, by the look . . ." Suddenly he remembered back. When he was ten? eleven? Berenet had had an accident while driving at his usual murderous speeds on an icy road. He had worn his arm in a cast for quite a while. . . .

"What is it *now?*" Grey demanded from above him.

James snapped out of his reverie. "You'd better take a look at this skeleton." He rose and stepped back. "Take a good look."

With a grunt and a perfunctory obscenity Grey dropped to his knees. "Pretty tall, wasn't he?" he asked of no one in particular.

"The skull and right arm," James prompted.

"Right." He picked up the skull, handling it with great care. "He really got his, didn't he?"

"With metal."

"The proverbial blunt instrument," Grey said drily. He looked up at James. "You're the anthropologist. You should be able to tell me what did this."

James knelt again, taking the skull from Grey. He turned it over slowly, checking the splintering of the bone. "I don't know, but I'd put my money on a hammer from the side. You see how this angle here. . . ." He touched the edge of the hole in the skull. "I think it's a hammer."

"And the arm." Grey had picked up the bone and touched it with some worry. "This. . . ."

But James tugged at his arm. "Yes. I want to talk to you about that, but not just here." He stood and drew Grey aside. "Do you remember the way Berenet drove? Didn't he have a bad accident about fifteen years ago, say a couple of years before he turned up missing?'"

"His arm was in a cast. The right one," he said reflectively. "You think that's Berenet?" he asked suddenly.

"It's not an Indian."

Grey sighed. "I'll check it out. I'll have to phone out. It might make it worse, if this isn't Berenet and Choffe or Yngvessen gets wind of it." He looked evenly at James.

The look was returned. "We've got to do this, no matter what. The body's got to be identified. There's a little time yet."

"Right." He stood, his weight slung into his hip, thinking. "You've got tools for sifting?"

"Sure. We were going to use them to be certain we got all of the effects in the mounds. Taken out with the bones and reburied in the new site — that's what we planned."

"So you're going to refute Yngvessen?"

"Not a chance," James said bitterly. "He's like Moby Dick. I'm not up to him."

"Gadfly?" Grey asked with a twinkle. "You can use those sieves now, to find out if there was anything else in the hole with that poor bastard."

"We'll get on it right away." He paused. "Can Grandfather buy us any more time?"

"I don't think so."

"Well," said James. "We can try. About half an hour, you'd say?"

"About that. Maybe William can hold them at the houses for a little while, but half an hour is the best I can guarantee." He shook hands with James and went off to the houses.

Twenty minutes later he had his answer, all the way from Regina. Yes, Agent Claud Berenet had had a bad accident; yes, it had resulted in a multiple fracture of the right humerus; yes, it had required surgery. Yes, a pin had been used. Grey fingered his notebook, lost in thought. If the skeleton were Berenet, then who killed him? Why did the whole tribe deny knowledge of it? Grey thought that he knew William well enough that he could trust the old man to leak information like that to him. True, this case was fifteen years old, but he hoped that William had been sure of him even then. . . .

He left the house, walking slowly back toward the mounds. Nicholson and Alyoisu were waiting for him, triumph in their eyes. "What have you found?" he asked.

Nicholson held out his hand. On his palm lay a tarnished silver crucifix and a St. Christopher's medal. "The chain was almost completely corroded. We found this under the head."

Grey touched the crucifix. "I see. Catholic." He stood still for a moment. "Where is Dr. Raven Feathers?"

Alyoisu cocked his head in the direction of the trailers. "He and Leon are processing a couple more things we found. It's all lab work for them."

"What things?" Grey asked, frowning deeply at the hole and then at his watch. There was very little time left.

"We found a few items that might have been caught in his clothes. Of course, they might be his, but they might be his murderer's too. Dr. Raven Feathers is waiting for you." Nicholson smiled benignly at him. "Should we fill the hole in, Captain?"

"Hum. Oh, certainly. Go ahead. The press should be along any minute now. Which trailer is Dr. Raven Feathers in?"

"The green one. You'd better knock before you go in. They're using some ruddy awful chemicals in there," Nicholson said happily. "Tell Dr. Raven Feathers we'll finish this up out here. And Mike Whiting will pitch them some guff about anthropology until he's free to talk."

"Good idea. Thanks for thinking of it." He kicked at the moist earth with his boot. "Make it neat, will you?" Before they could answer he had moved on toward the trailers.

Whatever chemicals James was using, they stank. Grey paused in the doorway as his lungs objected, then he went into the trailer, closing the door behind him.

James and Leon Sandenny were bent over the sink, each working with jeweler's pliers and small shards of metal. "Hi, Grey. I think we've found something."

"Yes?" He peered over their shoulders. "What is it?"

"Part of it," James said enthusiastically. "The rest is on the table over there. Be very careful with it."

Grey maneuvered to the table and saw there, on a strip of muslin, four or five tiny bits of metal like an incomplete jigsaw puzzle. "What is it? It looks like it had a chain."

"Right on the first try. It had a chain. It was under the left hand."

"Could it have been *in* the hand?" Grey held his breath as he bent over the table.

"Yes, it could have. There's a magnifying glass on the seat there. Have a look at that bottom line." James had not taken his eyes from the bits of metal in the sink.

As he picked up the glass, Grey asked, "What's on it? What am I looking for?"

"Look at it."

Curiously Grey moved the muslin into clearer light. As he did he could make out the lower halves of numerals. It was either 1936 or 1956.

"I'm betting on '36, myself." He managed a tight smile.

Leon Sandenny, hunched over a sliver of metal murmured, *"Mehr Licht."*

"Macht doch den zweiten Fensterladen auch auf," James said promptly. He remembered Yngvessen's fondness for the truncated version of Goethe's last words, and his anger at having the full quotation rendered, in quite acceptable German, by a poor Indian boy not yet in his teens. Then he realized. "What did you say?" he demanded.

"Look," Sandenny offered the scrap of metal to James. "That's what it says."

James let out a whoop of pure joy. "The watch fob. We've found the watch fob."

"So what?" Grey said. "It could have been planted. It might be Berenet's, if this is Berenet."

James scowled. "It might have been planted," he allowed. "But why? It's been

105

in the ground quite a while. If it is a plant, who planted it; Yellow Sky? No, I'll bet this is a souvenir of Nils Christian Yngvessen." He leaned on the table, bright intensity lighting his face. "This could almost make up for the book."

Grey put a restraining arm on James's shoulder. "If the tests prove you wrong, Jamie . . ." He didn't finish. He, too, wanted the guilty party to be Yngvessen. "It's not a lot."

"It's enough. He'll have to answer one hell of a lot of questions about this." He looked over his shoulder at his assistant. "How soon can you have this ready, Leon?"

"About an hour?"

"Good. Choffe will be here by then. Grey," he turned impulsively to the Captain. "Suppose Choffe finds out that Yngvessen did this. What will he do then?"

Grey answered drily, "He'll ruin Yngvessen."

James drummed his fingers on the table, smiling.

At this Grey was genuinely alarmed. "You can't accuse him, Jamie, not with so little proof. Especially in your position. If it turns out you're wrong it will look like a put-up job from the first. Yngvessen will pounce all over you. He'll destroy you. He can do it, too."

There was mockery in James's eyes. "I'm not going to accuse anybody. I am simply going to tell those nice gentlemen of the press what we found while digging in our own graveyard. They might not respect me as an anthropologist, but you said yourself they respect me as a la crosse player. They'll pay attention for that reason alone. I'll remind them that we do not allow digging within twenty feet of our burial mounds, and that whoever buried that man knew it. Then I'll have Leon produce these little displays, and put a few words in about the probable identity of the skeleton. . . ."

Grey relented. "It's Berenet. He had the fracture and the pin."

"Oh, we've got enough of a jaw to send along for dentals. That should take care of any doubting Thomases. Lincoln McCloud has taken some very interesting photographs, on Charlie's advice. And we've sent Henry off to meet Yellow Sky at the gates. So long as he is going to harangue the press we might as well get a statement from him. Without him, we'd never have found Berenet. I never thought I'd be happy for John's mischief, but I am now. I'll give him full credit for the find, if he likes. Publicly."

"But you can't be sure."

James smiled serenely. "That watch fob was a thing Yngvessen was very proud of. All the time he was here he boasted of it. It was a graduation remembrance from his family."

Grey nodded. "All right, Doctor, why did he kill Berenet?" Then, as he said it, he thought he knew the answer. "Berenet was writing a book, wasn't he? About the tribe."

James's smile deepened. "And Berenet didn't want Yngvessen's book published. He said Yngvessen was wrong. Talk about academic rivalry. Poor Berenet worked on that book of his for years. Grandfather said it was dreadful, but his history was right."

"There's the rest of it," Leon Sandenny said from the sink. "All we need is the bits around the edges and we've got it." He passed it over to James. "There you are, Doctor. 'Uppsala' and the date is 1936."

As his smile broke into a grin, "Great. Thanks," he said to Leon. "Well, Grey, care to wager what year Yngvessen graduated?" He put the missing sliver into the fob. "Aren't those nice reporters due here about now? It would be a crime to keep them waiting." He straightened up. "Coming, Grey?"

"You don't have a case yet."

"Oh, I'll leave it to you and Charlie to do that for me. There's certainly enough evidence to warrant a preliminary investigation."

"So you dump a case like this in my lap without so much as a by-your-leave?" He glanced at the watch fob and heaved a sigh of resignation. "Right. Lead on, James."

"Oh, no." Dr. Raven Feathers paused in the door. "After you, Liam."

They went out together.

Fugitive Colors

Like a scream falling he fell away from Earth down the long night. The roar at his back had been loud once, but loud only to him; a cry that would reach no ears but his own. In the beginning he had found some sense in it, in the demonic threads of sound that reached out to him through the spume of stars. How easy it had sounded when he had volunteered for the voyage, and how difficult, how impossible, it had turned out to be. The glowing promises and assurances were sufficiently far behind him that they could no longer reach him, and the chance to correct their earthbound expectations was lost to him forever.

The old days had been different — no one had gone very far, and the umbilical cord of sound and sight held the adventurer as securely as a leash. Centaurus was reachable and there had been a kind of glory for him when he was the second to make the voyage and the first to return alive. Then they had told him of their new discovery, the culmination of a dream, the wished-for faster-than-light drive that would make a mockery of time and scoff at distances. He had believed them. He had wanted to believe them. He would go farther and longer than any man living, and still have half a lifetime to call his own on his return. There would be hundreds of light-years to his credit, and a chance to enjoy his place in history.

Arcturus tomorrow, they had promised him. He had listened to their explanations and accepted them, prepared to wait through the endless hours, the neverending night. But the loneliness was too familiar and the dark a thing he had known before.

That was before the ship had changed, and now there were only impossible things in the ever-receding void. Strange splendor would occasionally rise in the dark and he would watch, thinking himself in the heart of a star. He remembered the change, that moment when his substance made the crossing which had robbed him of his sky, his light, of days that were marked with the position of those beacon stars that surged and faded and sang. Now he did not know the things that slid by him in the engulfing silence, for now they were not points of light, not the familiar mocking brightness, but strange elliptical vortices, showing colors that made no sense to him, colors for which he had no name. He thought of what he had known before, the wanderings of the traditional animals in the sky, and he longed, uselessly, to return to that place where things were as they ought to be.

One idea niggled at the back of his mind, an idea he refused to recognize, one that he would not face; for if it were true, then he would no longer exist, and would be truly and ultimately separated from himself, rushing away into the dark at impossible speeds. Over and over he insisted to himself that since he could think, he must be cohesive.

It did him no good to look back. Aft there were the others, lost in their awesome sleep that defied the clocks of mortality: hoary they were, without awareness of their adventure, their uniqueness — without any knowledge, without senses — and as far as he knew, now without life. They were stopped, held in a waiting they could not feel in anticipation of a landfall that would never come.

Behind the cargo were the dormant volcanoes of his engines, not needed now that the change had occurred. And beyond the open, silent mouths of the engines was the dark, always the dark.

An ineffable pull tugged at him, the unknown and unfelt tide of Sol, his sun, his home, his light. He had experienced its touch before, going to Centaurus, but now it was part of his being, mixed with his bones, and it wore at him like pain. The shapes around him in the luminous dark were all strange, and none of them were as real to him as the star he could no longer see. It was yellow, he remembered, and gold, burning orange at sunset. He dared not admit to himself that these were words only, and he no longer knew whether yellow was like summer hillsides or like old paper. He missed the touch of paper almost as much as he missed those summer hillsides.

He knew a kind of time was passing, that his body — if he still had a body — was tuned to its own finiteness, that there was a rhythm that lulled and waked him in seasons of its own while centuries flickered by. Looking out at the radiant

110

dark, he pretended he knew the shapes that lived there. He was determined to understand their strangeness, to make it part of him and so lose the sense of being utterly lost. If a dark spot in a glowing constellation could be called a Coalsack, then he, too, would make names to identify the things he saw.

That curving luminosity, shifting across the blackness, suggesting softness and depth — that, he decided, was Celia. Celia, the woman he had spent his last earthbound night with, Celia who had been a gift of a grateful and generous government, the best of their payroll. She was lovely, he remembered, the color of new sand with hair bright as ripe corn. What a last-night fling she had given him! He had been more drunk with her body than he had ever been with wine. Tangled limbs and rumpled sheets, these returned to haunt him in the long, long dark, and he saw her in the night around him.

At first he had wondered if she would be there when he got back, but now it no longer mattered. He would not get back; he knew this. Even if he did, time would have harvested her long ago.

To take his mind away from these things he had turned to the micro library and the recordings, until he knew the words and sounds so well that they made no sense and could not move him. What did white whales mean to him, when they were things of mortality and time.

When he had become desperate and so alone that he no longer thought of himself as human, he took women from the Cold Room, and superimposed his memories of Celia on them. They had been a delight at first. They were companionship, talk, soft touches and curling sleep. But they didn't last long, these women. For awhile, a very little while, they thrived with summer in their faces, but not for long. Eventually the shadow would come over them and they would wither, coming to hate him as they did.

So now he did not have the women. It was easier. Now Celia's image blossomed in his mind, warming him, touching him with the compelling bonds of Sol. It was better this way, he told himself, because this way his recollections were uncontaminated and complete, an entire picture without distortion.

He had the computer, though he had begun by resenting it, using it only for information. But as the distances grew more terrible, he hoped for company and understanding. He had Celia for his dreams, but even he could not dream forever. Once or twice he longed for his own kind with a longing that was close to madness, and he had asked the computer to find the others — the three other ships like his that had set out into the vastness at the same time he had. The other ships had been scattered like seeds, and logic told him that they must be somewhere. The machine could not do this thing and he blamed it for his isolation.

Time drifted on, sliding with the alien lights. For what may have been the tenth or fiftieth or hundred-thousandth time, he calculated the chances of finding Arcturus amid the wavering brightness. Would he, in the changed place, know if he were near it? Or would it be only another of the pools of shifting light that spread around him? He was enough of a mathematician to know that the chance was too remote to bother with.

He took to reverie as the ties of language forsook him, calling up the ghosts of his terrestrial life, seeing Cecelia, her pale skin, her hair like ripe grain, butter colored, falling softly on her rosy face. Her body was warm and filled with ripeness, a seedpod near its bursting. Was he mistaken, or had there been a light about her that imbued her with the brightness of the sun?

It troubled him that he might not remember clearly anymore, that this night had laid its fingers upon him and surely, secretly, plucked away his memories. For he knew that the days he had spent with Cecelia were special, that she had yearned for him and wept her distraction when they were parted at last. He knew that even now she would be waiting, a faded woman slipping into the quiet of the grave, wearing her sorrow like a banner. The limpid pools of her eyes would be muddied with age, deep crystal wells telling her story more surely than words.

How he longer for her, to lie with her, finite, at peace, in the tangible earth. Death was nothing here, where life itself eluded him. But there, with the grass and the rain, it would be fitting. No matter what happened to him, the ship, guided by the computer would fling itself endlessly through the night. It would be an easy thing to be like Cecelia, if only for a little time. Little or long, it would mean nothing to him now. He would put himself into the sleep that was not sleep. The shapes in the night would not bother him and the memories of Cecelia would be fresh within him.

So, clutching Sol and Cecelia to him as the last rags of his humanity, he offered himself to the oblivion of the Cold Room.

(Entity/vehicle/movement) around (us/this one): (we/this one) will (communicate/align with/associate with) (you/that one).

It was a day without number when he woke again. The thing was in front of the ship, as distorted as the stars and lights that pinwheeled in the dark around it. The thing surged and flopped like a beached whale. He watched it come and wondered what it was and why it had wakened him.

The alien thing drew nearer, coming languidly through the great speeds, growing. It loomed, bulged, crested like a wave. He stared at it and found in it all the bogeys of his aeons-lost childhood. None of the others in the Cold Room had heard it, and none of the others had emerged from sleep. He inspected the chatterings of the computer, and dreaded the stranger for no reason other than strangeness.

The habits of solitude were strong in him, and only Cecily was permitted to share in his memories. To have this thing he did not understand — a thing as distorted as the dark invading his place, his mind, manipulating him — filled him with disgust.

(Entity/vehicle/movement), (prepare/alter awareness) to (receive/participate) with (us/this one).

Frightened now, he waited. The thing outside, around his ship, throbbed steadily, beating like wings, or a heart, though there was no sound, and could be no sound.

(We/this one) will (detain/arrest/interrupt) (you/that one). (We/this one) will not (hold/keep/accompany) (you/that one) more than (we/this one) (find necessary/think important/consider reasonable). (We/this one) have (information/intelligence/data/insight) that (we/this one) must (impart/inform/adapt) to (you/that one).

The thing grew steadily nearer, dwarfing his ship and making him worry for the ones in the Cold Room, from which he had so recently emerged. In this alien place, with its uncharted tides and unpredictable occurrences, what might happen? He had been so eager for change, any change, and now that it had happened, he longed for the sameness he had disliked.

(We/this one) (request/insist/require) that (you/that one) (present/demonstrate) (your/that one's) (appearance/likeness/schematics).

He stared around his quarters, his living tomb, and could not remember what he looked like. What color was his hair? Was the strand across his eyes gray, or brown, or another color? Perhaps he was like Cecily: flower-faced, petal-mouthed, eyes like clear streams, body softly round with swelling fruit. Perhaps his hair shone like hammered gold that twisted and writhed in fantastic curls. He ached for the years they had spent together and the life they had shared. Even now, at this great distance, he could still remember the sad months before he left when he had tried to make her understand why he had to leave, and how she had begged him to stay, to turn away from the titles and honor and stay with her in the countryside, where the important officials could not find them. She had threatened to take her own life, saying that after so many years of devotion, she would never be able to go on without him. She had clung to him, breasts to his face, pulling at him.

Desperately he went to the computer, trusting that it had not forgotten its origins and would be able to communicate with the strange presence beyond the hull. A special display for such occasions had been programmed into the machine. He remembered how much thought and worry had gone into it. He waited as the unused circuits chattered into life, and then he saw a screen light up, and knew that there was a comparable display on the outer part of the ship.

A ball festooned with white rolled there, showing night and day marching

113

across it endlessly. He stared at it, refusing to believe that he was seeing his home. Earth was like that? No, Earth was quite different. Earth was like Cecily. The pale yellow thing in the sky was not Sol, could not be Sol. There was not sufficient brightness, certainly not enough majesty. Sol was huge: it blazed in a glory that rivaled the strange shapes in the dark. It was brilliant, shining, moving like glowing brass through the sky.

Now the screens showed other things. In front of a large building surrounded with thin, spiky towers more people than he remembered there were in the world jostled and gestured in the hazy heat. All wore engulfing clothes and had tiny, dark eyes. This was nothing like the people he saw in his mind — great splendid beings with faces like moons, like suns. On the screen a triangular cloth cupped the wind, dragging a wooden shell over a gray ocean. The man at the tiller bent to the list of the boat as he ran before the storm. Then that was gone and a boy — so small! — in bright, tattered clothes followed large, sleepy animals up the side of steep rocks. Beneath him there were valleys and small brown-roofed buildings like mushrooms. A woman like a cloud moved on the ends of her feet so that she seemed to float; her face was serene, masklike though beaded with sweat, and her long, taut body was bright as a flame. Lastly a man and a woman as black as their own shadows pushed their way through tangles of green toward a place in the rocks where water trickled.

"No," he said in a voice rusty with disuse. No, it wasn't like that at all. He remembered Earth, and it was not like that. The buildings were spires of many-colored metals and glass. The people were few and glorious.

(What/when) are those (demonstrations/appearances)?

"They're supposed to be . . . people," he said, watching the images flicker. Something must have gone wrong with the computer after all this time, to have got people so wrong. Where were the ripe bodies like Cecily's, rounded and filled with the bursting fruit that came from their life together? Where were the eyes, large and water-clear? How could the computer, with its superior logic, have drifted so far from the truth? He supposed that in all the vast time, there had been breakdowns — a bit gone here, a switch corroded there — until the picture it presented was no longer reliable or accurate.

(We/this one) (sense/perceive) some (discontinuity/confusion) in (you/that one). (We/this one) do not (appreciate/comprehend) the (cause/motivation/ reason) for it.

He shook his head, frowning. On the screen he watched the thing that hovered beyond the ship. Did it have tentacles? Did it have a face? Did it have anything he would recognize as being part of a living being? Fervently he hoped that the thing might, in some unrevealed way, be familiar, perhaps rounded like Cecily, with soft, petaled features and twining curls. Even if the alien were horrible, he

114

could bear it so long as the horror was something he knew and understood. A giant spider, a scorpion, any of those would be welcome.

Still somewhat fuddled from the Cold Room, he quickly ran a check on the computer, searching for those indications that would show the full extent of its damage. His fingers moved like sticks as he struggled to remember the proper way to form commands. Once or twice his eyes blurred. His attempt did no good. Whatever had happened to the computer had occurred while he was in the Cold Room with the others, and he could not find the malfunction in order to correct it.

(We/this one) (desire/insist) that (you/that one) (make known/explain) the (purpose/intent) of (your/that one's) (presence/business) (here/now/immediately). (We/this one) will (inform/evaluate) (your/that one's) (response/reply/demonstration) and (we/this one) will (decide/judge/assess) (you/that one).

He couldn't remember anymore why he had come into space. There had been a promise, and it seemed worthwhile at the time. In the control room of the ship he waited, not thinking as the thing moved outside. He wanted to find something, he was certain of it, but he didn't think it was in this blackness where creatures he did not know accosted him and demanded explanations. It would have pleased him to scream. Earth was too many years gone. Now there was only Cecily. Only Cecily, her ripened, seed-filled body shone in the dark places and rivaled the lights. Like Cecily, he had been sent to scatter seed, the seeds that were in the Cold Room. They were to be cast across the sky, making them like Cecily, making them things of space, not of Earth. They had lied, long ago, when they had told him that there were places he could land, where Earth could grow in soil and continue. There was no soil, and if, in the vast eternal night, one little dust mote longed for new life, perhaps the broadcast seeds would land there and take root.

(You/that one), (we/this one) are (aware/perceptive) of (your/that one's) (destination/resolution). (You/that one) are to find certain (bodies/solids) on which to (leave/deposit/plant) those others that sleep. (We/this one) (believe/surmise) that (you/that one) are from (not-like-this/[no concept]). (We/this one) are (sorry/dismayed/regretful) to inform (you/that one) that (you/that one) will be (unable/incapable/unequipped) to (return/reverse) to (not-like-this/[no concept]).

He tried to understand what the alien was telling him. Surely it did not mean that he would forever drift in space, and in all the vast years and distance to come, he would never find that dust mote he had been sent to discover.

(We/this one) (watch/guard/monitor) this (place/time/phenomenon). There have been (many/countless) like (you/that one). Never have any (returned/reversed/survived) into (not-like-this/[no concept]).

115

"But Cecily's back there!" He shouted it and the unused echoes rang through his ship. To be without Cecily forever, never to see her again, never to hold her bulging ripeness and feel the precious movements of the seeds as she brought them forth to scatter in the earth to grow. . . . Never to know the satin petals of her face, the tendrils of her hair, the pools of her eyes. . . . The loss hurt him as he thought of it.

(We/this one) do not (understand/comprehend) the nature of (your/that one's) (disturbance/upset/imbalance).

"It's Cecily," he said aloud, almost pleading with the thing that drifted in the dark. "We were lovers, Cecily and I, for years and years. Every day we were together. We never spent a day apart. It nearly killed her to let me go. I was everything she ever wanted, and I was foolish enough to let them persuade me to leave her, though I knew then that I was being a fool. Her eyes were clear water; when she wept, it was like oceans and it broke my heart to see that." He paused, trying to find words that the presence might grasp. "She carried ripe seeds in her, and her body was full." He cried out. "I must go back!"

(We/this one) must (inform/notify) (you/that one) that an attempted (return/reversal) would (lead to/result in) (your/that one's) (discontinuation/ nonviability/cessation).

Would he die? Was he stuck out here in this night with only the Cold Room and a computer to remind him of Earth? Mindlessly the ship provided him with food, but suppose he stopped eating it? Suppose he let himself drift with the time and forget the tides that drew him toward Earth, if only in his dreams. He clutched at his head as if his brain itself were bursting, making sounds that seemed like those of an animal, but he could no longer recall which one. The Cold Room tempted him more than death, because there it would not matter that eternity went by.

(Those/the others) are (terminable/finite). Yet (they/the others) have potential for (motion/life/actuality).

The observation penetrated his misery. "We were going to a star, or some-where near it. They called it Arcturus. It was an experiment." He no longer cared about Arcturus. The loss of Cecily blotted out the other, lesser disappointments. Forcefully, he shut her out of his mind so that he could express himself clearly. "The ones in the Cold Room are stopped. They can be started again. They are like clocks — all you must do is wind them up again to set them in motion. Then they will mark out the days with their lives in heartbeats." Did it understand, that thing in its dark, unfathomable speed?

(We/this one) have (empathy/understanding/compassion). To be (terminable/finite) is (undesirable/tragic/unfortunate). (We/this one) will (prepare/ initiate) the (others/third ones) for a (better state/greater opportunity/more successful adaptation).

He turned quickly. "What are you saying? You can't take them. They're mortal. They can't live out there!" Again words escaped him and he rummaged in the attic of his mind for ways to make matters clear to the thing. "Listen, listen to me. They have no way to live here. They're not like you — they're like me, but asleep. They are finite, as you say, and they need a place, a . . . planet, a solid where they can live." He waited for a response that did not come. "It's their clocks. They make rules, those clocks."

You/that one), do not (alarm/disturb) (yourself/that one). It is (possible/ accomplishable) to make the (others/third ones) like (us/this one).

"You can't!" he screamed in terror.

(You/that one), (we/this one) sorrowfully (inform/explain) that (you/that one) are (incapable/impossible) to (adapt/change/alter) to the conditions existing (here/now/at this place). (You/that one) will (destroy/negate) (your/ that one's) (body/conveyance/manifestation) in the (attempt/demonstration).

His tenuous link with humanity was near breaking. He could feel it pull away like the bandage from some ancient wound. Now there was only Cynthia and his memories, and she would fade, he knew, if he let her. He recoiled at the thought. Should he resign from life entirely? He had stopped eating — when? — it was too long ago to remember. The ship had taken care of that, nourishing him with strange tubes and other devices while he slept. He had lost too much, he thought. It would not hurt to lose it all.

(You/that one), (parting/separation/transformation) of the (others/third ones) will be as (swift/unprolonged/efficient) as (we/this one) can (manage/ perform/accomplish).

From the control room he watched as his ship was bled of its cargo, as the stranger drew the occupants of the Cold Room out into that vaster cold. As he watched, there was yet another thing before his ship, something like the first — a being, perhaps, a shape he did not recognize. The two things touched and intermingled, then began to drift apart. Spirals of light were around them, like storms or halos.

"Wait!" he called as he saw himself abandoned. "No! Make me like you. Change me, then! Don't leave me here." As he said it he could feel the freedom, to drift forever in the strange place where there were no stars and speed was so great that it had no sense of time. Then he could be as the water of Cynthia's eyes, deep and calm. There would be others like himself, and over the ages they would meet and see in each other something that was familiar, and he would recall his humanity.

The first thing turned back toward his ship, its shape fluctuating eerily as colors he had no name for surged and ebbed in the bulk of the alien.

(We/this one) are (unable/incapable) of (doing/performing/accomplishing) the (task/change) that (you/that one) (request/desire).

117

"But the others!" There was panic in his voice. "The others are gone! Surely you can change me if you can change the others."

(You/that one) are not the (same/like) (us/this one). Only (terminable/finite) (beings/entities/creatures) can be (changed/transformed). (You/that one) are not (like this/similar). (You/that one) are (fixed/set/locked) as (you/that one) are (now/here).

He stared dumbly out at the thing, wanting its companionship. The shapes that wavered in the dark, that might have been stars or might have been the shadow of time, glared in their glory, as they had done for unimaginable ages, and would for ages more. What could he, a man from Earth, have in common with them? Why must he be exiled among them? He was stuck here, the thing had said, and could not change to be part of it. Despair churned through him, potent as poison. He wished that he had listened to the pleadings of his Cynthia and not left Earth. He could see the writhing tendrils of flame-licked gold that clung to the drooping petals of her face. Her body throbbed with seeds and with her grief. He could see the seams on her body that would open to spew out the seeds sometime after he had gone, parts of himself that would take root and grow. She was cold and smooth and felt like ivory. Why had he left her? A woman like that, rich and fecund, how could he have left her?

Then he thought of the Cold Room. There was still sleep where he could wrap himself in the memory of her and with his dreams could relive her presence for all that was left of time. Involuntarily he took a step toward the Cold Room.

(We/this one) (opened/entered) the Cold Room. (You/that one) could not (sleep/survive/exist) there. (You/that one) must (remain/continue/stay) (awake/aware).

Awake. Forever awake. He reeled, then steadied himself. He could go into the Cold Room, and that would be the last of it. A sensation of freezing, an instant when breath caught in his throat, and then there would be sweet oblivion.

(We/this one) (changed/transformed/adjusted) the Cold Room. (You/that one) (cannot/are not able to) enter it.

His hands dropped. Yet there was not the same defeat. He could not recall dreams anymore. That was another one of his clocks that no longer worked. And without dreaming, there was no reason to sleep. So he could not enter the Cold Room. There must be other escapes. Once, long ago, he had heard that people who do not dream must go mad. Madness would take away his dream of Cynara, and all their love. He would have only the distorted sky for a companion, drawing him ever outward until he became, in his way, as alien as the thing that had wakened him. Trembling, he went to the screen and stared out, searching there for Cynara in the patterns of the dark. But she was not there. He could no longer discern the ripe lines of her, the twining coils of her hair and the layered petals of her mouth. Nowhere was there that radiance that came from her alabaster body, rounded, gravid as the moon. He tried to picture her, to recall the sound of her voice, the shape of her. To have to leave her after their lifetime together, after the years of fruitful unity, was too much to demand of any man. She had rent her flesh to show how her love of him tore at her soul. And now, in the terrible dark, he could no longer find her.

His eyes burned as he watched. When he closed them, he could see the ghost of her once more, and dream of the closeness of their bodies. How he longed for sleep, for the night behind his eyes where there was more reality. Sometimes he thought he dozed, but this was not the sleep he knew. There was too much of the nightmare in the sky around him, glowing with Cynara's lost body and her ephemeral flesh.

Then, out of his wishes and the night, she came to him and her vast arms opened, her body molten with the ripened young she would scatter into the aeon-long night for love of him. Her hair twined, writhed, twisted, its serpent's life reaching out for him. Her mouth, nearing harvest, dripped petals that showed a wide stamen among them, and the pistil, spiky with pollen. Her body, thighs, arms, breasts, reached out for him, drawing him to her and her glorious flesh that nurtured, that grasped. The hidden seed-pods were opening, and the spikes of them were filled with venom. Legs as implacable as stone spread to catch him in a vise that would destroy him, crush him, break him into fragments as incomprehensible as the sky. How much he desired her! How much he hated her.

Cynara moved toward him, closer, ever closer. Now the petals gaped wide and he could see the many rows of teeth that hid there, and the deep vortices of her eyes, where the madness and the whirlpools rolled. Her body gleamed, shone like pounded brass, sent off streams of brightness as she grew nearer, until the magnificent splendor of her filled the sky.

She was upon him.

Then he screamed.

Shuddering, he woke to look fearfully about the dark. Cyndra was gone; he was safe. Outside were only the oddities of the reaches of space. He sobbed with relief. It had been close, that time. The next time she might get him. He had forgotten how vindictive she could be, how possessive she was. But it was like that when you missed someone. You forgot the bad points and remembered the good. So far from Earth, it was not surprising that he did not want to remember the bad of her. Cyndra, he knew, was terrible when she was angry, and she had been angry when he left, though she had wept. She had not wanted him to leave her, and when she had clawed at him, there had been as much fury as love. He had seen venom in the petals then, and the dream had reminded him. How had he forgotten that?

But when he slept, if he slept again, she might return. He had to be on guard

119

always, for there was no easy way to tell the difference between waking and sleep, not where time meant so little and the years ran together like rain and rivers. Uneasily he turned once more to the viewing screen and searched in vain for the thing — the being that had stopped him and told him he would never return home.

The thing was gone, but Cymra was there, shining brightly in the dark — her face, her flesh brilliant, the luster of it spreading about his tiny ship until there seemed to be nothing but her. There was no place he could see where she did not appear, ready for him, poised, hoping for those dreams in which she might pounce on him for a last touching. Cymra beckoned to him.

He fled in terror down the sky, forever lost, his scream unheard, an infinite man seeking the embrace of death even as he flung himself into everlasting dark.

Coasting

There may have been an inlet or lagoon off to port, Courant was not sure because of the fog. It had come up a little more than an hour ago, first nothing more than a kind of fuzz over the water, then gathering into an insubstantial barrier that rose up between the sleek day-sailer and the shore. It muffled sound as if the coast had been wrapped in cotton, and forced him to keep silent in the wraithlike cocoon it made around his sloop. The occasional roar of the waves against the beach was distant, like gigantic yawns, and he feared he might be drifting out to sea, for although the tide was near turning, the wind had died away to almost nothing. Overhead the sail luffed, pulling the *ShangriLa* on with occasional languid jerks. The jib flapped once in a while. In time he would have to start the auxiliary engine, but he was reluctant to use it until he could discover how far away he was from the rocks and the beach.

It was late in the afternoon; in another hour the tide would be noticeably higher and if Courant could not find the coast by then, he might be in a great deal of danger. He did not like sailing blind, and he was well aware of the risks he ran. As the light faded, his situation would become more precarious. He listened to the quiet lappings of the waves against the hull of his thirty-two-foot sloop and gave a halfhearted tug on the shroud-line.

The ocean was eerie in its silence, and the mists seemed to merge with the water so that he felt he was floating in the greyness, apart from the world, isolated in a place he did not know.

121

Why hadn't he brought Sammy along? It would not be so lonely with Sammy here, and they would joke about their predicament, or set the running lights together. Maybe they could cook up a story the Coast Guard would accept if they came into port after dark. Sammy would enjoy that. And with no one on board but himself, he had to admit that he would welcome the sight of the Coast Guard. In a fog like this, they would have to stretch the rules a little for day-sailers that could not reach their berths before the sun was gone. Even the best of sailors got caught out once in a while, Courant reassured himself. Anyone else out in this fog would have the same feelings that plagued him now, and would take the same precautions, watching, listening to the water so that he would not run aground or have the bottom of the boat clawed out by the rocks along the shore. He imagined he heard the first scrape of the keel against submerged, jagged boulders: he braced himself for the shudder that heralded ruin.

In an hour, he reminded himself when several minutes had passed without the dreaded wreck, there would be the onrushing tide, and no matter how muted the sound of the beach, he would be able to hear the breakers where they gnawed at the coast. It would be safe then to begin his search for the entrance to the harbor at the mouth of Barranca River, or, barring that, to drop anchor.

He pictured in his mind the breakwater at El Pescador. It was little more than an extension of a sandpit on the south side of the inlet. Rocks had been piled up over the concrete, and there was a diaphone at the end of it with a revolving light on top that did not always work. Inside the breakwater there was a jetty and facilities for about thirty boats, with deeper moorings for the occasional large pleasurecraft that put in at El Pescador in the summer. Most of the boats out of El Pescador were commercial fishing craft and party-boats. On days like this, in the chill of autumn, they often did not put out to sea — there were no tourists to hire the party-boats and the fisherman set aside these days for painting and repair, anticipating the storms that would come at the back of the cold, taking a fearful toll on unprotected boats. Courant doubted that he would see any of the boats he knew, should there be a break in the fog.

El Pescador, San Jorge, Anderson, Port Talbot, Puerto Real, Bronley, Green River, Stella del Mar, Princeton Beach — he ticked off the little coastal towns in his mind as he held the tiller steady. He should be able to put in at one of them. He had an uncle in Port Talbot, a crusty old Welshman who had been in the first generation of settlers. The Bakers, in Green River, would let him sleep on their couch for the night if he fetched up there. He decided that he ought to stay away from San Jorge, since that was where the construction was going on at the harbor entrance. Tim, the bartender at *The Pelican*, was always willing to let him sleep in the back room, but he did not want to chance it, not since he had been heading into port there a month before and had been warned off by half a dozen men in a forty-foot cruiser that bristled with antennae and other devices. No, he would not make an effort to reach San Jorge. Better to try for Anderson.

He would not be able to call Sammy when he had said he would. Sammy was over with Kate today, with Kate and Barry. Courant was not used to his ex-wife's second marriage, and in his mind he stumbled over Barry's name. A nice fellow, he supposed, and if the circumstances were different, he might be able to like the man. He was pleasant enough, was generous with his beer and had pretty good sense about politics. But the way things had turned out, Courant was certain he would never like Barry. It was bad enough that the man had married Kate, but now he was starting to work on Sammy. The boy liked spending time with Kate in Santa Marisa, and Barry encouraged it. It was just that Santa Marisa was a good-sized place, with two high schools and four movie theatres, and much more to do than was offered in El Pescador. Sammy was eleven, and was eager for the excitement of a town and new friends.

Courant was distracted by a soft, scraping sound against the sloop. He looked over the side. Kelp floated around him, brown and leafy, the long fronds stretching out into the fog. For a moment it appeared that the seaweed was rising out of the ocean and winding its way up the striations in the mists, like ivy going up a wall. In the mild swell the branches appeared to gesture to him, beckoning him and reaching for him. He had seen kelp before, and knew it for the hazardous nuisance it was. If the engine had been on, the propeller might be badly damaged or perhaps even broken if entangled with the plants. There were kelp beds all along the coast, of course, but he had thought that the largest of them was off Green River. By the look of this — what little he could make out in the thickening fog — it was extensive. Had he drifted as far as Green River? Or was he farther out from the coast than he thought? Was the remote sound of the shore caused by distance and not another illusion of the fog? He did not let himself worry too much about that. There were more immediate problems, because if there was kelp looped around the propeller now, he would have to get it free or damage the engine when he started it at last. He had seen other boats, some of them quite large, with big engines powering them, come limping into port with their screws fouled by the long, trailing weeds.

He tightened the sails and pointed toward what little wind there was, in the hope that there would be enough power in the halfhearted gusts to pull the *ShangriLa* free. It meant that he had to aim his bow directly at where he thought the coast was, but he preferred that risk to remaining in the clutch of the seaweed. If only the fog would clear so that he could tell how far he was from the shore, and how much kelp was around him. Inadvertently he might put himself more deeply into the patch of floating plants, ensnaring himself inextricably, so that he would have to drift with the kelp as it moved.

The cold had begun to bother him, the clammy mist that held him insinuated its frigid breath into him. He had a peacoat down in the cabin, but he did not want to leave the cockpit, not with the kelp around him and the sails trimmed enough to give him some real speed once he was away. His sweater, however

123

inadequate against the fog, would have to do for the time being. Once he was safely away from the kelp and knew where he was bound, he would be able to take a few minutes to get warm. He might even break out the bottle of rum he kept under the hard bread in the food-locker. The rum would warm him up, and lend a festivity to this dull, terrifying afternoon.

The swell had been increasing as the tide made its first lunge at the shore. The *ShangriLa* rocked, and Courant eased it off the wind a point or two. He would bring the compass up from the cabin, too. In theory, it should always be in place near the tiller, but the brass had become encrusted and he had taken it below a few days ago to clean it, thinking that it was a good time to do it. He hardly ever used it anyway, and for that reason had not made much of an effort to put it back into place. He had been sailing along the coast here for more than five years and he knew almost all of it by heart. It was simple to navigate by the frowning, steep front of Steeple Rock, or by the arch of Green Point. He had boasted the year before that he could find his way from Sanchez to Hollyville by landmarks alone. A compass was redundant unless he was going farther, down to Guddiston or beyond to San Dismas. He recalled guiltily that the brass was not entirely cleaned and shined yet, but it was the compass itself that he wanted, not its housing. Once set in its place, he was convinced, he would feel relieved, and this worry that was growing within him would not be as nagging as it had become. There was something about having the compass in place that would give him a sense of ease that did not come entirely from the instrument's function; since he was a boy, he had always believed that if he had a compass, he could not be lost.

The wind picked up, and for a little while it gave Courant the vain hope that the fog would dissipate. But it only became thicker, blurring the water around the *ShangriLa* and making the boat itself appear ghostly. No wonder the old sailors had believed in ghost ships, he told himself, attempting to persuade himself that the idea was absurd. If he saw his own sloop gliding silently out of a fog like this one, he might easily believe he had seen a vessel that was supernatural. It was silly, he insisted, but that was the way that legends got started.

Sammy would not have liked the sail much, he admitted as he made a deliberate effort to turn his thoughts away from the myths he had heard all his life. The boy enjoyed the ocean, but this grey, enveloping mist, the persistent kelp and the slow, aimless progress he was making would have driven the boy to a state of frustration and annoyance that would soon have led him to whine and complain. He was glad that with all the other difficulties he had to cope with, his son's ceaseless demands were not added to them. It was not that he did not love his son. Of course he did. Of course. But he often lacked patience with the kid when he became obstreperous. It might be just as well that Kate had him for the afternoon. If the fog had drifted inland as far as Santa Marisa, she would have to deal with the boy's moping and smart back talk, just as he had done for the last three years. Then she would understand what he had been objecting to in Sammy on those few occasions when they had discussed the boy. And, for a change, when Sammy returned, he would be glad to see him, to be home with his dad, and would tell him all the awful things that had happened while he visited mommy and her new husband. It would be a pleasant change, he thought, allowing himself a hint of gloating. Then it would be Courant who would make the phone call, asking what Kate had done that had upset the boy so much. In the past, it had been her privilege to call with unkind inferences and innuendos. This would provide a good turnabout. It was high time that Kate learned that their child was not the most reasonable and intelligent kid in the world. He was okay, but he had his bad days, like everyone else. Then Kate would understand a little why he resented her phone calls and the notes she sent him, saying that Sammy ought to be taken to the dentist, or needed another pair of new shoes, or was not studying hard enough and ought to be encouraged. God, how he hated those conversations!

There was more kelp around him, and the *ShangriLa* wallowed through it, tossing on the increasing swell. He studied the water around him, and was more dismayed than he let himself know to see how thick the seaweed had become, and how densely it stretched away into the fog. He held the sloop steady while he searched for something that would help him clear it away. There was not much he could do by himself, that was plain. If Sammy were here with him, he could have the job of pushing the kelp aside as the *ShangriLa* got through the worst of it. One man, holding the tiller and minding the sails, could not take the time to sweep the kelp out of the way.

A wave slapped at the side of the boat and a frond hooked over the splashboard, for all the world as if it intended to haul itself aboard. Courant cried out in surprise and disgust, and reached out for the brown, wet thing to throw it back into the darkening sea. It was worse than any creeper growing around his house, he thought, and gritted his teeth as he pointed the prow back closer to the wind. The *ShangriLa* would pitch, but it was better than having that stuff all over the deck, he decided, cringing inwardly as he heard the slither of kelp brush the length of the boat.

His hands were stiff from the cold and the tension that gripped him. The tiller felt enormous to him, and as heavily leaden as his infrequent dinners with Kate. He tugged at it, dragging it closer to him, his shoulder beginning to ache with the strain of it. He stared into the whiteness that engulfed him, giving no light, concealing everything. Slowly the sloop moved forward, the aft setting lower in the water as if the *ShangriLa* were dragging something. He turned to look behind him. Christ! What was back there? His uncle in Port Talbot had told him stories of creatures that lived under the sea and would often attack solitary boats, pulling them down to hideous depths where the monsters could consume their catch

125

at their leisure. His uncle always laughed when he told such tales, and once or twice explained that it was typical of sailors to invent nonsense when on long hauls. Courant had always nodded his agreement, but now the fear came back to him without the welcome denial of chuckles. As if in confirmation of his anxiety, the *ShangriLa* lurched sideways, then righted herself and bobbed in the water. Whatever it was, it no longer held the boat. He swallowed four or five times in succession to keep from being sick.

The wind carried him farther, and he seemed to hear the rustle of waves on the beach. There was no break in the fog, and although he strained to listen, there was none of the determined, exuberant crash of breakers. He gathered up his courage and reached over the side of the boat, and to his relief, did not touch the brown leaves he dreaded. The water, in fact, was a bit warmer than he had expected. Perhaps he had inadvertently entered the long lagoon at Green River. If that were the case, he would find the first of two long docks not far ahead on the port side. He was pleasantly light-headed at the realization that his horrible afternoon was nearly at an end. Once he tied up, he would go into town for a drink and a hot meal with Sophie. He might even call Kate and tell her that she could keep Sammy another night. Cautiously he let down the jib, gathering it up as the *ShangriLa* drifted forward. A sudden gust of wind could send the sloop careening into one of the piers, and that would be the perfect end, after a day as bad as this one had been. He made his way back to the cockpit and took the tiller once more. He estimated that it would be ten minutes at the most before he found a place to berth his boat.

But the ten minutes went by, and nothing happened. He continued to move forward slowly, the wake behind the *ShangriLa* hardly more than a gentle ripple, the fog as thick as it was at the entrance to the harbor. What made him think he had got into the harbor? A hard, cold fist knotted his guts. If this were a harbor, any harbor, the reasonable thoughts went on, without remorse, then there would have been some sign of life. There would be a light, a diaphone, a signal of some sort that he had arrived. Other boats had to be protected, too, and there would have to be some evidence that they could use as a guide.

"*Hello!*" he shouted suddenly, very loudly. He heard his voice echo distantly, so faint and distorted that it might have been anther speaker entirely. "Hello!" he bellowed again. "This is the *ShangriLa*! Where do I tie up?" He half-stood, listening intently, and heard only the sigh of the water as it passed under the prow of his sloop. "Hello!"

Something came toward the boat, thudded against the side, rolled once and then submerged.

He stared at it. "It was a log," he said aloud, thinking that someone would hear him. It had to have been a log, for he could not believe that the distorted, blackened thing that he had seen turning in the water was a body. They were twigs he had caught sight of, not fingers. He pulled on the tiller, as if to bring the

ShangriLa about, so that he could pursue the thing he had seen, but the tiller did not respond, not even when he braced himself and pushed at it with the limit of his strength.

"It's the kelp," he said, still speaking loudly, hoping that someone would hear. "There's kelp down there. I can't steer because there's seaweed on the rudder." As if to prove this to himself, he gave one more push to the tiller and nodded grimly when the *ShangriLa* continued on her course without the slightest deviation. It would mean hauling her out of the water and having Pete at the boatworks give her a complete going-over. It was an expensive waste of time, he told himself, so that he would not have to say that he longed for the familiar boatworks and the genial rapacity of the owner.

If this was Green River, the harbor would be dead ahead, and he would ram a dock or a boat, anything. He thought of the damage with affection and hoped that the *ShangriLa* was enough damaged to justify replacing her with another boat. He would not be able to take her out again without recalling this endless fog and dead tiller.

How would he explain that to Sammy? The boy loved sailing, and thought of the boat with more affection than he often showed his father. Courant did not let himelf be distracted, but as minutes passed and there was no impact, no sight or sound to catch his attention and reassure him, he began to invent stories. There was a storm, he would say, or the sloop was wrecked in the fog. That was close enough to the truth that it would be acceptable to his son, should he ever learn the truth. The truth? But what was that? That somehow, while coasting, he had lost his way in the fog. It had happened to other sailors. His uncle had once been becalmed three days out from Tahiti and had almost lost his ship when one of his three crewmen had got crazy and said that they were damned for their sins, and that the ocean would punish them. He could not remember how that story ended, but he did not think this uncle had done much sailing since that voyage. Small wonder.

The water was growing warmer and more quiet. The *ShangriLa* drifted in the stillness and continued into the fog. There was a splash as something broke the surface off to starboard, then dropped out of sight before he could peer through the fog to make out what it was.

Sammy, he thought, would be running around the deck by now, demanding that his father do something about what was going on. Sammy, who would never understand why it was that Courant could not solve anything in a moment, who insisted that his mother and father vie with each other in giving him the things he wanted most. And Kate encouraged him. She did not have to live with him, and so it pleased her to set him at odds with his father, paving the way for her own generosity and bribes to convince the boy that his mother was the only one who loved him.

There were reeds off in the fog, taller and stiffer than cattails, standing at odd

127

angles, disappearing into the water. The wake of the *ShangriLa* when it touched them made them rattle strangely, but nothing more. The mists wreathed around them, making them turn into shadows, like an army with spears.

He released the tiller and moved to the far side of the cockpit, and dangled one hand over the side so that it dragged in the water, which was quite warm now, almost to a temperature that would provide a pleasant swim. He did not look at the sail, holding taut without his aid. He watched the little wake his fingers made until something, perhaps a submerged reed, cut his knuckles and he brought his hand to his mouth to suck away the blood.

The fog grew less dense, and a touch of wind heeled the *ShangriLa* over on its side, and in that short moment, through a gap in the mist, Courant saw a dreadful thing, and he recalled those men in the cruiser with all the equipment. But this was nothing so comprehensible. This was a machine, or a beast so huge, so monstrous, that his mind had no space for it. Objects were being discarded or dismantled, at a rate that was stupefying.

"It's the sawmill at Anderson," he said in a stifled voice, as if he did not want to tempt the thing he had seen to respond to him. It had to be the sawmill. He had been in the fog too long, and his eyes were playing tricks on him. That was it. Nothing was out there, taking the coast to pieces as easily as a stagehand pulls down a set. It was the sawmill, and the disorientation was because of the wind and the sloop responding.

The wind had stopped and the fog returned, thick; Courant welcomed it now, and stared ahead into the stiff, closing reeds, with their spearlike stalks, and the narrow path of warm, oily water that stretched through them, winding away in the mist, swallowing him up.

The Arrows

Slowly he took aim, concentrating on the target. His hand was steady, his mind preternaturally clear. This time, this time he would be right: he held his breath.

The brush moved, leaving a smear of raw umber beneath the vermilion.

Witlin stood back, frowning at the canvas. "Shit," he muttered as he glared at the result of his work. God, would it never be right? He wiped the brush on an ancient rag already stiff with encrustations of color, then poked it into an old coffee can half filled with turpentine that had absorbed so much paint that it was the color and consistency of wet silt.

Afternoon sun slanted across the untidy room he called his studio, turning it glaringly bright. He rubbed his face with both hands, wishing he could afford another place, one with north light instead of this western exposure. But such places were expensive and he was almost out of money. Better this than doing charcoal sketches for the tourists down at the waterfront, he told himself, as he had every day for the last six weeks. Better this than doing lettering for the advertising agency where he had slaved for three years before getting the courage to work on his own. And far better this than those wasted semesters at the community college, where all they taught were better ways to make messes in oils.

He wandered over to the window and looked down on the playground, three floors below. Children were playing there now that school was over for the day.

They ran and shouted, making a racket that gave him a headache as he listened. He leaned his forehead against the glass and sighed. Another day shot, and the painting worse than ever. When he had asked for a six-month leave, it had seemed to be a luxurious, a voluptuous amount of time, but now he knew it was completely inadequate.

A baseball thunked against the side of the building and Witlin jumped at the sound of it. The world was full of aimed missiles, he thought. Baseballs, ICBMs, arrows; it made no difference. He turned away from the window, cursing the noise that erupted beneath him. They did not understand what he was doing, how important it was.

When Witlin had finished cleaning his brushes it was almost sunset and the children were gone from the playground. He studied his canvas as he prepared to go out for the cheapest meal he could find. It wasn't right, not yet. Some ineffable quality of reality and suffering continued to elude him. The canvas itself was big enough — almost eight feet high — and the figure slightly larger than life. That wasn't the problem. He brought out the sheaf of sketches that had guided him through his work for more than five months.

Brakes squealed in the street; horns clamored.

Cursing, he got to his knees to gather up the paper he had dropped. One of the sketches had torn: it was a study of heads and necks and the jagged division neatly decapitated the best of the heads he had done. Conscientiously he pressed the sketch back together though he knew it was a futile gesture. He would not be able to look at the sketch again without seeing the damage and feeling it had been compromised in his vision as well as ruined on paper.

Why was it so difficult? That question had plagued him for weeks, haunting him as he strove to bring his work to fruition. Why should the bound figure of a man transfixed with arrows torment him this way? He had already done half a dozen iconographic drawings, but that had been early in his leave of absence, when his confidence had been high and nothing seemed beyond him. That had changed; oh, yes, it had changed.

The smell of frying foods drifted up from the floor below and Witlin felt his stomach tighten. Hamburgers had become as rich and exotic as Chateaubriand in forcemeat had once been. Now he had to content himself with soup and hardrolls at the local cafeteria. On such a regimen he might eke out his funds for another two weeks. As it was, he barely had enough for the extra tube of thalo green that he needed; food would have to wait until he had the supplies he required.

A television blared, driving music and an announcer's voice proclaiming the superiority of a particular tire over all others.

"Scum." He was disgusted with it all, mostly with himself. He had been so sure that he would be able to paint the Saint Sebastian that he had done only the most cursory sketches of the subject. Doubt had come to him three months ago, when he had made his first attempt at the work. The canvas lay against the wall, the face turned away from him so that he would not have to look at it. That first effort had been small, as most of his work had been up to that point. When he was less than half finished with the underpainting, he knew that he had not allowed adequate scope to his ambition, and that a larger canvas would be needed. That had led to the second attempt which he had burned more than three weeks before. Now he was working on the fifth version, and knew it, too, had failed.

"It's not possible," he said to the canvas, defying it. "I'll do it. I swear I'll do it." He could not stand the thought that all his efforts had come to nothing. He scowled at his palette, as if seeking blame in the colors or the scent of the oils. He was using the highest grade of paint available, he had stretched, sized, sanded, and sized the canvas again, taking care that the surface was right and the paint would not crack. "But painting must have worth," he muttered as he scraped his palette clean, putting the used bits into an old milk carton with the top cut off.

When at last he had cleaned the dismal attic room , he went out, taking great care to lock the door and pocket the key.

A week later he was in despair. He took his pocket knife and jabbed it at the painting, seeking those places where he had shown arrows entering the flesh of the saint. "There! There! Be wounded, damn you!" In his frenzy he kicked over the table where he kept his supplies; brushes, paint tubes, turpentine, linseed oil, gesso, all went flying and skittering and spreading over the bare wood floor. Witlin knelt down, weeping, hardly noticing the new stains on his faded clothing. "Damn you, damn you, damn you," he crooned in a rapture of defeat.

There was a sharp knock at the door. "Mister Witlin? Mister Witlin!" came his landlady's voice, querulous and timid at once.

It was a moment before Witlin came to himself enough to answer. Awkwardly he got to his feet and stumbled toward the sound. "Missus Argent?" he called after a moment of hesitation.

"What's going on in there, Mister Witlin?" the woman asked, trying to sound demanding and achieving only petulance.

He blinked at the shambles he had created. "I . . . tripped, Missus Argent."

"Are you all right, Mister Witlin?" It was more of an accusation than an expression of concern.

"I think so," he answered, wishing she would go away and leave him to deal with the wreckage around him.

"What's that smell?"

Witlin sighed. "I guess it's turpentine," he said, sounding like a chastised child.

131

"It . . . spilled." He knew it was the wrong thing to say as soon as he had spoken.

"I think you'd better let me in, Mister Witlin," his landlady said in whining determination.

Reluctantly he opened the door and stood aside.

Missus Argent had a pointy, rodent's face, not endearing like a rabbit but pinched and mean, more like a rat. She held herself like a rat, too, he realized as he watched her survey the damage: her hands held up close to her chest, drooping, her head with its receding chin thrust forward. He could almost imagine her nose twitching. Belatedly he found something to say. "I was going to clean it up at once. I didn't know it would disturb you."

"Good gracious," was all she would say, but there was condemnation in every line of her. "What have you been doing up here, Mister Witlin?"

"Painting, as I told you when I rented the . . . " He almost said attic but stopped himself, since he knew she disliked having this room called that, though it was.

"Clean it up? But look at the floor. Does any of that horrible stuff come out? What if you've ruined it? Well, at least there isn't a carpet up here, but this . . . Mister Witlin, I don't know what to say. Yes, you will clean it up, and if there is any sign of staining or other . . . problems, we'll have to review your responsibility and make some financial adjustment." She folded her arms across her skinny chest.

Witlin was filled with anxiety. He did not have money enough to move, let alone pay for a new room. Recognition of this spurred him to a defense that he might not otherwise have used. "Look, Missus Argent, if there's any problem, any problem at all, I'll take care of it. If you don't think that the stains are out of the boards, well, I *am* a painter, and I can paint a floor as well as a picture. I'll do a good job, Missus Argent. You won't be disappointed. And it would be easier to take care of a painted surface than bare boards." He could not tell what she thought of this offer; her face suddenly puckered closed and she watched him closely.

"Mister Witlin, I won't have shoddy work in my house."

"No," he agreed at once. "Of course not." He thought of the bedraggled plants in the front garden, the frayed carpets on the stairs, the loose bannnister supports, the cracked and peeling paint on the windowsills. "It would be a good job, Missus Argent. And," he added, inspired by his own fear, "I'd . . . pay for the paint myself."

Her face relaxed a bit. "I'd have to approve the quality and color of the paint," she said at once.

"Oh, yes. Well, yes." He could hear himself blither in relief, but it no longer mattered to him that she thought him an irresponsible fool. He was far more concerned about the cost of the enamel for the floor. He could manage it if he gave up lunch at the cafeteria and confined himself to one egg and toast in the morning.

"You come downstairs to get me when you've cleaned up here," Missus Argent said with decision. "I want to see what you've accomplished." She looked around the room disdainfully. "Those drawings of naked men . . . and you call yourself an artist!" She glared at him in triumph, then slammed herself out of the room.

Witlin set to work restoring order to the attic; he could not get the memory of Missus Argent's expression of fascinated revulsion out of his mind.

Painting the floor took more than two days, and another day to dry. During that time Witlin spent as much time as he could in the nearby park, escaping from the fumes which made him lightheaded. His eyes stung, and when he tried to draw, his vision wavered so that all he put down on paper were vague and awkward lines, not the sweeping gestures in his mind. Twice policemen told him to move on; when he protested that he lived in the neighborhood, they threatened to run him in for vagrancy or something worse. He had not dared to object, though it galled him to be mistaken for one of those derelicts who dozed on the park benches and pestered the more affluent strollers for quarters. Not, he had to admit, that he could not use a few quarters. He had not been able to afford new razor blades for more than a week and his face showed scrapes and stubble in proof of this. Perhaps, he thought, he ought simply to grow a beard. So many other artists did. There was nothing wrong with it — in fact, it was almost expected.

At such moments, he would think of Saint Sebastian, who was almost never shown bearded. Saint Sebastian, the youth, the archer killed by his own men, his body quilled with arrows. How it haunted him, that vision! So he continued to shave, and each day the results were a bit more crude.

Once the floor was dry and Missus Argent had grudgingly approved it, Witlin set to work again, this time choosing the highest grade of canvas and taking more time than usual to stretch it over the enormous frame he had made for it. His arms ached with the work. Twice he skipped breakfast and bought a chocolate bar instead, hoping that the rich candy would give him more energy for his task. When he was satisfied that the preparation was of archival quality he took charcoal and began, once again, to sketch.

This time it went better, or so he told himself. The enormous scope of the painting, its sheer physical size promised an impact his previous efforts had lacked. No matter that the canvas itself had to be canted and braced in order to fit under the low ceiling, no matter that he had to stand on a drafting stool to reach the top of it, this time the work would be perfect: he would achieve his masterpiece.

*　*　*

Witlin stood back to look at the painting, which was almost complete now. It was better, definitely better, he thought, than any of his previous efforts. Yet it was not up to the quality of the image he had held in his mind for all these months. Working large had helped, no doubt of that. He had been able to show the torment of the saint, the arrows lodged deep in his body, his features at once resigned and agonized. That much he believed he could be proud of. But the rest . . . the rest was another matter. He wanted to show how heavy the body was, hanging from its bonds and the arrows, the languor of approaching death, the finality of it. That was still not on the canvas, for all his work and thought. He had been able to find it only in his mind.

The attic was stifling this afternoon in May. The sun pressed at the windows and made the air hard with heat. He felt lightly ill, but he was determined to ignore it, to persevere. He had to finish. At the end of the month he would have run out of money and would no longer be able to pay his rent; he knew better than to suppose Missus Argent would permit him to remain here if he could not give her the seventy-five dollars she demanded of him. So he had to be prepared to move, though where he would go now he could not imagine. He would think of it later, when he was through with Saint Sebastian.

He glared at the painting, trying to think of ways to correct the lifelessness of it that so dissatisfied him.

The wounds, that was it, he decided. They were not real. Anyone looking at them would know that what they saw was paint, not blood, and the holes made by the painted arrows appeared equally false. This was not holy flesh rent by metal and wood, it was pigment. "It's hopeless," he muttered, sitting down on the drafting stool and wiping at his eyes with the last comparatively clean corner of the rag he held. He could not think of what to do. He could not concentrate any more, no matter how he forced himself to clear his thoughts of everything but the painting.

Was it the color? Was that the problem? With the light so glaring and hot, had it changed his perceptions so that he could not see as clearly as he needed to? Was the glare from the windows so strong that he was no longer able to weigh the hue and value of his paints? Would a stronger shade of red have more impact? Did he have to make the flesh a pastier shade, suggesting Sebastian was in deep shock? Was that what was lacking? Had he been misled by the angle at which he had to paint so that he had unintentionally distorted the work? Or was it something deeper, something more profound? Was it a failure not of the canvas and paint, of the medium, but of himself as an artist? Did he shy away from the reality of the saint's suffering, and had that aversion found its way onto the canvas? He could not bring himself to examine his feelings too closely, for fear he would discover how much he was lacking.

He decided he would attempt to fix the colors first. That he could do with comparative ease. The rest he would have to consider later, when he was more prepared to examine the state of his soul.

Green for shadows in the skin, then, a mustard shade for where the direct rays of the setting sun struck it. Acidic orange to make the blood shine more — was it true that blood was more the color of rust than rubies? — and five kinds of brown for the shafts of the arrows. And white, great amounts of white, for the feathers, for highlights, to mix with other paint, to lend radiance to the canvas. If only oil paints could be truly transparent, like stained glass, and still have the force of their opacity. Other painters had achieved it, that luminosity; why couldn't he? What prevented him from doing with his hand what his mind conceived so totally?

Sunset came, and with it the scattering colors that usually irritated him, but now he paid it no heed. He could not be distracted by the sunset, by alterations in the colors around him, by shifts in the light. Those were excuses, not valid reasons for his failure. Surely if he had the right to call himself an artist, he also had the obligation to put himself above those intrusions that had no part of his work.

When the night came, he continued to work, illuminating the cramped studio with two bare bulbs. He felt like an acolyte proving his calling at last.

"I'm sure I'm sorry, Mister Witlin," said Missus Argent in a tone that revealed she was nothing of the kind. "If I could, I'd keep you on a week or two. But there, it isn't as if you have a job. If you were looking for work, Mister Witlin, it might be another matter. But you're a . . . painter."

"And my work is important, Missus Argent," he said in a remote way. He no longer worried about how or where or if he would find a place to live. "Saint Sebastian is immortal. That's more than either you or I can say."

She gave him a puzzled glare. "Well, I'll have to ask you to be out by the end of the week unless you can pay the rent. And I won't have excuses."

"Of course not," he told her, thinking that it would take care of itself. "I'll tell you what I've decided to do by Wednesday."

Her expression grew sharper and a whine came into her voice. "And you'll have to clean this place proper. No more nonsense about painting the floor. The way it smells, I don't know who'd want to rent it. You'll have to set aside one day at least to scrubbing it."

"If that's necessary," Witlin agreed.

"It is," she insisted with a sniff. "You've been up here for months with those paints of yours. You may be used to it, but there are others who . . . ." Her eyes traveled over the room, pausing accusingly at paintings and brushes as if identifying incriminating bits of evidence. "It's bad enough you wanting to paint things like that, but the smell is more than I can bear."

135

He drew breath to protest, then let it out in a sigh. He could not explain to anyone how he felt about the smell of paint, that it was as rich as the scent of food to him, and in many ways more necessary. He only nodded. "I'll do my best, Missus Argent. And I'll try to get the money. I will."

"Well . . . " She stared at him dubiously. "you're not quite the sort of tenant I usually have, Mister Witlin. If there is another place you can go, it might be better if you . . . " She let the words dangle, as if asking him to spare her the necessity of saying anything more.

"Missus Argent, I don't want to move. I haven't the money. I haven't the time. Don't you see? I'm getting close to the work I want to turn out. I know it doesn't look like much yet, with only the underpainting and just a few of the colors, but this canvas is the best I've ever done. It is." He extended his hands toward the surface as if warming them at a fire.

The landlady sniffed. "It isn't the sort of picture I'm . . . used to." She gave it a grudging look. "And your face on it, too," was the only comment she was able to muster, saying it so condemningly that he dared not question her, though he did not agree at all with her observation.

"I'll talk to you tomorrow, Missus Argent. I . . . I want to work some more." He pointed toward the windows. "This isn't the best light for an artist, but I need to make the most of it. Especially if I have to find another place. It won't be as good." It was not an accusation because he was inwardly certain that would not happen; he would be here to finish his work.

"All right, Mister Witlin," she said, making no attempt to hide her disapproval. "I don't want any excuses if you can't find the money for this project of yours. Pay or leave." She stepped back preparing to close the door. "And I don't want to have you working all night. It disturbs the rest of the household to have you do that."

"I don't work on this phase of the painting at night, Missus Argent," he told her with an austere glare. "You have to have clear light at this stage."

She sniffed once to show her doubt, then left the room.

Witlin hardly noticed her going; his mind was on the painting again, and there was nothing in his thoughts but the glorious suffering of Saint Sebastian.

His head ached, a combination of hunger and fumes gnawing at him from the inside. He had risen just after dawn and set to work, and now sunset was distorting the colors on his canvas. And what colors! Finally the glowing, pain-wracked figure was emerging from the flat surface, taking on the kind of reality he had only dreamed of having until now. Witlin was dizzy with it, and his pulse raced. He paused to squeeze out a little more paint onto his palette, thinking vaguely how appetizing it was, that thick, rich worm of color. It was enough to make him hunger for the taste of it, as if the hue carried a special savor all its own. He touched his brush to it, and felt a thrill go up his arm, as electric as a caress. The first pressure of the brush on the canvas made him tremble; he held the wooden shaft in eager, quivering fingers, almost afraid to move for fear of bringing the wonderful sensations to an end.

When he had worked for another hour, he drew back, seeing that the sky was already fading. It astonished him to discover how much he had accomplished, and how swiftly the day had gone. His thoughts were dizzied by what he saw, for at last he perceived some shadows of the vision he carried. Nothing could ever be as vivid, as overwhelming as the impressions that drove him to paint, but he saw that an approximation of that powerful gleam was within his grasp. He contemplated the twisted, lean features of the saint, wondering if Missus Argent had been right, and that he had somehow put his own likeness on that countenance. It had happened before, he reminded himself: Michelangelo had painted himself in his "Last Judgement," Gauguin had included himself in his tropical groves, the likenesses of Rembrandt, Tintoretto, Cezanne, Van Gogh, Botticelli, Giracault, and the rest of the illustrious roster blazed, frowned, smiled, peeked and stared out of their work. Witlen dared not number himself with the others, but he wished to be their equal in integrity if not immortality. He would have to study his face more closely the next time he attempted to shave.

Because he knew he had to see his face more clearly, Witlin began to search through trashcans in the night, hoping to find bits of discarded food and once-used razor blades that would tide him through his last few days. He knew that he was becoming gaunt from his hunger, but that was no longer important to him — as the bones showed more distinctly in his long features he detected a definition of line he had not found there before, and it pleased him. If he was indeed using his own face as his model, it was now more worthy of that honor than it had been before, when indulgence had blurred and softened the angles and planes to a formlessness that could never serve Saint Sebastian in his travail.

Satisfied for the first time in more than a week at his appearance, he decided to bring a small mirror into the studio. Earlier he had disdained such methods, but with his time so short and the painting so near to completion, he took a chance that this intrusion would not interfere with what he had accomplished already. It took him the better part of an hour — and he begrudged every second — to place the mirror so that he could see himself without throwing unwanted light onto the canvas by reflection. He set to work feverishly when he had accomplished this, for he did not want to waste another instant on such considerations. The odors of paint and turpentine were like drugs to him now, the fumes filling his senses more intensely than wine ever had.

He was so caught up in his work that he was not aware of the knocking on his door until it became a pounding. He stepped back, one hand to his forehead to clear his mind enough to respond.

"Mister *Witlin!*" Missus Argent shouted, using both fists now.

He reeled back from the canvas, reaching out for a sloping beam to steady himself. "Yes, Missus Argent!" he called back. "I was . . . napping."

"Open this door at once!" There was nothing tentative about her, none of the whining hesitancy he had come to expect, and it jarred him a bit to realize she was truly angry with him.

"I'll be here in a moment," he told her, fumbling toward the door. "Just a moment."

"*Now,* Mister Witlin," she ordered him, and poked her flushed, pinched face at him the instant he had the door wide enought to permit her to do so. "I have to speak with you, Mister Witlin."

"Come in," he mumbled, setting his brush aside. "I've been working and . . . "

"I know you've been up here," she said, refusing to use the word work for what he did. "We can hear you all over the house, with your muttering and climbing and moving."

"It's necessary," he said, trying to find a way to get rid of her. She distracted him, with her greedy eyes and rapacious little hands. "I don't mean to disturb you when I . . . "

"That's all very well," she interrupted, her hands going to her hips. "But there are complaints. Do you understand that? I can't run this house if everyone is complaining to me about my tenant in the attic."

"Missus Argent . . . " he began, but could think of nothing to say to her that she would understand or accept.

"Well?"

"I have work to do. I'm almost finished." He could hardly hear his own voice, and knew from the way she looked at him that she was not paying attention to what he said.

"This place stinks!" she announced with more irritation than she had shown so far. "What have you been doing up here, Mister Witlin?" She cast an eye around the room. "You haven't cleaned the floor, have you? You told me that you'd attend to cleaning up this place before you move . . . "

"Missus Argent," he cut in, goaded to protest by her behavior, "I will clean the room, such as it is, the moment I'm finished with this painting. To do so before then would be a fruitless waste of time. Don't you see? I have only a little bit of work to do, and it will be . . . " He indicated the canvas. "Look at it, Missus Argent. I want you to see what I'm doing. You've got to understand what it means to me."

Once again the landlady glared around the attic. "I see the painting. But daubs and smears of paint . . . Well, I don't know anything about art. I'm too busy taking care of the people in this house, Mister Witlin. I haven't time for art. Or whatever that thing is."

He did not hear most of this; his mind had caught on one particular phrase.

138

"Daubs of paint!" he demanded of her. "You think this is nothing but daubs of paint? Don't you see . . . no, of course, you don't. People like you throw eggs at the 'Mona Lisa'. You tear down a Rivera mural to make way for a glass box full of offices. You think you have a right to ignore me because I don't go off to a regular job. You think that makes me nothing but a bum and a sponger! But that's not true." He turned away from her, convinced that she would never comprehend him, no matter what he said or how he strove to explain himself and his work to her.

"You're crazy," Missus Argent whispered, drawing back from Witlin, one arm up as if to brace herself against him. "You're just crazy."

Witlin sighed. "I suppose I am, to you."

"You're dangerous," she went on, not hearing him.

"Missus Argent, don't talk . . ."

"I want you out of here. Never mind the rent. I want you out of my house tomorrow night." Her eyes had turned glassy, her face was fixed in a ghastly smile. "You've got to leave."

He scowled. "I have a few days more, and I've already promised I'll pay my rent." He could feel a headache forming in his skull, driving out the sense and the comfort he had felt only a few minutes before. "I have to finish the painting, Missus Argent."

"Sure. You finish it. But not in my house." It was her final word, every detail of her posture, expression and tone of voice emphasized it. She stalked to the door, angular and cautious as an insect. Witlin was reminded of a mantis or other delicate and predatory creatures waiting to devour hapless victims.

"You'll get your rent," he said in what he wanted to be a reasonable tone.

"I don't want it. I want you out of here." If anything, she was more determined as she slammed the door.

Witlin stared at the knob, wishing he could think of the whole encounter as a dream. He resisted the urge to follow her down onto the lower floors where she undoubtedly was regaling the others with lurid tales of what he was doing in the attic. His work was more important than her petty lies, more important than money or time or anything else.

He waited in silence for hours, watching the light disappear and the eerie shadows of night claim the attic, bleaching first and then covering Saint Sebastian with an indigo gauze. The air was very still, so that he thought that the motes were endlessly suspended like little planets in the heavy air. Night engulfed him, leaving him feeling empty and without form. He could not say what he was any more, with the color gone from him and his world sunk into darkness. Idly he felt for his pulse, and was mildly surprised to feel it beat. Under his hand his chest rose for breath; he was still alive, but he no longer believed it, not when there was so much night around him.

139

Around midnight he left the attic, stealing softly down the stairs, freezing at the faintest noise. He let himself out of the house and trudged off through the streets toward the liquor store where he could get day-old sandwiches at half price. Testing the bristles on his face, he wondered if he had nerve enough to steal a packet of razor blades. He wanted to be neat when he finished the painting.

In the end he barricaded himself in the attic, all his old, unsatisfactory work serving now as jamb against the doorknob. He had no intention of leaving now, when Saint Sebastian hovered so tantalizingly near fruition. Twice he had heard a voice, loud and blustering on the other side of the door, but now he had been left in peace to do the work he had to do.

He was almost out of paints, and that should have troubled him, yet it did not. There would be enough. Saint Sebastian would not let him down. Only the reds were precariously low, the tubes giving up mere dollops of color. He touched his finger to the rosy nippple of pigment he had put on the palette. The act consumed him with a pure sensuality that left him breathless. If he had dared to waste the paint, he would have pressed the paint flat and felt it squidge out around his finger, more yielding than flesh ever was.

Witlin hesitated. That was the trouble with paint, he realized, and the recognition shot through him hideously. It was soft and pliant, malleable, a substance without strength beyond the power of chroma and hue. With a cry he dropped his brush and brought his hands to his face to shut out the enormity of his failure. Saint Sebastian was not real, would never be real. He could not finish it. Anything he put on that canvas, though each work was bigger and of brighter colors and more emphatic shades, would always be nothing more than a pale, timid reflection of the might of his vision.

His hand slammed down into the paint, smearing all the colors into a blur as he deliberately twisted his hand. The paint had failed him, would always fail him and would betray his talent in every conceivable way. He had sold himself to a fraud!

He made an effort to stop sobbing, but there was no way to keep from that anguish and after a little time he no longer tried. His body shook and trembled, his hands turned to talons, weapons to eradicate the travesty he had seduced himself into creating. He went from palette to the painting itself, clawing at the paint, smudging the surface with other pigments now the color and texture of mud. It was a Pyrrhic satisfaction, but the only one left to him. There was no way he could avenge himself adequately. He had brought himself and Saint Sebastian to ruin because of the bright promise of chemicals suspended in oils. How many others had been similarly undone! The idea staggered him and he howled with the pain of it. And how many of those realized before they died how they had been compromised?

140

Suddenly he stood upright, the grief stilled in him. There was a way, there was still a way. He would show what art was, not this insignificant imitation that had masqueraded as art for so long. Yes, there was one way, and what was needed was a little resolution. Surely that was easier to face than this ultimate despair. He wiped his face with the edge of his paint-fouled sleeve, paying no heed to the reds and yellows that were left behind on his skin. That was nothing, less than nothing.

He had to search for the better part of an hour, but at last he found his pocket knife under some discarded rags. He seized upon it with urgency, then went to find his brushes, his eyes filled with anticipation. Those who never tested themselves never learned the terrible joy of dedication, and over the lonely months he had felt his devotion grow from ill-defined hope to profound certainty. Only his focus had been misguided, and he would now remedy that and vindicate himself. He began to carve the ends of the handles of his brushes, taking great care to make them symmetrical and sharp before going for the pack of razor blades he had taken from the liquor store, remembering to reserve one or two for cutting the lying, deceitful canvas into strips.

When the door was finally broken in, Witlin could barely lift his head. It was not possible for him to see who was there, for the room had already faded into dusk. He heard a shocked exclamation and appalled swearing, which disturbed him. He had not done this to disgust them, but for art.

"Oh, my God," Missus Argent burst out before stumbling out of the room to keep from retching at what she saw.

"No," Witlin protested, but he had not enough voice left to be heard. Besides, when he breathed, the arrows sunk deep in his flesh hurt him. They had been excruciating at first, when he had thrust them, like the arrows of Saint Sebastian, into his thigh, his shoulder, his arm, his side, his abdomen while he hung in the hastily constructed canvas bonds. Then he spasmed once, twice, pulling his canvas restraints from the beam. But no matter; he had used only his longest and best brushes for his arrows and it pleased him to think that he had achieved something of merit at last.

The End of the Carnival

> Radiation mama, shine your light on me, I said
> Radiation mama, shine your light on me.
> I need your loving, and I need it bad —
> The hottest, longest, lastest love that I have ever had. I said
> Radiation mama, shine your everlasting light on me.

Big Hank Cassidy stood at the door of the Risen Sun and peered upward at the radiation symbol that was painted in the brightest Day-Glo colors with straight rays projecting around it like daggers. It was a couple miles out of town, this Risen Sun, a big lump of a house with nothing but room to recommend it to the fright-wigged woman who ran it. People in town preferred not to mention the Risen Sun, though it brought more than half the business done to the town: no one liked to admit it was a brothel that kept them alive.

There was a figure in the second storey window, a tall, angular creature like a mud-daubed scarecrow, who looked down at Big Hank. "We can't let you in yet. Becca isn't here!" The voice was raspy and gratingly loud, certainly not the soft and persuasive accents usually expected from a working whore, but those blandishments were not part of the Risen Sun, and no one expected them.

"How long do you think she'll be?" Big Hank shouted up at the window.

"Hard to tell. You know how folks are in Norlens. They don't take to her much." She waited. "You can keep on the porch, if you like. Elijah will bring you coffee, but it's extra."

"Fine with me," Big Hank said wearily as he stepped up to the elaborate screen door that was made to withstand much more than insects. He found a place on a small, dusty bench and sat down.

Madame Becca rarely came into town, but when she did she was accorded a precise kind of courtesy that usually is reserved for those who are unwelcome. She was not deceived and occasionally admitted that she did not feel any more comfortable with the townspeople than they did with her. Even with her wig and half a mask on her face, there was no hiding what she was and nothing that would adequately disguise the extent of her deformity. Over the years, she had grown worse and her compensations more outrageous. Today she had donned a voluminous robe of metalic brocade that made her appear more enormous than she was and did little to conceal the wide swaths of scar tissue on her blotched arms. Her wig was a ridiculous shade of blue. The eyes behind her mask were intelligent and bright, more keen than compassionate, riddled with grinding pain.

"What can I do for you?" Mister Taylor asked her when she came into his store. He kept his face averted from hers, addressing a shelf of canned goods instead of the middle-aged, deformed woman in front of him.

"You know what I always get, Taylor. I'll take the same thing." Her voice was harsh, more of a wheeze than speech.

"Sure," he said to let her know that he understood her. "Last week they said that you'd had another . . ."

"Accident?" she supplied when he faltered. "It was no more an accident than anything that happens at the Risen Sun. Nothing's an accident there."

"Unh . . ." was all the response he could manage. He looked at Madame Becca and tried to conceal his dislike of her, but there was a turn to his mouth or some other quirk that she could read, and she scoffed at him. He had the grace to look away.

"Mister Taylor, if you like, I'll leave my wigs and dresses on the shelf and come here just the way I am. *Just* the way I am. Would you like that?" She grinned, showing her blatantly artificial teeth and laughing at the expression on Taylor's face.

"Miz Becca, I . . ."

"That's Madame Becca," she corrected him sternly. "Madame. That is my title because I run a whorehouse, Taylor." She picked two items off the shelves and held them out to him. "You better start ringing these things up, Mister Taylor, sir, or you aren't going to get me out of here before sundown."

"That . . . sure." The prospect of having Madame Becca in his store any longer

144

than absolutely necessary horrified him. "I'll just take your list while you . . ."

"And I'll want some of that good candy you stock. Lots of it. Some of my girls like candy. The drug list is at the bottom." She sighed. "We need more of those drugs, Taylor, but we can't let you . . ." It was rare that Madame Becca showed any emotion but scorn; now her face drooped near despair. "They keep promising to arrange for the drugs. Cat needs it, she needs it worse than ever, and those bastards don't know that she has to have it. They won't come to see us any more, not now that we're making a little money. Look at what . . ." She turned abruptly as the door banged open.

"Saw your car, Becca," said the mayor, her moon face sweating from the effort of climbing three stairs. "I wanted to have a word with you."

"About what?" Becca demanded, her sarcastic smile once more affixed to her painted mouth. "We're gonna get hassled again?"

"No, I don't plan on it," said the mayor, her large, soft hands fiddling with the catch on her tiny purse. "I heard what you said about the drugs. I had to talk about that." She was embarrassed now, and motioned to Taylor to leave them alone.

"I can see you ladies want to be alone," Taylor said at once, grateful for the excuse to leave the room. Madame Becca was bad enough, but the mayor was infinitely worse.

"I been on the phone to that fool in Macon," the mayor said when the door to the back was firmly closed.

"You better talk low, Cindy. No telling what Taylor's doing back there, but I bet he's listening to us." Madame Becca pointed to a barrel of screws and nails. "Sit down. You look worn out."

"I am," the mayor admitted. "The job's a killer. No one'd take it but me, and I got all of this to lug around with me." She sighed heavily and took her place on the barrel, hoisting her enormous thighs onto the uncomfortable surface with a resigned indifference.

"Now, what did you hear from Macon?" Madame Becca inquired. As she listened, she looked over the nearer shelves and occasionally took items from them to add to the pile on the counter.

"I heard that they're phasing out the drug program for the Swanee survivors." She did not mumble — it was not her style.

"Phasing out the drug program?" Madame Becca repeated. "Who're they kidding?"

"They say that there aren't all that many of . . . you left, and that local agencies can deal with . . . you." She gave a delicate little cough which seemed to come from some other, much smaller, body.

"You mean they're writing us off. They don't want to waste their time on us. We remind them of what happened just by breathing, and they don't like it, so they're setting us aside. Don't remind me it's happened before." She brought up her heavily-ringed hand and stared over at the mayor. "Is that it?"

"Aren't you going to say anything?" Cindy asked.

"What? What more is there to say? You've told me that my girls are being forgotten, and I'm doing what I can to . . ." She clapped her hands over her mouth as if she were about to vomit. "Oh, shit!"

"Becca," the mayor said, attempting to get down from her perch on the barrel. "What is it, honey?"

"Nothing. Nothing." She had regained control of herself. "Well. Local agencies, they say? What local agencies? We got any local agencies set up to deal with my girls?"

"No, we don't and you know it," the mayor said. "The nearest local agencies are over two hundred miles away, and they're already too busy. I checked." She put her hands on her hips. "I'd like to find whoever made that decision."

"And what?" Madame Becca waited to hear.

"And sit on him!" This was no idle threat, since the mayor tipped the scales at over three hundred pounds.

"Wouldn't wish that fate on my worst enemy," Madame Becca said with a hint of jeering laughter.

"Well, I would!" the mayor insisted, then stared at Madame Becca. "Don't, Cindy."

"You gonna be all right? I mean, you and the others?" There was real concern in her piggy eyes and she could not conceal her fear. "I told Pa that we'd stick together, and I won't go back on my word just because he's dead."

"I didn't think that you would." Madame Becca seized haphazardly on a few more boxes and two glass bottles.

"You tell me what you want me to do, sis, and I will." It was rare that either of them mentioned their relationship, but once in a great while, the words would escape them, and then both of them would be silent.

"What is there to do?" Madame Becca demanded of the air. "They don't want us around any more, and so they . . . no more drugs and it isn't too long before the problem, the little reminder, disappears." She let one of the glass containers drop and there was a sudden, intense smell of old perfume.

"I'll find a way to stop this," the mayor said to Madame Becca. "There's got to be some way."

"What would you suggest? You read about how those other survivors committed suicide in a bunch. The authorities must have danced for joy over that one. Too bad that they killed themselves in public with half the cameras in the world covering it. That way, no one could pretend about them dying. But you can't tell me they don't heave a sigh of relief every time one of us dies." She folded her arms as if to brace herself against onslaught. "I ought to get ahold of someone and . . ." She stopped. "That's what I ought to do, all right."

146

"Becca, what are you talking about?" the mayor asked, frowning with worry.

"I'm talking about getting even. If they're going to do this to us, we've got a right to fight back." She started down the aisle, then stalked back toward her sister. "I think I know a way. It will probably take a little time, but I can do it. If I have enough time, and if I can get some drugs from somewhere, just long enough to keep my girls going, then we could . . ."

"Could *what*?" the mayor exclaimed. "What are you talking about, Becca?"

"And they wouldn't have the chance to cover it up, not this time." She deliberately broke another two bottles of perfume, ignoring the overly-sweet stench that filled the room. "You know what they're like. They pretend that there was no real trouble when the plant failed, and when they couldn't pretend any longer, they said it didn't matter."

The mayor frowned at her sister. "You're not going to do anything . . . reckless, are you, Becca? I know what you're like when you get mad."

Madame Becca laughed, making a sound like a rusty saw on green wood. "What ever gave you that idea?"

> *You can close all the porno houses*
> *but the one in your mind;*
> *You can say that you're disgusted*
> *at the things that you find;*
> *You can say you're vindicated*
> *when they leave you behind;*
> *But the fires are burning closer.*

Inside the Risen Sun it was cool, not a degree over seventy. Nine of the women who lived and worked there lounged about in shapeless housecoats, their faces without adornment, the wreckage of their lives horrible and familiar.

Lucille, thirty-four and scarecrow-thin, was the least deformed of the group. She sat stroking an auburn wig in her lap as if it were a cat. On the floor, two of the women were measuring out pills into little paper cups, like children's party candy.

"Hurry it up, you two," said Jody, who was in pain more than most of them. "Can't wait much longer. It's bad today."

"You just take it easy there, Jody," Noreen told her as she concentrated on her counting. "You'll get your stuff in a couple minutes."

"I got to have it or I can't work," Jody reminded them.

"Yeah, well, who's any different?" Ellen said, nudging Lucille. "You notice that Big Hank Cassidy is outside? D'you reckon he wants to come in?"

"He calls Becca sometimes," Ellen said, then fell into brooding silence.

"Big Hank?" Lucille asked distantly. "I knew him in college. He got Ben's job." She fell silent, her hand still on the rich curls of her wig. "What's he doing here now? Why now?"

147

"Maybe he's tired of it all," suggested Jody in so resigned a tone that the rest of them were slightly embarrassed.

"Why else do they come, if they aren't tired of it all?" Noreen said, as if to restore a little lightness to them. "Who comes to the Risen Sun but guys who are . . ."

"Ready to check out," Sandra finished for her. She had been reading a book, paying no attention to the work going on before her, as if she were unconcerned with what the others did. Many times the women would do that, pretending that the drugs were as important as extra vitamins — beneficial but not essential.

"Becca should be back in another hour. We'll know more then, I guess."

None of them responded to that, each of them feeling too vulnerable. It was always frightening when Madame Becca went to town, to find out about the drugs and what might become of them. They were nervous even at the mention of it.

"I think I'd like to have a go at Big Hank," Jody said dreamily. "He was at the main office when the plant went. A pity he wasn't . . ."

The others nodded. "I heard that he tried to get the power company to provide maintenances for us," Noreen ventured.

"If he did, he sure as hell didn't succeed," Lucille said, getting to her feet. "You gonna be all day with that?"

Noreen swore as one of the cups overturned and pills rolled across the faded carpet. "Almost done. Anyone here need uppers or downers while I'm at it?" She noticed that most of the women refused these drugs, preferring to have their minds clear for their work. "All right. Jody, you first. I put in a touch of morphine for you."

"Thanks, Noreen." They all knew that she daily used enough of the drug to kill a horse, but she had developed a tolerance for it, and lived in dread of the day that there would not be enough of it to hold her pain at bay.

"We're gonna have Elijah bring in the tea now, and we can get dressed when we're through." She took up her own paper cup. "Well, here's to another day of harlotry."

The others copied her toast without irony.

Madame Becca got out of the battered old Plymouth station wagon that she had driven for the last nine years. There were large bags in the back of the car and she took two of them out before going up onto the porch.

"Afternoon, Becca," Big Hank said rather sheepishly from his seat.

"Madame Becca to you, Big Hank," she said stiffly as she tugged on the bell-rope. "You here on official business?"

"No." He looked down at his hands. "I guess you might say pleasure."

148

"You might say," Madame Becca chuckled unpleasantly. "I hear that your company got its way at last. The mayor tells me that they're cutting off our drugs." She started through the door that Elijah held open for her, then looked back at the large man on the porch. "I don't imagine there's anything you can do about it, is there, Big Hank."

"I don't know, Madame Becca," he answered. "They don't pay much attention to me down at the office. Since the plant blew, well, you know what it's been like there."

Madame Becca handed the bags to Elijah. "I'll be in in a moment. You tell the girls to start getting ready." She gave her attention to Big Hank. "I don't have any idea what it's like at the plant. I haven't had since . . . it blew. I'll give 'em this: they stopped the meltdown, all right, with a blow up. Fine planning there."

"Now, Becca . . . Madame Becca. You know there was no way for them to anticipate that," he protested but his voice was a whine and he would not look at her.

"Sure, Big Hank. And we're all here because it's where we want to be." In disgust she went through the door and slammed it hard.

Elijah did nothing but shake his head: he had seen Madame Becca in these moods before and had learned to keep silent when she behaved this way. Without protest, he set about his work.

"Elijah," she said over her shoulder to him, "there are more bags in the car. You bring them in, will you? Part of it's groceries, but there are a few other items. I have to talk to the girls." With a wave of dismissal she headed for the back drawing room, trying to think of a way to tell the women what she had learned.

"It's Becca," said Noreen as the madame came through the door. "Glad you're back from town. How'd it go?"

"You might not be so glad when we through talking," was her somber reply as she waded toward the flowered settee where Jody was just finishing her coffee. The discolorations of her ravaged face were less obvious because of the greater animation in her deep-set eyes.

"It's good you're here, Becca. The coffee's still hot. So's the tea."

> *The Risen Sun, come Mardi Gras*
> *Is shining, yeah, it's shining.*
> *There ain't no place, not near or far*
> *Shines out so bright at Mardi Gras;*
> *Makes fools forget what fools they are —*
> *The Risen Sun is shining.*

"What are we gonna do?" Lucille asked in dismay when they had all heard Madame Becca out. "What *can* we do?"

"Nothing, that's what; same as always," Jody answered with disgust. "They want us to die, and they're making it damned easy for us to do it. No more of this piecemeal shit, no sir, just the straight fun of radiation poisoning." She leaned her head back and laughed terribly. "I shouldn't've been so greedy about the morphine."

"Jody, you cut that out!" Noreen said sharply. "If they want us to die, then we got to find a way to stop that. There's got to be other ways to keep us going." She turned hopeful eyes toward Madame Becca. "You thought of anything yet, Becca?"

"Not yet." It had occupied her mind all the way back in the car and now there was a tiredness in her face that appeared almost to be defeat.

"Can we keep going?" Jody asked. "Is there anything we can get, or do?"

"Not that I could find out about in town. . . . Well, it doesn't matter right away. So far as the mayor knows, there's nothing any of us can do, officially, and we'll have to fend for ourselves. That was the way the boys in the power company see it, and that's what they've got the government to believe, and that's the way we have to deal with it." She leaned back against the cushions as if ready for a nap.

"But how?" Lucille asked. She had put on her wig and now she fingered the tumbled curls as she had once done with her own hair. That had fallen out soon after the blow-up and she did not like to remember what it had been like not to be bald.

"That's what we have to figure out," Noreen said as reasonably as she could. "Isn't there anyone we can write to or call? There's newspeople, and . . ."

"They aren't interested in us any more," Becca reminded the girls. "We're old news. And look what we're doing for a living. Why, one of those power company men could say a few words and make it look like we're nothing more than a bunch of greedy, crazy whores trying to take advantage of their generosity. You know what they did to that family in Coleville who tried to get their fields tested for contamination. By the time the power company got off the TV screen, those poor farmers sounded like the worst sorts of opportunists and zealots. They'll do the same to us if you let them."

"No news, then. Besides, any of you want to see your faces on the news?" Jody slapped her thigh at this and two of the women looked away from her.

"Jody's right," Lucille whispered. "The way I look now . . ."

"We've got to think of something," Noreen insisted, verging suddenly on tears. "There's more to . . ."

Elijah stopped in the door, clearing his throat before he spoke. "Beg pardon, Miz Becca, but Big Hank is getting terrible impatient. He's pacing around the porch."

"You tell that man . . ."

Though Madame Becca was rarely interrupted, this time Jody cut her short.

"Can't he wait to die? Can't he spare a few minutes for us to figure out a way to live?" Jody pointed to a little case on the floor. "Hand me the make-up, will you, Sue?"

The girl did as she was asked, but kept her attention on Madame Becca. Sue was sometimes thought to be the most interesting of the girls at the Risen Sun because she occasionally glowed in the dark. She was soft-spoken and shy with people, wearing her contamination as a saint wears a halo. "Madame Becca, you'll find a way. You always have."

Madame Becca swallowed back tears at Sue's faith and said with heroic nonchalance, "Why, sure we will, Suzy. We're not stupid women, no matter what the power company and the government think of us. We're not going to let them just forget about us."

"Damned right," Noreen muttered. "I figure we got enough drugs to get us through next week, and then we're going to be in trouble." She had not wanted to say this, but the knowledge burned in her with acid heat and she could not hold it back.

"So soon," Madame Becca said softly. "Then we got to work quick on this one." She knew as well as the others did that once the sustaining drugs were gone, there would be nothing they could do but suffer and die.

"They can wait us out," Noreen said. "It wouldn't take long. No phone calls for a couple of days, no letters read for a week, and they got no more troubles." Jody was hiding her fury under a preditory smile.

"Neither do we, for that matter," Lucille said. "Can't we just let it go? Or get some of that stuff they gave the survivors whose skin wouldn't grow back? They say it's quick and painless."

"But then they'd be getting *away* with it," Noreen protested. "Don't you know that?"

"Well, sure, but they're going to get away with it in any case." Lucille had tugged her wig askew and now busied herself in righting it onto her head.

"Not if I have anything to say about it. They got our men, and that's enough!" Madame Becca rose from the settee. "They gave my husband some of that stuff, and at the time I was grateful. He was out of his head with pain and he looked like he'd been dipped in sulphur. I thought it was mighty nice of them to help him end it. That was then. Now I know that they didn't do it for any decent reason like that. They wanted him out of the way, like they want us out of the way. We embarrass them." She folded her arms. "I won't go along with it. If any of you want to check out, that's all right with me. I don't blame you for wanting to, and I'll do what I can to make it easy for you. But if you want to fight them, then we got a lot of work to do and a real short time to do it in." She began to pace, glowering down at the carpet with its pattern of cabbage roses. "We have to think about what they want, and then we got to do what *we* want. Fast."

"But what do we want?" Jody asked. "I know I want out."

151

"Sure, Jody," Madame Becca said, stopping in front of the woman and reaching down to put a hand on her shoulder. "You got the best reason of any of us to do it. I'll see if the mayor will get us some of . . ."

"Thanks," said Jody, and went back to applying her garish make-up.

"The Mayor's got her own worries," Sue cautioned them.

"Can the mayor help? Really?" Noreen asked. She was frightened enough to be skeptical, and blushed, being ashamed of her fear.

"The mayor'll help. She'll help." Madame Becca spoke with total confidence and the girls felt it come from her like heat. "You tell me what I should ask her to do."

"The drugs . . ." Noreen began.

"She'll be working on that already. If anyone can turn some up, she can." She could sense the doubt in her girls, but she said nothing more. "Not all fat women are lazy slatterns," she remarked with a nod toward Myra, who was even more enormous than the mayor, and who did all the carpentry around the Risen Sun when she was not tending to business.

"You know," Myra said in her thread of a voice, "I used to know Cindy pretty well, years ago. She's not the kind to say she'll do something and not do it." Myra did not often talk, as it was a tremendous effort for her as well as painful. When she did speak, it was usually only a word or two. The number of words she volunteered were eloquent testimony to her trust in the mayor's capabilities.

"Well, then, we'll let her get to work on that," Noreen said, nodding to the others.

Jody was half-done with her maquilage, and paused in the outlining of her scarred mouth to say, "I used to know a doctor in Fayette, a good man. Maybe I'll give him a call. He might know where we can buy supplies, temporarily."

"Thanks, Jody," Madame Becca said, and resumed her pacing. "There's two avenues already. You see, they aren't going to sweep us blow-up survivors under the carpet quite as easy as they thought they would."

"They're gonna try," Sue pointed out unnecessarily.

"But we aren't gonna let them," Madame Becca vowed.

"How?" Myra asked, and her question was echoed by the others.

"I don't know quite yet," Madame Becca admitted. "But we'll find a way. They killed our husbands and we are . . . what we are because of them and the blow-up. So we'll find a way. We'll get them where they live." She paused and her hard eyes grew thoughtful. "Where they live."

> *Like Juliet and Isolde, girl, to love you is to die,*
> *And I'm searching for oblivion to end my pain, all right;*
> *So I'll tell you that I love you, babe, it's just a little lie*
> *For the time we'll spend together for the carnival's last night.*

"They're gonna remember us," Madame Becca promised Big Hank as they sat in the sunny morning room, glasses of lemonade on the dainty round-topped table between them. "If they don't, then it was all for nothing, and those bastards will do it again."

Big Hank reached over and put his hand over Madame Becca's. It was like covering a filet mignon with a rump roast. "You know that they won't forget you. You're letting all that scare talk fool you," he said, trying to comfort her.

"Scare talk? Big Hank, Cindy knows they're doing it. We all know they're doing it. They don't want any more of us around, that's all. When the men died, they were relieved, and you know it's true."

He met the challenge in her eyes with reason tempered by fatigue. "Sure, they were relieved, because there weren't any more victims than . . ."

"Just what the fuck do you think *we* are?" Madame Becca demanded. "Because we weren't near the plant when it blew, it doesn't mean that we weren't victims of it, and you know that's the truth, Big Hank." She pulled her hand away.

"But Becca . . ."

"*Madame* Becca," she corrected him at once.

"All right, Madame Becca," he conceded. "You wives, you didn't know that it was so dangerous to be with your men. No one knew."

"Want to lay a bet on that, Big Hank? I sure used to think that, yes I did. But not any more. Not since they cut off our aid funds, and now with the drugs . . . Why'd I have to start up this house, anyway? Because there was no one who would let us work for them, that's way. We didn't have jobs, the insurances the power company provided did not cover deaths from nuclear accidents, such as explosions, and the pensions weren't available when less than the full term of employment had been served. No one in government would care for us unless we went into vegetable farms" — Becca winced at the current euphemism for mental wards even as she said it — "and none of us are ready for that. So what else was there? Most of spent what little money we had to make sure our kids were safe, the ones that weren't dead. We have to get by somehow, and Big Hank, there are a lot of men out there, believe it or not, who don't mind spending a lot of money to have one last night of love with one of my girls. We're getting by now, but without the drugs . . ." She reached over and picked up her frosty glass of lemonade. "I don't have to tell you what will happen when the drugs stop."

"You can arrange something," he said with a hint of desperation in his tone now. "You're not being fair to the power company, Madame Becca. You aren't trying to see what they want to do. They don't like to see you here, your girls, well, being whores. They were married to power company men, and it's . . ."

Madame Becca put her empty glass down so hard that the table rocked. "It all comes back to embarrassment. The blow-up was an embarrassment. The deaths

153

were an embarrassment. The drugs and publicity were an embarrassment. *We're* an embarrassment. And so something will have to be done to make them feel better." She shoved her chair back from the table with a sudden, abrupt motion. "You listen to me, Big Hank. You were a good supervisor and I know that my husband respected you. It was just chance that you didn't end up the way he did, but that's how it goes. You came here because you want something, and I've listened to you, but if all they want is for you to try to get us to keep from *embarrassing* them again, you can tell them that they can forget it. We're a lot more than embarrassed, we're contaminated and dying. Our men weren't embarrassed, they were killed by massive doses of radiation. So it isn't my place to salve their consciences."

"I didn't come here for them, not entirely," Big Hank said, staring down at his huge, meaty hands. "I felt real . . . rotten when the blow-up happened and my men all . . . died, and I wasn't there with them. I should have gone with them." He looked up at her quickly, then stared at the lace curtains where the sun came through them in a dappled pattern. "I've been trying to live with it for pretty long now. It isn't working, Madame Becca. I don't want to do it any more. I just want to get away from it."

Only the faint rattle of ice in their glasses disturbed the silence.

"You want to get away from it? Are you leaving town?" She hardly dared to believe that Big Hank really wished that of her. "You're the only one from the power company who's kept in contact with me and my girls. I thought that it was on orders."

"No. They don't know about it." He cleared his throat. "I hear that the girl to get is Sue, since she shines so pretty at night."

"Sue." She nodded slowly. "You know what happens, don't you?"

"Sure. I get the sickness, just the way you've all got it. In a little while, my hair and teeth will fall out, I'll stop being able to eat and I'll die." He got up. "And you got those pills, to make it faster. The rumor is that there's a euphoric in the pills, to make it better while you're going."

"Yeah. There's a euphoric." She started to leave the room, but Big Hank caught her by the wrist.

"Becca, if you got those pills, how come you and the girls don't take them? A lot of the other wives did."

"I guess they weren't as mad as we are. I guess they wanted to forget as much as the power company wants us to forget." Their eyes locked, and he released her arm. "Sue will be ready in an hour or so. She's got the room on the third floor with the bay window. Think you can find it?"

It was the carnival week, Mardi Gras, and the Risen Sun was ready for it. Bunting and banners draped the front of the house like a muumuu on a dowager.

Ribbons festooned the porch railings and sparklers marked the walkway. Speakers blared out taped music — few musicians came there willingly — and every window was shining with candles.

Madame Becca stood in the vestibule rigged out in her most outrageous clothes. Her towering wig was magenta and there were sequins pasted over the scars on her cheeks. Her wide smile seemed sincere enough and her manners were impeccable. "You did your job well, Big Hank," she said to the silent man in the wheelchair behind her. "You did a real, real good job for us."

Big Hank did not reply. He had lost the ability to speak the week before but so far had refused that last, delicious pill that would bring him the oblivion he desired.

"You sure this is free?" asked one of the men in an undervoice as he took Madame Becca's proffered hand.

"You paid the initial fee, and that's it," she replied, beaming at the casually dressed young man. "You might have to wait an hour or two to be alone with one of the girls, but you can go into the drawing room. Ellen's serving tea and Myra is tending bar for the time being. Later, they'll trade off with the other girls." She beamed at him, showing her delight.

"You short-handed?" the man's companion asked, a bit surprised.

"Of course not," Madame Becca said, wagging an admonishing finger at the man who asked the question. "My girls work hard. They work real hard, and they've got the right to enjoy part of this carnival with you. Serving tea and canapes and drinks gives them a chance to socialize a little. And tell me the truth — wouldn't you rather that one of my girls wait on you, so you can have a look at her before anything more . . . involved happens, than have to look at servants in short jackets? Ellen likes a little conversation. Myra, though . . . she doesn't talk much."

Big Hank rolled his wheelchair back a few feet, out of the line of traffic. He had seen what he wanted to, and now he was ready to leave. He rang the bell hanging from the arm of the chair and attracted not only the notice of Elijah but of Madame Becca, who left her place at the door to come to his side.

"Oh, Big Hank, I am grateful to you. You've done so much." There were tears in her eyes, and she paused to blot them away before she bent down to kiss his cheek. "You done more for me, for all of us, than anyone ever did, and I hope, if there is a just God in Heaven, that He will take you and bless you for what you've given us." Her voice was more husky than usual.

Elijah came hurrying up to the two of them. "I heard the bell. You ready now, Mister Big Hank?"

Slowly, agonizingly, Big Hank nodded. It was all he could do to lift his hand a few inches to show he understood what Madame Becca had said to him.

"Good," Madame Becca acknowledged. "You go along with Elijah now, and spend a little more time with Jody. She's waiting for you, just for you. Elijah's got the pills, and it won't take too long for them to work. You . . . rest easy, Big Hank." She kissed his forehead, then turned away to greet the new arrivals.

"I'm so pleased you came," she said three hours later when the last of the invited guests arrived. "I was afraid that some of you might refuse, considering."

The young men exchanged doubtful looks. One of them tried to laugh. "Your place is pretty famous, Madame Becca. People talk about it. A lot."

"That's right," another chimed in. "When I started college last year, there were two songs about it already. You've got a famous place here." He gave one of his companions a shove in the arm. "I told my dad about the invitation, and he got mad about it, but . . . well, it *is* free, and it's worthwhile to come here, since it's so famous and all."

"I hope you won't be . . . disappointed," Madame Becca said, then turned as Noreen tapped her on the shoulder. "What is it?"

"There's a call for you — your sister." Noreen nodded toward the young men. "While Madame Becca is busy, will you let me take you in and buy you a drink?"

The young men exchanged nervous, eager glances and one of them said yes for all.

"Fine," Noreen said, and looped her arm through the elbow of the nearest of them. "You'll like Myra's way with bourbon."

"What the devil is going on out there?" the mayor demanded of Madame Becca when she picked up the phone. "I been getting calls all evening."

"I'm holding carnival. It *is* Mardi Gras, isn't it?" She chuckled once, ending on a cough.

"Sure, it's Mardi Gras. You haven't done this before." The mayor's initial outburst gave way to worry. "Damn it, Becca, what are you up to?"

"Exactly what I told you I'd be up to," came the patient answer. "Who's called you, anyway?" She was pushing her luck with the mayor and knew it, but the victory was sweet and within her grasp.

"Mostly men from the power company." She paused. "They don't tell me much of anything, except that I've to close you down."

"And what have you told *them?*" Madame Becca asked, wishing they still had enough drugs to keep the pain away from all of them.

"You're not in town. There's nothing I can do. And the sheriff is fifty miles away." It was an uneasy answer.

"No, the sheriff is here. They can't reach him, even if they wanted to." Yes, the victory was good, she decided, in spite of the pain.

"They aren't upset about the sheriff," the mayor said decidedly. "Who else is there? Power company men?" Before Madame Becca could answer, the mayor went on. "No, of course not. They wouldn't come within a mile of your place, would they?"

"I don't think they would, no," Madame Becca said.

156

"Sis, will you tell me what's going on out there? And don't say Mardi Gras again, or I'll scream, so help me Jesus."

Madame Becca sighed. "I'm having a very select party. Everyone invited paid an initial fee of fifty dollars, and now everything here is free. Drinks, girls, pills, everything." She wheezed and her eyes watered. "Big Hank got the names and addresses for me, from the power company."

"But you just said that they're not . . ." the mayor began, then fell silent.

"I had to think of some way to get back at them. They killed our men, they killed our kids and they tried to forget about us. They just . . . threw us away with the rest of the contaminated garbage. Well, I couldn't bear it, Cindy. I couldn't. I told you. . . . You remember."

"Yes, I remember." Her voice was soft now, and very kind.

"It was more than an insult, it was worse than death. They made us *worthless*. All right, then." Her voice got harder and louder as a burst of laughter erupted behind her. "Listen to me, sis. Okay?"

"Sure, Becca," said the mayor.

"We got enough pills for all the girls. It won't matter that we're almost out of drugs, not after tonight, because we'll take them all. You know what will happen to the men here. I don't have to tell you about that. Well, it was the only thing I could think of, and with Big Hank's help . . ."

"You've got to have power company men out there, or government men, Becca," the mayor insisted. "Who else?"

Behind Madame Becca, the party was growing rowdy, and she had to raise her voice.

"Not them — their sons." She laughed with an emotion that was too sad to be malice.

"Their sons?" The mayor was horrified. "But . . . God, why?"

"You know why," Madame Becca said just loudly enough to be heard over the din.

"But they'll die," the mayor protested.

"Yes. But they'll be famous, won't they? Remembered in song and story, honey. That's why they're here." And before the mayor could speak again, Madame Becca put the phone down and went back to the excitement and debauchery of her last Mardi Gras.

> *I said,*
> *Radiation mama, shine your everlasting*
> *everloving*
> *neverending light on me.*

"Sis, will you tell me what's going on out there? And don't say Mardi Gras again, or I'll scream, so help me Jesus."

Madame Becca sighed. "I'm having a very select party. Everyone invited paid an initial fee of fifty dollars, and now everything here's free. Drinks, girls, pills, everything." She wheezed and her eyes watered. "Big Jack got the games and addresses for me, from the power company."

"But you just said that they're not . . ." the mayor began, then fell silent.

"I had to think of some way to get back at them. Those damn men, they killed our kids and they tried to forget about . . . us away with the rest of the contaminated garbage. Well, . . . Mindy, I couldn't, I told you. . . . You remember."

"Yes, I remember." Her voice was soft now, and very kind.

"It was more than an insult, it was worse than death. They made us worthless."

"All right, then." Her voice got harder and louder as a burst of laughter erupted behind her. "Listen to me, sis. Okay?"

"Sure, Becca," said the mayor.

"We got enough pills for all the girls, it won't matter that we're almost out of drugs, not after tonight, because we'll take them all. You know what will happen to the men here. I don't have to tell you about that. Well, it was the only thing I could think of, and with Big Hank's help . . ."

"You've got to have power company men out there, or government men, Becca," the mayor insisted. "Who else?"

Behind Madame Becca, the party was growing rowdy, and she had to raise her voice.

"Not them -- their sons." She laughed with an emotion that was too sad to be malice.

"Their sons!" the mayor was horrified. "But . . . God, why!"

Radiation mama, shine your everlasting

AFTERWORD

In his introduction, Charlie Grant remarks that I write out of the dark side of my perceptions, and in large part, I think that he's right. But I also think that's where most of the strong stories come from, and so I go looking there first. Naturally, this is kind of short hand for whatever it is that goes on in the alchemical centers of a writer's mind. Things surface and bubble and ferment and percolate, and sometimes they end up on the page and sometimes they don't.

For me, almost all the time, the stories begin with the characters. The characters are what interest me more than anything else. And part of the payoff for the process of writing as I experience it, is the way that characters come to life, become more than a sketch, or a collection of descriptions and behaviors turn into themselves, separate from me, doing what they have to do with their lives which are lived out on the page.

To me, that coming-to-life aspect of writing is not only the most interesting part of what I do, it is the very core of my job, because if characters can not come to life for me, they are never going to be real to anyone reading the stories. I think that the attraction of fiction (and theatre, for that matter) is the reality of the characters who inhabit it. In the long run, an elegant turn of phrase of a magnificient use of language will not sustain a work in which the characters of the story have nothing in their veins but printer's ink.

Of course, this can lead to some confusion for the reader who is determined to "psyche out" the writer on the basis of the stories he or she writes. So let me get this out of the way right now: I am not my stories and my stories are not me. I have my whole life to be real in, my characters have only the length of the fiction about them to have their lives, and I owe it to them, and to the readers, to make their lives as vivid and valid as I am capable of doing. When reading a story it is the story that should be important, not the writer, just as in a symphony the music is what matters, not the composer, or in a work of art, the work of art, is more important than the artist, if the artist, or composer, or writer is any good at all.

I very much doubt that the characters are the demons Charlie was talking about back at the beginning of this book, but certainly they are in league together. Which probably is why I ended up writing instead of doing one of the other arts, for at the very base, I think all arts are probably the same thing — a baker can turn the same yeast dough into bread and coffee cake and flapjacks. Like Charlie (no matter what he says) I love my demons, and I would be immeasurably lonely without them. I cherish them. I treasure them. Yet more than that I love my people (for they are all people, never mind the packaging) and their "reality." And once they form themselves, they do not leave until they have finished saying whatever it is they have to say, which is where I put the word *end* on my manuscripts. I've had it happen that whole booksfull of characters will remain in my mind, in a kind of antechamber, waiting for the chance to get onto the page. And occasionally I have the experience of a character who shows up without a story attached. One of them took almost a decade to bring the rest of his story and fellow-characters along.

For me, a story needs to offer not only resolution of the conflict, whatever it is, but it must also provide some insight into or revelation of character that shows some sort of change in the characters as a result of what they've been through. That's probably left over from all those years of working in plays both backstage, onstage and out front in the box office. I am intrigued by the consequences of the action of the characters, not simply for the action, but for what the ramifications of those consequences are for the personality of the character in question. How much of this actually gets onto the page, I have no way of knowing.

Perhaps this sense of ramifications has something to do with my fascination with the objects of horror, and my penchant for finding ways to turn the critters around, or upside down, or inside out, to find out what it is that makes them work. I've also wondered over the years in my reading of horror stories — and I've enjoyed reading horror stories since I was about seven years old — what it is like for the object of horror to be what he or she or it is. Is there something intrinsic to the beastie itself, or is it a matter of reaction? And assuming such things did exist, how would they manage in the world? How would they escape detection and what would their lives be like? As Charlie has already mentioned, I've devoted well over a million words to characters of just that type. These, while not necessarily strictly within such limitations, are certainly cousins with no more than a couple of removes.

There has been another bonus from writing, and one that I did not anticipate when I was much younger and writing the first dreadful attempts at fiction that all of us produce when we start, and that has been the pleasure of knowing my colleagues. It would be stretching things much too far to say that I am on marvelous terms with every writer I know; as a group we're much too diverse and opinionated for that. But there are quite a number of friends I never thought to have who are writers I would not have met without my own work to serve as an introduction. (By the way, Charlie, we met briefly, by phone, for the first time in Boston about fourteen years ago, but didn't do any serious face-to-face talking until about four years later.)

Writing by its very nature is isolative work. For the most part, you spend your time alone in a room at a typewriter or computer keyboard, thinking up things. The work is draining and peculiar because there are very few people out there who actually understand what it is to write a story, to have all those people running around in your head, or to be baffled by the perceptions of the world at large about what it is we think we're doing. At times like that, it is truly wonderful to be able to pick up the telephone and talk to someone who knows precisely what you are doing. There's a lot more to it than that, but that is the part that is private between friends, like the special anguish of having non-writing friends make assumptions about you based on their interpretations of your writing. We've all had that happen; it's one of the things we call each other up to talk about. We cheer each other up, all my friends and I, offer encouragement and commiserations and pep-talks. When Charlie gives me lectures, he always begins by reminding me he's older than I am — he is, by three days.

As I write this on a clear, breezy afternoon in March of 1984, I am forty-one years old, sharing this house with a Leslie-Howard-style cat named The Pimpernel. I have two new projects in the hatching stages, (since writing this afterward, both projects have sold) which means that I spend a fair amount of time making obscure notes to myself and assembling information about the background from which I will be working when I start preparing the proposals and samples for submission. There are a number of new characters starting to separate themselves, telling me what they're like, who they are and why their stories will get onto a ms page and then the proposal-and-portion of each can go out into the world to seek a home.

There are those who compare the submission of stories to sending children out into the world, but I don't think it's quite that simple. It may be because I don't haved children, but I always feel that I am sending out a pet. No, the story is not my pet, nor is it likely to be a pet of some editor. I intend the metaphor in this sense: a child, whatever else it is, has its humanity in common with the editor, and therefore can appeal to the editor on that basis. A pet, on the other hand, has no grounds for appeal unless it happens to be the kind of pet that the editor actually likes, and is not allergic to, or can't stand. To me, that's the basic worry any writer faces in submission. Far more than how much might be paid or how long it will take to get into print; a writer worries about the editor's allergies.

As an editor, Charlie's allergies must be fairly similar to mine: of the ten stories appearing in this book, eight of which are reprints, Charlie bought four of them.

Every book is an end-product, and this collection is no different. All these stories have begun wherever it is they begin, perhaps with the demons Charlie describes, perhaps with something else. The characters have come, more or less successfully to life and have lived out their lives, which are the stories on these pages. They have survived all the pitfalls — submission, contract negotiations, copy-editing, galleys and print, to end up here, where you, the person reading this page, can have a chance to bring your perceptions and experiences to them, and get out whatever is there for you to find. What you find is not always what I put in; what a story says to you is not necessarily what it says to me.

Charlie is right about a writer's temerity in assuming that anything we might want to tell you can be interesting to you, but without it, none of us would ever get a single word on paper. There is a curious humility that comes from writing as well, for we succeed or fail not in what we, the writers, do or say, but in how willing we are to let our characters be true to themselves, to live their lives and meet their dooms on their own terms. Which is just as it should be. Ultimately, the people in the stories are what matters. If you have got this far in *SIGNS AND PORTENTS*, I am very complimented because I am asuming some of the people in the preceding pages who became so real for me, became real for you as well. On their behalf as well as my own, I thank you.

Chelsea Quinn Yarbro

162

Printing and binding for this volume by
Braun-Brumfield, Inc., Ann Arbor, Michigan,
through the agency of Paul de Fremery, San Francisco, California.
Production services by Colleen Timmerman, Merry Belgere, Mya Kramer,
Cyndi Stubbs and Metro Typography.
Book text set in Palatino, acid free paper used throughout.
Book design by Glen Iwasaki, Los Angeles, California.

A 250 Copy Boxed First Edition—signed by
author and artist—has been produced of this work.